T3-BXA-481

PROXY BRIDE

The Lindstroms #1

Katy Paige

For my parents,
Diane and George Gilliam,
who always believed in me.
Some as good, but none better.
I love you both until the end of time.

Chapter 1

There are some things you should never agree to do, even for your best friend.

Jenny Lindstrom drummed her fingers on her knee and glanced, for the hundredth time, toward the double doors at the entrance to the county courthouse. From the bench where she sat in the back of the small lobby, she had a good view of incoming traffic.

The doors opened, and she gulped with anticipation, but instead of the young man she expected, an older man rushed in, followed by a whoosh of snowy Montana wind. He brushed off his snow-covered sleeves and stomped his boots on the large black mat in front of the doors.

"Getting bad out there," he muttered.

Jenny checked her watch. *He should be here by now, for heaven's sake!*

Maybe the snow was slowing him down. It had, after all, taken her over an hour to drive up to Livingston from Gardiner. But didn't Ingrid write that he would arrive yesterday? If so, wouldn't that have left him ample time to be punctual for their appointment?

Jenny took the printed email out of her purse and reread Ingrid's instructions:

Your appointment with Judge Hanlon is at 2:00 p.m. on December 1.

Kristian's cousin Sam is tall, blond, and hot, Jen. He's going to stick out like a sore thumb in Livingston—you shouldn't have any trouble finding him. He promised he would fly in on Thursday night, so he should be able to meet you at the courthouse on Friday afternoon.

We can't thank you enough for what you are doing for us. Baby Svenson thanks you too, *Aunt* Jenny. We know it's inconvenient, and you'll have to skip a day of school. We just couldn't bear the thought of strangers...

The door whooshed open again, and Jenny looked up to see a young couple enter the courthouse, holding mittened hands. They wiped their boots without a word, taking off their mittens. The man used his hands to sign something to the woman, an expectant look on his face. She smiled at him and nodded, signing something back. He kissed her cheek and took a folded piece of paper out of his pocket, lacing his hands through hers and pulling her toward the stairs. As they passed the bench where Jenny sat, she could just make out the bold-type words on the top of the form he held: "Marriage License."

Jenny watched them go up the steps, tears stinging the backs of her eyes. She thought of Ingrid and Kris—so far away, so very much in love—and shook off the sudden loneliness that made a thick lump form in her throat. *Silly sentiment. You have a good life, Jenny Lindstrom.*

She glanced at her watch again and sighed. An hour late! The courthouse would close at four. She had quizzes to grade at home and Monday's lesson yet to plan. Something she hadn't told Ingrid was that she wasn't one hundred percent comfortable with this plan: having to wait for him as the seconds ticked by was shredding her nerves.

Craning her neck to look through the windows that flanked the double doors, Jenny guessed the thickness of the falling snow had doubled in the last hour. Maybe tripled. It was only dusting when she had arrived, and now it was coming down in thick white flakes. When she drove home, the sun would be setting and the roads would be slick. Dark and dangerous.

If only Ingrid had given her a cell phone contact number so she could call this Sam and give him a piece of her mind for leaving her waiting like this. But everything was thrown together so last minute, she'd barely had a chance to ask her principal for an emergency day off.

It never occurred to her to say no to Ingrid. She was raised, like the rest of her kin, to honor servicemen and women…and anyway, Ingrid was like a sister to Jenny—they'd grown up together.

She ran her palms flat against her lap and smoothed out the skirt of her simple gray dress: she bought it online from JCPenney last winter to wear to her cousin Linnea's wedding. The irony of wearing the dress again today for its second time wasn't lost on her.

The doors opened again, and she sat up straighter, but a disheveled, older woman entered, her arm held by a younger man who looked to be in his midthirties. The woman brushed off her snow-covered skirt and thanked him profusely for his assistance.

Jenny's eyes narrowed.

She hadn't seen another single, young man enter the courthouse all afternoon.

This must be him.

He had a kind face, rather more filled out than Ingrid led her to believe, but perhaps he'd changed in the years since her friend was deployed. He was about five foot five, with a protruding round belly, and while his hair may have been blond at one time, there was so little of it left, it was hard to tell. Jenny's heart thumped uncomfortably as she walked briskly to where he stood in front of the double doors, stomping his thick, black boots.

Focused on the gentlemen, she didn't look down to see the wet patch of slush and melted water on the marble floor.

At the same time her high-heeled shoes lost all traction, the double doors whipped open again. She couldn't stop the forward motion of her body—feet sliding and arms flailing. The short, stout man leapt out of her way just before she barreled into him.

Which meant she barreled into someone else instead.

Slamming into the broad, hard chest of the man entering the courthouse, she felt his hands catch around her waist and steady her. But her adrenaline had fired too forcefully for her to recover quickly. Dazed and limp, she clutched at his snowy coat like a drowning woman clinging to a life raft.

"Are you okay?" rumbled a deep voice.

It snapped her out of her coma, and she lifted her

cheek from his lapel.

"Y-Yes. I'm…I'm so sorry!"

Finding her footing, she stepped back from the stranger, smoothing out her dress and sliding her purse back onto her shoulder. Only once she'd regained a semblance of order did she muster the courage to meet his eyes.

"Oh!" She gasped.

Tall. Blond. Impossibly handsome.

There was no doubt in her mind:

This was Sam—the man she was going to marry.

***

Sam Kelley blinked back at her in shock.

One minute he'd been rushing to open the doors of the old courthouse, anxious about arriving so late, and the next, a cute blonde was barreling into his arms. He took off his gloves and ran his fingers through his cold, wet hair, checking her out.

She had her hands on her hips, long blonde hair framing her face. A simple gray sweater-dress accentuated her small waist. She was taller than the average woman, and he guessed she was in her midtwenties, but it was hard to tell with the irritated expression that was souring her otherwise pretty face.

Wait a second. Tall. Blonde. In her twenties.

"You're Jenny!" he said, beaming at her.

"And you're Sam," she said, her voice decidedly less enthusiastic, her cheeks still flushed from her fall.

For no good reason in particular, he'd been expecting a Brunhilde-type: a thick-waisted, big-boned Scandinavian country gal.

She's cute. Huh. Kristian failed to mention that…

"You're *very* late," she chastised him, adjusting her purse again.

Then she turned sharply, crossed the lobby with hurried steps, and started up the stairs, leaving Sam no choice but to follow.

"I'm late," he said, catching up with her halfway up the marble staircase. "Sorry about that."

"Humph," she pouted without looking back at him. *Click, clack, click, clack.* Her shoes echoed up the stairs. "I've been waiting for over an hour."

"Sorry about that…*again*. There was a mountain pass, and a plow—" He stopped, realizing how adolescent and ridiculous he sounded. His next excuse would be about how the dog ate his homework.

"Mmm," she murmured, still marching straight ahead. Her voice dripped of condescension when she added, "It's *Mon-tan-a*. In *win-ter-time*. Mountains and plows should be expected and anticipated."

Sam wasn't accustomed to this sort of dressing down and found that he didn't like it very much.

"You're Kristian's cousin but not from around here?" she asked.

"My folks left Montana before I was born. I'm from Chicago."

She smirked at him over her shoulder, her expression cool. "The big city. Of course you are."

Stopping at the end of the corridor before a door that

read "Clerk," she turned to face him. He stopped short, watching as she closed her eyes, inhaled through her nose, then exhaled loudly like she was practicing a Buddhist relaxation ritual. Finally, she opened her eyes and lifted her chin.

"Let's start over." She smiled woodenly and put out her hand. "I'm Jenny Lindstrom. I'm Ingrid's best friend. Thank you for meeting me today. Sorry I…fell into you."

A mulligan. Okay.

When she smiled—even though he supposed it wasn't genuine—it brightened her face quite a bit, and she didn't look as harsh and angry. Mustering his most charming smile, he enveloped her smaller hand in his.

"Nice to meet you. I'm Sam Kelley, Kristian's cousin. And you can fall for me anytime."

She stared at him stone faced, then blinked, pulling her hand away. An unmistakable flush of pink deepened the color on her cheeks.

Just from shaking hands? Whoa. He tried not to grin. *So, Miss Snippy isn't quite as cool and confident as she seems.*

"Um." She cleared her throat. "Right. Good. Let's do this."

He winked at her. "Ready to get married, Jenny?"

"Proxies!" she blurted out, her cheeks turning scarlet. "We're just proxies! *We're* not actually—"

Sam chuckled. He couldn't remember the last time he met someone so uptight and ripe for teasing.

"Oh, well, thank heavens," he said, putting a hand over his head. "It would have been pretty forward of you to ask me to marry you. We barely know each other, and you may have *fallen* for me already, but I'm not that kind of guy…"

Her expression was positively glacial.

Sam cringed for her benefit, trying not to grin but losing the battle. "Oh, come on! I'm just trying to lighten up the mood."

She blinked at him and appeared about to say something, then must have decided against it because she turned sharply and opened the door in front of her.

"Good afternoon. We're here for the Svenson-Nordstrom proxy wedding." She glanced in annoyance at Sam and then back at the secretary. "I apologize that we're so late."

The woman behind the counter straightened her glasses and gave Sam a cross look before offering Jenny a sympathetic nod.

"Well, now, that's a problem." The secretary squinted at the computer screen in front of her. Typing something on the keyboard, a loud, angry beep answered back. "Judge Hanlon left for the day and won't be back until Monday morning."

"What?" Jenny stepped forward, her hands landing on the countertop. "No! He can't! We—we're proxies for the Svenson-Nordstrom…they're counting on us…"

She looked back at Sam, her face a mixture of anger and panic.

He cleared his throat and stepped up smoothly beside her. Finally, a chance to show her that he wasn't some bumbling kid.

"Surely there must be *something* we can do." Pushing aside his cashmere coat, he reached into his back pocket and took out an expensive crocodile wallet. "Perhaps we could call Judge Hanlon and explain the situation? I would make it worth his while to come back in. I'm more than happy to pay a...surcharge."

The secretary glanced at Jenny, then stood up, directing her full attention to Sam.

"Put that wallet away."

He grimaced at her tone. "I only wanted—"

"You only wanted to fix things by offering money to a public servant? Well, that's just not our way, son." She straightened up to her whole five feet, lowering her glasses to take a hard look at his face from across the counter. "I don't think you're from around here, so I'll explain this as fair as I can: Judge Hanlon is gone for the weekend, deep into Yeller, and he's only coming back in time for the 9:30 Sunday-morning service at All Saints in Big Sky. So if you two want to step in for your friends and make sure they get married, you'll come back Monday morning *on time* and we'll forget this silly wallet business even happened."

"Yes, ma'am," whispered Sam, duly chagrined. Now *his* cheeks tingled with an uncomfortable flush.

The secretary plunked back down on her stool and turned her attention to the computer screen in front of her. "Monday. 10:25 a.m. That's the earliest I can do."

Jenny nodded. "Yes. Thank you. Yes, ma'am. We're grateful."

"No," said Sam. "Monday won't work. My plane ticket

is for tomo—" Faced with two sets of furious eyes, he took a deep breath. "Monday it is."

The secretary pursed her lips, narrowing her eyes at Sam with disapproval. "Wouldn't hurt you a bit to stick around for a day or so, son. I imagine it might even do you some good."

"Mmm," hummed Sam, "I can't wait."

***

Jenny was *not* happy.

She click-clacked back down the corridor in her uncomfortable high-heeled shoes, clenching her jaw in anger. The way he took out his expensive-looking wallet made her quake with embarrassment. *Big-city ways.*

"Well, that was…unpleasant," she muttered.

"How do you think *I* feel?" he griped. "I have to reschedule my flight."

Not my problem, thought Jenny. *And definitely all your fault.*

"Good luck with that," she snarked, stopping at the lobby coatrack and pulling her parka from a hanger.

It surprised her when he took the coat from her, holding it by the shoulders to help her. She paused for a beat, annoyed that he wanted to help her. But heck, the faster she got her coat on, the faster she could go home. She punched her arms into the sleeves, and he tucked the collar around her shoulders, lifting her hair off her neck, where it was trapped.

"Hey!" She whipped around, surprised by such an intimate gesture.

He put his palms up in the universal sign of surrender,

though his eyes flicked briefly to her chest before skimming back to her angry face.

"Sorry, ma'am…" he drawled. "Just trying to help."

Oooo! He's so danged full of himself!

He was doing that "charming" thing again that he'd tried with the secretary, and it wasn't working any better with her. She zipped up the coat and crossed her arms over her chest, her brows knitted in consternation.

"I think you've done enough to *help* today. I'll see you back here on Monday."

She turned away from him and started for the doors.

"Wow!" he called from behind her, his voice practically reverberating in the small lobby. "You're *something*! Without me, you would have been sprawled out on the floor twenty minutes ago. I don't remember a 'thank you,' come to think of it. Since the second I arrived—"

"Well!" she said, spinning around to spear him with a furious glare. "Maybe if you'd been on time, I wouldn't have slipped on the floor, which got progressively worse while I waited for you. You want a thank you? Thank you for *that*."

"Ohhhhh. I see. It's *my* fault you fell into me."

"*You* were late!"

"You're a real piece of work, lady. I said I was sorry for being late. Like, a thousand times."

"Well, that and a dollar'll buy me a pop."

He recoiled as though smacked. "Have you even *noticed* how bad the weather is outside?"

"Yes!" she cried. "Yes, I have. In fact, I was *watching* it get worse while I sat on a bench *waiting* for you, and now I'm real *excited* to drive home in it. So *thanks* for that too."

He whistled low, shaking his head back and forth. "Okay. For the last time, I am *sorry* for being so late. Sorry. Sorry, okay? Last thing I'd want to do is let Kris down."

"Well, I'd hate to know what the *first* thing you want to do is!"

"Wow, you're—" He ran a hand through his hair, his face finally as irritated as hers. "You're *snippy*. And *bitter*. You are a snippy and bitter person!"

Snippy. Bitter. Ouch.

She took a deep breath, too mad to feel hurt.

"Actions have consequences. I missed a day of school. My students missed an important review for their midterms. We missed the appointment for Kris and Ingrid. It was hard enough to come up here and do this in the first place, and now it's just going to hang over me all weekend. And I'll have to miss another day of school on Monday doing it all again."

He stared at her with his hands on his hips and his brows furrowed. "I didn't realize…"

"And if you want the truth," she added, "I'm embarrassed that I slipped and crashed into you, and I don't *like* driving in bad weather if I can avoid it." She gulped, her fury losing steam. "For the record, I'm not *bitter*. I'm just…*upset*."

He raised his eyebrows, about to say something, then shook his head.

"Listen, we got off to a bad start, right? I think we can both agree on that. Let's start over. Again." She had been expecting a snappy retort, so she was surprised when he offered her a small, genuine smile. "How about I take you to dinner? To make up for everything? Looks like I'm staying the weekend."

Jenny eyed him warily. "I don't think so."

"Come on," he cajoled. "I'm Kristian's cousin. I can't be *that* bad. I'm just...unaccustomed to your aggressive Montana weather patterns. Dinner. It's the least I can do."

"I'm not hungr—" she started to say, but just at that moment, her stomach—*traitor!*—growled, so instead, she rolled her eyes with a sigh, conceding defeat. "Okay, fine. Besides, we need to write to Ingrid and Kris. They probably think they're already married."

"I'm sure there's somewhere around here to have dinner. I have my iPad with me—"

"Oh, I can't stay *here*. I have to get home. I have a puppy, and she's been alone too long. She needs a walk. We can have dinner after that."

Sam shrugged. "That's fine. I'm a free agent. I checked out of my hotel in Bozeman this morning. I guess I could come stay in—"

"Gardiner."

"—Gardiner...for the weekend."

She cocked her head to the side and looked—*really looked*—at his face for the first time. When he wasn't trying so hard to be charming or funny, his eyes were kind. He was several inches taller than she—as tall as her brothers, even—but his hair was a redder blond than theirs. Long lashes gave his brown eyes a softer look than the rest of his face, which was angular and chiseled.

He's handsome. Really handsome. Ingrid was right about that.

She inhaled deeply, closing her eyes as she held the breath, then opening them as she exhaled.

"Okay," she said. "It's not far. You can follow me. I'll take you to the Lone Wolf Lodge on the way home. It's the…nicest."

"Sure. And we can meet up after you walk…"

"Casey," she said.

"Sounds good."

She would expect someone from the city to complain about how staying the weekend in off-the-beaten-path Gardiner, Montana, was inconvenient or cramped his style. But here he was, asking to take her out to dinner, not raising any objections to following her back to her hometown.

Maybe she didn't have his number, after all.

And that single thought made her smile at him for the first time—like he was someone *worth* smiling for. Then she turned and headed out the door.

***

Sam's pulse quickened.

Well, *that* was unexpected.

He was totally caught off guard by the impact of Jenny's smile.

From the moment he'd met her, she'd been snippy, prickly, bitter, and punitive—a cold, uptight schoolmarm who, he was *quite* sure, didn't have a man in her life, warming her bed.

But then she smiled. And it was impossible not to see

the potential behind the sudden transformation.

When Jenny Lindstrom wasn't pissed off? She was a knockout.

He watched as she made her way down the courthouse steps. Her long blonde hair fell halfway down her back, and his hands tingled, remembering the silky softness when he lifted it off her neck.

Why did I do that?

He hadn't even realized what he was doing until she whipped around, her eyes shooting daggers at him. At the time, it had somehow seemed the most natural gesture in the world.

Once in his rental car, he made a mental note to call Hertz and extend the contract for another few days, then pulled up behind her in front of the courthouse. She waved to him in the rearview mirror, and they started the trip to Gardiner.

Turning on the radio to some Carrie Underwood wannabe, he tried to get his head around the events of the past half hour. Nothing had turned out as he'd expected.

He had *expected* to meet some meek country gal, stand politely next to her, say whatever words were required of him, shake her hand good-bye, then drive the two hours back to Billings to catch his flight home to Chicago in the morning.

Instead, Jenny Lindstrom had literally fallen into his life, and now he was bound for someplace called Gardiner with a woman who was—in her own fresh-faced way—one of the prettiest girls he'd ever met.

Prickly and pretty.

Well, it's only for a weekend. Maybe she'll chill out a little. Anyway, it's for Kris. Be nice. Maybe the—what was it?—the Lone Wolf Lodge will have Wi-Fi.

The vocalist on the radio stopped screeching, and Sam grinned when Patsy Cline's honeyed voice filled the car. His parents had often played her music on long car trips when he was little, and he loved her husky voice. While Patsy sang about falling to pieces, he thought about what he would say in his email to Kris.

When he'd received Kristian's email last week, asking that Sam stand in as proxy for Kristian's wedding to Ingrid, there was no way he could say no to his favorite cousin. Sam had a ton of vacation time piled up anyway, and it was a slower time of year at the investment firm where he had worked since graduating from college seven years before. People rarely made significant financial investments before the holidays, so it was one of the better times to take a day off.

After he read Kristian's email, Sam had consulted the internet to confirm that "double proxy marriage" actually existed. It sounded like the implausible plot of a bad movie: two people who couldn't be at the same place at the same time could be married legally if they designated two other people—proxies—to take their vows *for* them.

Sure enough, Wikipedia had confirmed that double proxy marriage was a real thing, though Sam had to reread the article twice to understand. Apparently, it was a completely legitimate, little-known legal loophole that existed only in Montana, almost exclusively utilized by servicemen and women—like Kristian and his fiancée Ingrid—deployed to different parts of the world. With Kristian in active service in Afghanistan and Ingrid serving at an army hospital in Germany, their only option for an expedited marriage would be a double proxy ceremony in Montana.

For the young couple, it was a welcome solution to a *growing* problem: a short, passionate weekend leave two months ago in Germany had resulted in the happy but unexpected news that a baby was on the way, which meant a wedding needed to happen. Immediately. Kristian's family wasn't exactly the modern, understanding prototype when it came to matters of propriety: right is right, and if you're having a baby, then you'd *best* be married.

Kristian had explained that generally the lawyer expediting the marriage would "supply" proxies, but Ingrid was beside herself with the thought of strangers taking their vows for them. He asked if Sam would stand in for him and said Ingrid would find someone to stand in for her. Sam had replied immediately that he would be happy to go to Montana to help out. Aside from the fact that he loved his cousin, Sam was living it up in Chicago while Kristian was putting his life on the line in Afghanistan. Without calculating the cost, making travel plans, asking for the time off, or figuring out any other details, Sam said yes right away. Refusing to help simply never occurred to him.

Of course, that was *before* meeting Jenny Lindstrom.

Chapter 2

Jenny flicked a glance to her rearview mirror.

Sam's rental car followed at a reasonable distance behind her.

She turned her eyes back to the road, but her shoulders slumped in self-reproach, and she shook her head. After having a few minutes on her own, she was wishing she'd handled things differently with Sam.

Bitter.

What an ugly word.

She sighed, frowning at her reflection in the windshield. She'd made assumptions about Sam, merely based on the fact that he was from Chicago. He was right: she'd acted like a snippy, short-tempered priss, and in retrospect, she wasn't positive he'd deserved it.

"Oh, God," she moaned, cringing at the thought of plowing into him, then hanging onto his coat like a lunatic.

Yes, she'd been genuinely irritated that he arrived so late, but he had apologized right away.

And after all, it wasn't *his* fault the judge had decided to leave early for a weekend in the park.

He wasn't accustomed to Montana's version of winter, apparently, but what out-of-towner could be expected to know how quickly the weather could change here?

The bottom line was that he came here to do a favor for his cousin and had traveled a long way to see it through. He certainly hadn't set out to annoy *her* as his life's mission, and she'd treated him as though he had.

She cringed at her behavior, wincing as she remembered enunciating the words Mon-tan-a and win-ter-time as if he were a moron.

Badly done, Jen. Unkind.

If she was honest about it, the whole business of taking someone else's wedding vows on their behalf was extremely unsettling to Jenny and had been from the first time Ingrid mentioned it. In Jenny's mind, vows *that* sacred should only be said once, and certainly not on behalf of someone else. But she was stuck between a rock and a hard place. She couldn't refuse Ingrid's request for help, no matter how much it bothered her.

Anyway, the bottom line was that she had no right to take out her misgivings on Sam. She shook her head, as much in anger toward herself as in frustration for the entire situation.

The setting sun out her right window colored the sky with oranges, pinks, and lavenders. Usually she would take a moment to admire the beauty of another stirring Montana sunset, but it was entirely lost on her this afternoon as she muddled through her thoughts.

If she forced herself to be honest, there was another reason that she was uncomfortable around Sam: the handsomer the man, the sharper her prickles. And poor Sam was very, very handsome.

Despite the fact that Jenny had three older brothers—*or maybe because of it*—she'd never been totally comfortable around boys. As an awkward and painfully shy teenager, Jenny admired the boys in her high school from afar, having unknown, unrequited crushes, but she was too introverted to actually date anyone. She preferred the safe embrace of her small-town church and protective, loving family over the uncertainty and potential heartache of actually falling for someone.

As a college student, she had let her guard down a few times, only to be disappointed by clumsy embraces and grabby touching. Part of her craved an intimate relationship, but it seemed that her blonde, blue-eyed looks; larger-than-normal breasts; and curvy hips attracted the wrong sort of guy.

And immediately after college? Well. Her whole world had suddenly changed. Her family became her top priority, bar none, and any interest in dating dropped from cautious to nonexistent. She became a turtle person, scared of the world, hiding in a prickle-covered shell that was increasingly uncomfortable and claustrophobic for her but had become so much a part of who she was and how she saw herself, she didn't know how to escape it.

That didn't mean, however, that Jenny was content to be alone. She wanted someone to love her. She wanted to have children. She longed for those things with an almost painful yearning.

But those things are hard to find when your first instinct is to push eligible men away.

And nobody ever really called her out on it. She'd protect herself by being snippy, and men would stay out of her way. Until now. Sam was *in her way*, literally following her home. He had pushed back. He had stood up to her and called her "bitter," that awful, terrible word reserved for dried-up spinsters who have lost hope—and worst of all, she deserved it.

He thinks you're bitter, but inside you're not.

Inside, you're soft, like a turtle's tummy.

Inside, you're warm, like a favorite down comforter.

Inside, you want someone to love you, but you're scared that if you love someone, they'll leave you…and experiencing that kind of pain again would break you.

But I've been protecting what's in inside so dutifully, for so long, my prickly shell is the first thing that people see.

Is that what I want?

She looked back in the rearview mirror and could almost make out the shape of his head inside the car through the glare of the setting sun.

No. It's not.

Swallowing over the lump in her throat, she sat up straighter.

Can I change?

Yes, I can.

How strange that someone she barely knew could hold a mirror before her with the use of a single, sad word.

I can show him that I'm not…bitter.

How mollifying that she had a whole weekend to prove

21

him wrong.

***

The small, silver-blue SUV in front of him was about the most uptight, girly SUV he had ever seen.

He could see her blonde head poking just an inch or so above the headrest, the result of impeccable posture, no doubt. She was probably that no-nonsense type of woman who always sat like there was a rod in her spine.

And possibly up her ass, he mused, recalling her sour face and clipped manners.

Not that he didn't admire her backbone. Grudgingly, he had to admit he did. Most girls he knew didn't speak their minds as directly as she did. Women were enigmas to him; they'd say one thing and mean something completely different, and he often had a difficult time reconciling the two. But he got the feeling that Jenny said what she meant and meant what she said. It was refreshing—no wasting time trying to figure out if a coy yes really meant *yes* or some cryptic version of *maybe*. After years around more sophisticated, urban girls, he found her candid manners intriguing.

He attributed her persona largely to her small-town upbringing. She was a country girl through and through: honest, fresh, wholesome, and extremely uptight. She didn't seem very worldly, but she sure was genuine.

He thought of her standing there in that shapeless, fake-fur-adorned, puffy parka while she gave him hell and smiled to himself.

She's a corker, that's for sure.

He thought about her barreling into him as he walked into the lobby of the courthouse. Through his wool coat, he could feel her full breasts pressed against him, all the more pronounced because she had fallen into him with such force and was taking gulping breaths to steady herself. And while her sweater-dress had been perfectly modest, the material clung to her chest in such a way that it—*blessedly*—hadn't left much to the imagination.

In fact, before she had turned into a cross between the Pillsbury Doughboy and Nanook of the North in the space of one zip, he'd taken a quick look at her *heavenly handfuls*. His palm twitched with the way his thoughts were headed. Her breasts would be soft and real. She was all natural, from the color of her hair, to her trim waist, to her perfect rear, which had proved a pretty unsettling distraction as he followed her up the courthouse stairs.

Too bad she was so sharp tongued, because he could think of some better uses for that tongue other than slinging barbs at guys she barely knew.

Yes, he appreciated that he'd messed up her day—and her Monday too, for that matter—but it wasn't as though he'd intentionally arrived late to screw up her weekend.

Then again, Sam thought of her cheeks coloring bright pink as they shook hands. There might be a lot of bluster to Jenny Lindstrom, but she wasn't quite as tough as she wanted him to think she was. He wondered if she was just tightly wound or a little crazy, and if he had to spend the weekend around her, he hoped for the former.

As he turned up the volume for the next Patsy song, he

caught sight of her red taillights zigzagging in his peripheral vision and—

WHOA!

Oh, crap!

Suddenly, Jenny's SUV was spinning out in front of him.

"No! Oh, God! Oh, my God!" Sam yelled.

He clutched at the steering wheel with a white-knuckled grip, watching her car spin across the outside lane. Once. Twice. She gained momentum, and he watched in horror as she slid sideways closer and closer to the guardrail. "Stooooooooop!"

Thank God the snowy grass slowed her down, and he watched as the car rumbled to a stop just inches from the thick, metal rail separating the highway from a dense forest.

Help her!

He slowed down, shifted lanes, and pulled over.

Stopping his car behind hers—*her car is facing the wrong way*—he unbuckled as fast as he could, threw open the door of his rental, and ran the few snowy steps to her car, peering in through her window.

She stared straight ahead, hands clenching the steering wheel, unmoving.

"Jenny!" he shouted. "Jenny, are you okay?"

She didn't move. Didn't even flinch.

She's in shock.

Opening her door as slowly and calmly as possible, Sam tried to steady his own worried breathing. He squatted down on the ground beside her. In case she was in shock or disoriented, he didn't want to frighten her.

"Jenny?" he asked quietly, urgently. He cleared his throat softly, then wrapped his hand around the wrist closest to him. "Jenny, can you hear me?"

She gasped loudly, breathing in audibly, painfully, as though she hadn't taken a breath since her car stopped moving, as though his touch had woken her up from a living nightmare. She exhaled a sob, which released the stiff tension in her shoulders, and they started shaking.

He covered her hands, gently loosening her claw-like grip from the steering wheel.

"Are you okay?"

He wished he knew her better so he'd best know how to help her, what to say to comfort her. Holding her hands in his, he tried to rub the warmth back into them. She was crying now, sobbing in a heartbreaking way that made Sam feel even more helpless.

"It's okay. You're okay," he said, squatting beside her, still holding her hands in his.

She shook her head back and forth, as much from shivering as in answer to his question. He gently let go of her hands and shrugged out of his heavy coat in one smooth movement, leaning back down to drape it clumsily across her chest and lap.

"You're shaking."

"I—I couldn't stop."

"I know. It was black ice." He patted her shoulder. "You spun out. Did you see it?"

She breathed in deeply, shakily, her sobs finally

subsiding.

"N-No. I d-didn't know what happened." She sniffled, looking at Sam to her left and wiping tears off her cheeks with her palms. She took another ragged breath, then sighed loudly, leaning her head back against the headrest and closing her eyes. "I'm sorry."

"For what? You didn't…die. I mean, you—you didn't hurt anyone. There's nothing to be sorry for!"

Jenny stared at his face for a moment and then crumpled, shoulders shaking all over again.

Nice job, Sam. Way to be a comfort. Mentioning death. Yep. Terrific work.

He reached out to stroke her arm and realized with a start that the noises she was making didn't sound exactly like crying. *Hold on.* It sounded like a cross between crying and…*laughing?* Yeah. She was…laughing. And crying, of course, but laughing. Too.

"I meant—I meant the way I treated you at the courthouse," she clarified. "That's what I was thinking about right before my car—"

"Oh!" Sam's forehead wrinkled. *She almost had an accident, and that's what she's concerned about? Being snippy at the courthouse? Hmm. Could she have a concussion?* He spoke slowly and carefully, patting her shoulder. "That's okay. Don't worry about that now."

"I was awful."

"I was late."

"I was unforgiving."

"I shouldn't have called you names."

"Maybe I deserved it," she said, sighing softly.

"You know what, Jenny?" he suggested. "We'll take a mulligan, okay?"

"A-A mulligan?"

Sam nodded. "In golf. If your first shot stinks, you're allowed to take a second shot. A second chance. It's called a mulligan."

"A mulligan." She took a deep, shaky breath. "Okay. That's good. I'd like a mulligan."

"You got it. Fresh start." He stood up and stared down at her. "Are you okay? Did you hit your head at all? Did you—"

"No." She sat up a little straighter and clicked the seat belt to finally release it, rubbing a spot on her chest where it must have pressed hard into her skin. "No. I'm okay. I didn't hurt myself. The airbag didn't even…I'm fine, Sam. Just a little—"

"Shaken up." He offered her a sympathetic smile.

She nodded, and tears filled her eyes again as she bit her lower lip. "You're being very kind, and I was so terrible…"

"Jenny. I was an hour late. We missed the appointment, and the weather got worse. You had a right to be upset, okay?" His face softened. "Anyway, we're taking a mulligan, remember?" Suddenly, his fear for her came out in a rush. "I was worried. It happened so fast. You could have—" He paused. "You were lucky."

Jenny swiped a tear rolling down her cheek and nodded again.

Sam leaned closer to the car and took her hand from

her cheek. It wasn't as tense now. Almost pliant, but still cold, he rubbed it between his until he realized she was trying to gently but firmly pull it away. The blotchiness on her face was deepening to an even pink.

She swallowed, pushing his coat away. "Let me give you back your—"

"Are you sure? It's warm."

"It is. Thank you for it. But I have my own. In the back."

Moving quickly, Sam opened her back door and grabbed the parka from the floor where it lay tossed and crumpled.

"Easy now," he reminded her as she stood up. "You could be in shock. Maybe we should have your car towed, and I'll drive us both back to Gardiner."

"No. I'm okay, Sam." She spoke clearly and decisively but softened her delivery with a smile, then stepped into the coat as he held it for her. She zipped it up and pulled the hood over her head. The white fur framed her face, and her eyes were even bluer after crying. "I've spun out before. Lots of times. I don't know why it got me so upset this time."

"Hey, it's pretty upsetting to lose control like that. You're entitled to some nerves. You think you're okay to drive?"

Jenny nodded. "I do. Truly."

"Sure?"

She gave him a small smile and nodded.

"Okay, then. We'll take it slow." Sam turned, heading to his car.

"Sam?"

He faced her, eyebrows raised.

"I'm grateful to you," she whispered, her face soft and vulnerable, her eyes earnest.

He smiled at her again before returning to his car.

***

It took Jenny a few turns to get her car pointed back in the right direction. Back on the interstate, she took it easy, driving slower than she normally would.

She *was* shaken up.

She couldn't remember the moment she had lost control of her car, but she had let up on the gas and remembered not to slam on the brakes as soon as she realized that the car wasn't responding. Mostly she just held onto the steering wheel with an iron grip so that regardless of what the car was doing, she wouldn't make it worse by jerking the wheel.

Her heart was finally slowing down, and her breathing was returning to normal, but the adrenaline rush left her eyes heavy and thick, and she rolled down her window, thankful for the bracing gust of cold air against her burning cheeks.

Jenny had been in several spinouts in her life. No one could live her whole life in Montana and not hit a patch of black ice now and then, but truth be told, she hadn't had an accident in several years—certainly not since her mother's death. The thought of her father and brothers having to face *her* loss after suffering so brutally through the loss of her mother made her wince. Stinging tears sprang back up, unwanted, in her eyes.

No more crying, Jenny. Nothing happened. You're fine.

She looked in her rearview mirror and was comforted to see Sam following behind.

He probably thought she was a crazy woman: crying, then laughing, then apologizing for her behavior at the courthouse, all while clutching onto his coat on the side of the road.

But, Lord, she couldn't let him think she was the snippy, acidic person he thought she was, and apologizing seemed more important than anything else in that moment.

The sound of his rumbling baritone saying her name had imprinted itself on her brain, and she listened for his voice in her head, savoring its warm concern. He had spoken to her so gently, his brown eyes so earnest and solicitous of her. Holding her hands. Giving her his coat. Giving her a mulligan. *I was worried.*

Jenny shook her head, ashamed of herself. She had misjudged Sam from the start.

She promised not to make that mistake again.

Pulling into the parking lot of the Lone Wolf Lodge, Jenny idled for a moment as Sam parked his car and walked the short distance over to her. She rolled down her window.

"You sure you're okay?" he asked.

"Yes. I was just a little shaken up is all. My car's fine. I'm fine. Really." She kept her voice as polite and controlled as possible, offering him a poised smile. Certainly he had had enough of her hysterics for one afternoon. "Thanks for everything, Sam."

"No problem." He cocked his head to the side. "Do

you want to call me after you walk Casey? When you're ready for dinner?"

"Sure," she said, handing him her phone. "Put your number in here."

He pressed in the digits, then hooked a thumb toward the motel office, swinging his bag onto his shoulder with masculine ease. "I'll see you later, okay?"

"Sounds good."

She rolled up the window and pulled out of the parking lot, trying to ignore the butterflies in her stomach as she watched him amble away.

Sam. She had a quick flashback to Sam's concerned brown eyes, to the way his hand circled her wrist to pry it off the steering wheel. A shiver went down her spine as awareness spread warmly through her middle. Although she would trade the reason it ended up there, she *liked* feeling his skin touching hers.

Once home, she took off her heels and stockings and carefully hung her gray dress on a hanger and put it back in her closet. She took out her favorite jeans, a white turtleneck, and an old Norwegian sweater that used to be her mother's. It felt good to be out of those Sunday clothes, and besides, she needed a hug from her mom after the day she'd had. Wearing her sweater was the only way Jenny would get one.

Noen elsket meg en gang. Jeg er velsignet.

She crossed her arms over her chest, opposite hands touching opposite shoulders, and breathed deeply in and out, taking her time, finding her mother's face in her mind and focusing on it. She closed her eyes as she inhaled and reopened them as she exhaled, just as her mother taught her. She whispered the Norwegian words over and over like a mantra or a prayer.

Noen elsket meg en gang. Jeg er velsignet.
Someone loved me once. I am blessed.

Calmer and more centered as she headed into the kitchen, Jenny slipped her feet into thick rubber snow boots while Casey whined from her pen.

She adopted the golden retriever puppy shortly before Thanksgiving and was still amazed by how much having a pet had changed her life. She had to come home from school at lunch to walk her, and days like today, when she was out of town, meant finding someone else to look in on her. Housebreaking the puppy was proving challenging, and at least one of Jenny's slippers had been ruined by Casey's razor-sharp baby teeth. But there was nothing quite like coming home to a puppy, whose wiggly body and wet hellos took the edge off of a bad day and just made a good day better.

"Come on, Casey," she said as she lifted the puppy out of her pen, rubbing their noses together with delight. Puppies' paws always smelled like Fritos. Jenny loved that.

Casey wriggled and squirmed, trying to lick and gnaw on Jenny's nose, thrilled to see her owner but angry to have been left alone so long.

Jenny giggled. "Quit it, you! Mamma's had a rough day, Little Bit!"

She pulled Casey's bright red leash from the hook and snapped it securely to her dark-green collar. She would have to change out the colors after Christmas, but for now, Casey looked like the perfect little Christmas puppy she was.

Jenny snapped a tiny plaid jacket around Casey's wiggling body and then shrugged into her own parka. She didn't bother zipping it up; it was only 35 degrees, unusually balmy for early December in Montana.

As puppy and owner started down the stairs from their apartment above the Prairie Dawn Café & Bookstore, Jenny looked out onto Main Street. The sun was low in the sky now and gave an Old West, sepia tint to the small town of Gardiner.

Jenny had lived here all her life, like her parents before her and grandparents and great-grandparents before them. A small town located in the southernmost part of Montana on the Wyoming border, Gardiner was also the northernmost entrance to Yellowstone National Park, which meant a brisk tourist business year round, but especially from May to September. Jenny's father owned and operated a small but highly reputable tour-group business that took small groups into the park for custom-designed excursions, depending on the interests of the tourists. Hot springs groups, wild animal–viewing groups, hikers, leaf peepers. Her father's schedule was always busy.

The town itself offered more amenities than other places in Montana as a result of its connection with and proximity to Yellowstone. There were several shops offering tackle and bait for fly-fishing on the Yellowstone River, a saddler's shop, a camping and outdoor store, a bookstore, an internet café, and several boutiques and restaurants. There was only one pharmacy in town, but it carried DVDs if you wanted some entertainment.

As they strolled, Jenny's attention was captured by two men arranging a banner between streetlights on opposite sides of the street and read the words "Gardiner Annual Christmas Stroll Saturday, December 2."

Tomorrow night! I'd almost forgotten!

Jenny loved the Christmas Stroll, but she'd been so distracted with Ingrid's news and request, she had forgotten all about it. She smiled with anticipation, enjoying deep gulps of clean mountain air.

She passed Joe's Lodge on her right and waved to her brother Erik, who was working at the bar. Erik was the youngest of her brothers, though still older than Jenny by sixteen months. She briefly considered stopping in to tell Erik about the spinout. Yes, she'd get a big hug's worth of brotherly sympathy, but it would just worry him unnecessarily. Plus, the boys didn't know about Ingrid's proxy wedding, and she wasn't ready to explain all about it. He gestured for her to come in, but she pointed to Casey, shook her head, and shrugged. He mouthed, "See you on Sunday," and she nodded and waved, continuing on her way.

Casey pulled her across the Yellowstone River Bridge and by the Grizzly Guzzle Grill, where she briefly admired the cheerful blinking lights and Santa scene in the window. Her brother Lars suddenly appeared on the other side of the window, surprising her with a funny face. She shook her head and giggled, waving a quick hello as Casey pulled her forward with puppy enthusiasm. As they neared the arch to

Yellowstone, Jenny was breathless, begging the puppy to slow down.

At the Roosevelt Arch, Casey obediently turned around to head home—she knew the routine—but Jenny regarded the monument for an extra moment, trying to see it through the eyes of a visitor instead of a lifelong resident.

President Teddy Roosevelt himself had laid the cornerstone of the massive stone arch in 1903, as Jenny had been told many times by her parents, grandparents, and even great-grandmother, who had lived until Jenny was six years old and remembered attending the ceremony on the actual day with lifelong pride.

What will Sam think of Gardiner? she wondered.

Jenny loved Gardiner—and all of Montana, for that matter—with her whole heart, but she had no illusions about where she lived and would make no excuses for it. With just shy of one thousand citizens and a downtown area smaller than Soldier Field, Gardiner was a universe away from Chicago. But it was a good, solid place to live with kind people who cared if you lived or died…and didn't that matter more than the bright lights of a big city?

She walked home at a leisurely pace, making Casey heel so she can mull this over. It's not that she wouldn't like to see other places. She had visited Billings many times, of course, and she had attended college at the University of Great Falls, where she had spent four memorable years. But even Billings and Great Falls couldn't compare with Chicago, which was fine with Jenny.

It didn't really matter what Sam or any other visitor

thought about Gardiner. Deep in Jenny's heart, she knew: Montana would always be home.

Chapter 3

Sam stood in the doorway of his room and made a face as he thought of the Four Seasons, where the company put him up whenever he was out of town on client business.

This room, at the best spot in town, according to Jenny, was small and drab with a polyester patchwork bedspread covering the double bed and very little in the way of amenities or decoration.

"Whatever," he muttered, telling himself to be grateful there was a room available at all.

He plopped down on the lumpy bed, lying back and shuddering as his mind replayed Jenny's car spinning across the highway lanes. She could have been seriously injured or worse.

My God, what if—what if—

The flashback came on swiftly.

He hadn't been as fortunate as Jenny.

His car had crashed into a guardrail on a major highway in October, and he had suffered two broken ribs and a concussion, which required several days of hospitalization for observation. Luckily, aside from being a little banged up and pretty sore at the time, he was good as new now. He only felt a slight, occasional twinge in his chest as the rib healed completely.

The accident itself had scared him, though, and had additionally acted as a wake-up call, making him rethink his life and the path he was on.

Suddenly, Pepper's face flashed through his mind.

He and Pepper had broken up soon after the accident, five months shy of their two-year anniversary. He'd known all along that she wasn't "the one," but he'd held onto her because she was scorching hot and he knew a breakup would be messy.

Besides, he'd loved the looks from other men as they walked into a posh gala or entered a club or bar of her choosing. He could feel all those chumps eyeing Pepper, then turning their gazes to him in wonder. What did he have that they didn't? How come he could get a girl like that?

The truth?

Sure, Pepper was stunning—like, just-walked-out-of-a-magazine perfect—and insanely sexy…but she was also an expensive, whiny, demanding girlfriend, with a little added sprinkle of crazy for the up-close viewer.

Sam had stayed with her for so long because he liked the powerful way he felt with her on his arm. He had been promoted to vice president while dating Pepper, and although the advancement was outwardly based wholly on merit, Sam suspected that his girlfriend's local celebrity status hadn't exactly hurt his business prospects. The firm seemed to like having a young associate dating such a well-known local news and Instagram personality.

And if Sam was totally honest? He'd have to admit that

the sex was explosive, especially in the beginning. Pepper was adventurous, and they got a little rough sometimes in a hot, exciting way. But after two years, even *that* part of their relationship had gotten mechanical and stale. Toward the end, those nights lying next to Pepper were the emptiest of his life.

He sat up, thinking about the girl he met today and chuckling softly.

Jenny and Pepper couldn't be more different.

He thought about Jenny sitting in the driver's seat staring straight ahead after the spinout, looking more like a scared teenager than the pinched, snippy schoolteacher who'd dressed him down repeatedly at the courthouse. She'd looked so young, so frightened.

His need to comfort Jenny had thrown any initial feelings about her out the proverbial window. And when she'd apologized for her earlier behavior, it had definitely thrown him for a loop. It didn't change the fact that she was still, essentially, an uptight, small-town bumpkin, but she wasn't as bad as he thought. Small town or not, she was prettier every time he looked at her. Sam looked down at his hands, remembering them spanning her tiny waist and then shook his head, willing thoughts of her away. He wasn't interested in letting her under his skin.

He changed into jeans and a sweat shirt, grabbed his laptop, and decided to make his way back to the small lobby, which had a sitting area with a fireplace. Nothing fancy, but he could catch up on some emails using the hotel's Wi-Fi there. Anyway, even the lobby sitting area had to be better than his dumpy, depressing room.

Walking outside, he noticed a sign with an arrow pointing to the back of the motel that read "Yellowstone River." Hmm. Why not take a look before the sunlight disappeared completely?

Sam had grown up in Chicago, yes, but he'd also spent just about every New Year's Eve of his childhood at his aunt and uncle's Montana lodge betting Kristian whether or not they'd get a glimpse of the northern lights.

It had been years since he'd thought about New Year's Eve in Montana. New Year's in Chicago always included a reliably flashy party, complete with too much champagne and loud, blinding fireworks, a far cry from the simple New Year's Eves of his childhood, spent stealing sips of glögg and looking for Mother Nature's fireworks dancing soundlessly across the inky Montana sky like a high-tech laser show in impossibly vibrant pinks, blues, and greens.

Around the corner of the motel, after a short walk through a brief patch of woods, he found the river, white water rushing over the rocks in a hurry to get somewhere. He could *just* make out the mountains in the distance, black peaks in the dying lavender light.

It was a long time since Sam had visited Montana, but strong, nearly forgotten memories of a happy childhood engulfed him as he breathed in the crisp, fresh air. It was almost as though he was suddenly in the presence of a long-lost friend, whom his heart and mind instantly recognized, despite years apart, and he smiled, looking up at the myriad stars developing in the increasingly dark sky.

He probably should have felt more inconvenienced by the unexpected change in his travel plans, but he didn't. In fact, he was pleased to be back in Montana again, grateful for its timeless, unchanged majesty. He would always have an affection for this wild, untamed state, where seasons and geography were dramatic and intense, demanding respect and attention. So different from Chicago or any other city, where the seasons and geography barely impacted more than your footwear.

It's in my blood, he thought, *this love for Montana. Like my mother and her folks too. It will always feel good to return.*

***

When Jenny and Casey got back to her apartment, Jenny checked herself out in the mirror, chastised herself for vanity, and then called Sam.

"Hello?" his voice rumbled, deep and clear on the line.

"Hi, Sam, it's me."

She was nervous. Aside from her brothers or the occasional father of one of her students, Jenny didn't talk to men on the phone very often, and certainly not single men as handsome as Sam.

"Me who?"

"Oh! Um, Jenny?" Why in the world she was phrasing this like a question was beyond her powers of deduction. "Jenny Lindstrom. From today. From th-the courthouse."

"Not ringin' a bell."

"Really? But, um…we—"

Then she heard him chuckling and grimaced. He was teasing her. Again.

41

"Oh! Jennnnnnnnnnny. Yeah. Right. What's up?"

Didn't he say he wanted to take her out to dinner? Or had she just imagined that?

"Um, did you want me to pick you up?"

"Pick me up?"

Jenny bit her lip. *Had she somehow gotten this wrong?* "Are we going, um, to go out to dinner?"

"Are you asking me out?" he asked.

"N-No! No! I thought you asked to—never mind. Crossed wires. I'll just—"

He chuckled again. "Jenny Lindstrom, of course I know who you are, and I would love to take you out to dinner. If you're still free tonight, that is."

Dang, but his laughter was contagious.

"Well, now I don't know if I am," she said, hoping he couldn't hear the smile in her voice.

"Aww, Jenny. Come on. I promise I won't tease for the rest of the night."

She jumped on that. "Really?"

"Really. No more teasing. And if I do, you get to choose a punishment for my bad behavior."

"It's a deal. I'll be there soon."

She smiled merrily, thinking of "punishments" to fit a big-city blowhard and hanging up before he could take it back.

***

Sam was unexpectedly pleased with the quaint downtown area of Gardiner, walking alongside Jenny on their way to dinner.

The village had a surprising variety of restaurants, probably owing to the proximity to Yellowstone. In certain places, it even felt like a movie set out of an old cowboy picture updated for the twenty-first century. Neon signs cheerfully beckoned folks into western-styled saloons and grills, and storefronts were so authentically Old West, he would have sworn they had been regenerated from abandoned ghost towns.

Jenny seemed to know everyone they passed. He couldn't count the number of times he heard "Hey there, Jenny" or "Hi, teach!" from passersby. Jenny always answered with a cheerful smile and wave, often answering back more personally: "How's the ankle, Clive?" or "Wonderful singing in church last week, Mary Beth."

He also noticed the curious looks *he* received, walking next to her. Some approving, mostly from ladies, who nodded or simpered. Some suspicious, mostly from the men, at least one of whom tried to stare him down as they walked by.

Only one older lady stopped to ask, "Now who's this a'walkin' with you, Jenny?"

Jenny looked up at Sam, then answered the lady with a friendly smile, "Kin of Ingrid Nordstrom's fiancé."

Without another word, the lady stuck out her hand and offered Sam a beaming smile. "Thankey for what your kin's a'doin' out there in Afghanistan."

Sam was caught off guard by her kindness yet was confused by her intimate knowledge of his cousin. Kristian was from a small town five hours north and, as far as Sam knew, had met Ingrid at college and never spent much time in Gardiner. It seemed unlikely the woman would know him.

After she walked on, he looked at Jenny quizzically. "How does she know Kris?"

"She doesn't know him personally." Jenny grinned at him. "But we always remember Kristian and Ingrid at the Grace Church Prayer Circle. We pray for them every week with special supplication for Kristian's safe return."

"That's nice," said Sam.

"It's just what we do," said Jenny matter-of-factly.

It's a wonder that small towns like Gardiner still exist in modern America, thought Sam. Places where everyone knew and looked out for one another.

Beside him, Jenny strolled along, hands in her parka pockets and white earmuffs covering her ears. She was kind to everyone they passed and so effortlessly pretty in her jeans and furry boots. That uncomfortable feeling rolled around in the pit of his stomach again: the beginning of a foreign, instinctually inconvenient feeling he wanted to ignore. He glanced at her again, and it eased.

"Here we are!" Jenny exclaimed, gesturing to another western-styled storefront where a royal-blue neon moon wearing a bandit's mask blinked jauntily overhead. The Blue Moon Raccoon Saloon.

He raised his eyebrows at her and followed her inside.

***

Sam is behaving himself.

It was a shame too, because she had thought of such a terrific punishment for him. *Oh, well*, she sighed, *the night is young.*

"What?" he asked.

She peeked at him over the menu. "Huh?"

"You sighed…nothing look good?"

"Oh." She set down her menu. "No, I love it here. The pizza's very good."

"I tell you what, Jenny." He smiled back at her and closed the grease-stained paper menu, placing it on top of hers. "Your turf, your choice. You order. I'll go along with whatever's good."

"Then I choose pepperoni pizza. It's good. I promise."

A chubby, blonde waitress in a too-tight uniform came over to take their order.

"Heya, Jennnn," she drawled with a guarded expression, chewing her gum like cud. Her bovine eyes flicked to Sam sitting across from Jenny and brightened. "Well, now. Who is *this*?"

"Hi, Missy." Jenny's nose turned up a touch, and she pursed her lips, ignoring the question. *Easy Missy.* She was not introducing her to Sam. Nope. No way. "Large pepperoni and two Cokes, okay?"

"Oh, I'd like a beer, please," Sam interrupted. "What have you got?"

Missy turned her entire body to face Sam and gave him a thousand-megawatt smile.

"I got what-ev-er you want, sugar."

She straightened up and threw her shoulders back, pushing her double-Ds toward his face like twin torpedoes seeking a close-range target.

Sam looked down at the table in embarrassment, and Jenny tilted her head to the side, rolling her eyes and giving Missy a disapproving look…which Missy ignored.

"*Hei-ei-einey*-kin…*Bu-u-u-sch*…" she drawled flirtatiously, drawing out each word as suggestively as possible while she batted her eyelashes and snapped her gum.

"Heineken!" said Sam quickly, looking anywhere but at Missy's bust. "Great. Hei-Heineken is great. Thanks."

"*Heiny*-kin. Mmm-hmm," Missy groaned. "Coming up in a jiff."

She winked at him and lingered for a moment until Jenny cleared her throat loudly.

"Thank you, Missy."

The waitress narrowed her eyes at Jenny, then *humphed* once before she sauntered away.

***

Sam grinned at Jenny's expression.

Her pursed lips made her feelings clear as she watched the eager waitress head over to the bar.

Good girl versus bad girl, he thought, studying Jenny.

Jenny didn't know it, but Sam had no interest in Missy's come-ons. He'd seen it all before. What he hadn't seen in a long time was someone like Jenny—a nice girl, in the traditional sense, like his mother or sisters. And her exasperation with Missy was completely adorable.

"I'm sorry about that, Sam. She is just—"

"It's fine, Jen," he answered, his gaze briefly dropping to her lips as they relaxed.

"No, it's not. It's *disgraceful.* She's always—I mean, she

has just *always* been like that. When we were in seventh, she came to Wednesday-night fellowship with me, but I couldn't find her at the end. Well, when I finally did, she was *doing things* in the coat closet with two boys from Big Sky. She just—I don't know. Some girls are just like that, I guess."

"I guess. Unless boys from Big Sky are especially racy?"

She looked at him, he supposed, to see if he was teasing her, but he kept his face carefully neutral. *No way I'm getting busted for teasing.*

"Not especially," she answered, thinking it over. "I mean, maybe. It's more built up there. No. No, I don't think so. Mostly I know some very nice people from Big Sky," she decided. "Anyway, those two never came back to Wednesday-night fellowship."

He glanced down at the table grinning and swallowed back all the teasing comments he wanted to make, most of which included the observation that they may not have *come* to Wednesday-night fellowship, but Sam was fairly certain they *came* somewhere else. He had promised not to tease her, after all. He didn't realize how tough it was going to be.

"Maybe we could write those emails while we wait?" she asked, stealing his attention.

Missy returned with their drinks, and although Jenny's icy expression didn't invite further conversation, she winked boldly at Sam before sauntering away. He just nodded curtly in thanks. *No point in ruffling Jenny's feathers.*

"Sure. What should we say?" he asked, placing his iPhone on the table.

She sipped her Coke and considered, drawing

concentric circles with her finger on the table. Her blonde hair was pulled back in a low ponytail, and his eyes followed it across her shoulder to where it ended right above her right breast. His eyes lingered there, distracted, until her voice jolted him back to their conversation.

"We don't have to tell them it was your fault. We could maybe tell a little white lie"—her face colored—"and say Judge Hanlon left early for the park. Sun sets so early now, he'd have to leave midafternoon to have a few good hours." She paused, shrugging sheepishly. "I wouldn't want them to be mad at you."

He looked up at her pretty face, big blue eyes wide with a mixture of chagrin and compassion.

There you go surprising me, Jenny Lindstrom.

She certainly didn't owe him anything. His late arrival at the courthouse had upset her and inconvenienced her life. Heck, if he hadn't been late, it would have been lighter on the drive home, and she wouldn't have hit the black ice patch.

Her kindness touched him.

She looked down, no doubt uncomfortable under his scrutiny, and he watched her draw circles on the table with the pad of her finger before impulsively locking his index finger around hers, forming a link. He rubbed his thumb lightly over her finger.

"Thanks, Jen."

Jenny looked up, her face flushing as she met his gaze. She wet her lips with her tongue, and Sam felt a small jolt of awareness pass through him, watching her, wondering what it would be like to—

She straightened her finger to draw it back gently from his. "Maybe I like you better teasing than serious…"

He chuckled to cover up the direction of his thoughts, then took a long sip of beer. "Does that mean I don't have to watch myself? Teasing is okay now?"

"A deal's a deal." She smiled back at him easily and shook her head. "I wouldn't try it if I were you."

"Such moral high ground from the person suggesting white lies!"

"Are you teasing me?" she demanded playfully.

"Nope! Nope. Just an observation." *Huh. She can be pretty fun when she isn't being so prickly. She's smart. Quick.* Before he found himself roped into washing her car or walking her dog, he decided they should get going on that email. "Okay. We'll say Judge Hanlon left early for 'Yeller' and I was running a little late. The two circumstances left us without an option, and we're headed back on Monday to get married instead."

"To get *them* married instead."

"Of course. That's what I meant." His phone was dark on the table, and he pressed the start button on the bottom. Nothing happened. He pressed it again, and then it dawned on him: he had tried to use it to map himself an alternate route from Bozeman to Livingston while behind the snowplow and must have forgotten to turn off the roaming signal. The battery had died sometime during the afternoon. "Shoot!"

"Dead battery?"

He shook his head back and forth. "'Fraid so."

Could he get nothing *right around this woman? He perpetually looked like an unprepared student.*

She smiled at him. "It's okay. I'll just send them an email from my laptop after dinner."

Of course he trusted Jenny to send something completely appropriate, but as he checked her out across the table, he realized he didn't want their evening to end so soon. "Mind if I come along and we write it together?"

"Don't trust me?" she asked.

"No, it's just—"

"It's fine!" She put her palms up and turned her face away. "Big-city ways. Can't trust anyone."

He thought about telling her the truth: that he didn't want to go back to his cold, dumpy hotel room when he could possibly spend some time with her in what he was sure would be a warm, homey apartment. He pictured somewhere cozy and bright with—

Wait a minute, brother! What's going on with you? She's a prickly little schoolteacher from a tiny town in Montana! Why exactly are you plotting ways to spend more time with her? Are you interested *in her, Sam?*

She was looking around the bar with that pinched expression back on her face.

Interested in her? *No! No way! She's just the only person I know in this one-horse town. And the email! We need to write that email. That's all. Interested? Please. No way.*

Missy returned with their pizza and licked her lips at Sam, her tongue lingering on the corner of her mouth. She sure was trying hard, but she simply wasn't his type.

Jenny took a slice of pizza, and Sam did the same.

"So," he said, because the silence between them was getting uncomfortable, "you grew up with Ingrid?"

Jenny nodded. "Ing's family moved here from Wyoming when she was a baby. I don't ever remember a day of my life without Ingrid in it. We were in the church nursery together, preschool. I was homeschooled, but she always told me the public-school gossip: which boy liked which girl, anyone who got in trouble…" She chuckled lightly. "Even if it was her."

"You were homeschooled?"

"Uh-huh. Me and Erik, my youngest brother. Well, not *the* youngest. *I'm* the baby, but he's the youngest of my three older brothers."

His eyes shot up to her face. "Wait! You've got three older brothers?"

She nodded while wiping at her lips with a paper napkin.

"Cheers to you, Jenny." He raised his beer to her and took a big gulp. "You don't drink alcohol?"

"Not really. Seems like liquor just causes problems."

"If you drink to excess."

"Which so many do."

"Well, no need to be worried on my account. *I* just enjoy a glass now and then."

She mumbled something under her breath.

"What was that?"

"Men will have their vices."

"What does *that* mean?"

"Just something my mother used to say. *'A woman chops and dices; still a man will have his vices.'*"

Sam thought for a minute and then looked up at her, perplexed. "What in the heck does that mean?"

"Actually?" Jenny looked up, her eyes sparkling with amusement as she giggled. "I have no idea! She always said it, and I *never* understood it! But I didn't want her to think I didn't get it!"

Her face was transformed by her merriment, and he chuckled with her, leaning closer. "Is it, like…a woman cooks while a man carouses?"

"Or a woman criticizes while a man indulges?" countered Sam.

"Or a woman works so hard making dinner and then a man doesn't show up for it?" asked Jenny.

"Or a woman threatens the man with violence, but he drinks anyway?"

Jenny was snorting quietly between giggles. "S-Stop. Please. I'm going to ch-choke."

Sam sat back and watched her, his cheeks starting to ache from smiling so much. He pushed her Coke closer to her, and she took a big sip, then wiped her eyes with the back of her hand.

"People are always saying things like that around here. Half the time, I have no idea what they're talking about."

He shook his head at her. "Why don't you ask?"

"I should! No, I can't. I mean, I grew up here. I'm supposed to know what these things mean. Heck, I've even *used* that expression before, and other women have nodded at me like I'm very wise." This confession made her start giggling again, and she looked down at the table, shoulders trembling, trying to compose herself, but Sam heard tiny snorting sounds and knew she was losing the battle.

Sam couldn't quite figure her out. She seemed kind of stuck-up sometimes, but someone who was truly haughty wouldn't be able to laugh at herself like this. Frankly, he couldn't remember the last time he'd had dinner with a woman who just laughed—really *laughed* with genuine amusement—at something funny and self-deprecating.

He couldn't imagine Pepper laughing at anything until tears slipped out of her eyes. Her eyes were always perfectly made up; she wouldn't dare mess them up with a stray tear. Anyway, Pepper didn't find things *funny*; she found them *amusing*. She took life—*her* life, especially—so seriously. Laughing at herself would be unthinkable.

"I'm sorry, Sam." She sniffled and chortled once more, still trying to compose herself. Her eyes were bright and shiny and still full of mirth, and he knew she was on the verge of giggling again, just holding herself back. "You must think I'm crazy."

Actually, I think that under those prickles, you're completely genuine and absolutely adorable.

"Nah, it's okay." He leaned back in his seat, watching her until she sobered under his perusal. "It's nice to hear someone really laugh."

"Oh, I love a good laugh." She cocked her head to the side. "Your friends don't laugh?"

He considered this. Yes, they laughed: at a well-constructed barb at someone else's expense, the shared delight in someone else's misfortune, or a droll observation with a sophisticated, witty delivery. They laughed. But it was different. It was night and day from Jenny's good-natured giggling.

He shrugged noncommittally, turning his attention back to the pizza.

"It's good, right?" She smiled at him shyly, biting into her third piece.

"Yeah," he agreed, smiling at her. "It sure is."

***

It only took fifteen minutes to walk home from the restaurant, but Jenny pointed out various Gardiner points of interest on the way: the restaurant where one of her brothers worked, the road that led across the river to the Roosevelt Arch, and the high school where she worked. They walked over to the bridge, and she paused, holding onto the railing, looking up at the sky.

"I love Montana," he whispered.

"What? You *do*?"

"You never see this many stars in Chicago," said Sam. "Never see this many stars anywhere."

Jenny sighed, nodding in agreement. "When I see a sky like tonight, I always think of early ship navigators, you know? Looking at the sky, trying to figure out where they were headed." She leaned her elbows on the railing, putting her hood up, grateful for the thick down between her arms and the icy, cold iron. "It must have taken such courage, such faith to set sail, relying only on the stars to see them home." She smiled at him, then turned her glance back up to the sky, pointing. "There's the North Star. Polaris. See it? The brightest one that way. If you can find that, you can always find your way."

"Always find my way, huh?"

"Uh-huh. It's a fixed point. If you prefer Shakespeare, it's an '*ever-fixed mark*.' It doesn't move. It doesn't change. If you can find north, you can find your way."

"Shakespeare?"

"It's from one of his sonnets."

"One that you know well, I'm guessing. Go ahead..." His smile encouraged her.

She chuckled nervously and shook her head but spoke the words quietly, staring out at the black river before her. "'Love is not love which alters when it alteration finds, or bends with the remover to remove. O, no. It is an ever-fixed mark.'"

He leaned beside her. "So I'm guessing you teach English."

"No." She shook her head. "Science."

When he chuckled, she gave him a quizzical look. "What?"

"Suits you."

"Are you laughing at me? Teasing me?"

"No! Not at all! Just...stars, navigation...you threw me with the Shakespeare. I had figured science, but then..." He looked back up at the sky. "Sure is pretty."

"The sky or the Shakespeare?"

"Both. Either." He shrugged and smiled at her. "I can't remember the last time someone quoted Shakespeare to me. An 'ever-fixed mark'..."

"Well, maybe there's a frustrated English teacher in here after all." She touched her heart with her hand and grinned at him. "Or maybe just cold winters mean lots of time for reading."

"Reading. Hmmm. I can think of better ways to pass the time—" He cleared his throat. If she didn't know better, she might wonder if he covered a chuckle by clearing his throat. She could hear the controlled humor in his voice when he asked, "And science?"

"Always loved it. I spent a lot of time in the park growing up, and my pappa was always teaching us something about the hot springs, the geography, the animals. Natural fit, I guess, being from here."

He looked back up at the sky. "There's *nowhere* like here."

She turned to him, staring at his profile. "I didn't realize you had such an affection, you know, for here. For Montana. I just assumed—"

He blew into his bare hands, then rubbed them together and stuffed them in his coat pockets. "Sure. I mean, I live in Chicago and my life's there, but I love it here too. Maybe I wasn't clear before, but we drove out to Choteau twice a year like clockwork my whole childhood. Spent a lot of time in Montana as a kid. My mom and Kristian's mom are sisters, and they didn't think a twenty-four-hour drive was reason enough to keep them apart."

"Whew! Twenty-four hours!"

"Yeah. With two older sisters heckling me in the backseat."

"You're the baby too." She smiled at him, fascinated to find they had a bit of common ground when their lives seemed worlds away.

"My aunt Lisabet and her family drove out to Chicago for Thanksgiving and Easter. And we drove out here for *Midsommardagen* and New Year's. Never missed either my entire childhood. No excuse was good enough for my mother, you know? I may not have always loved the drive, but I *always* loved being here."

"You celebrate *Midsommardagen*?"

"Of course! My mother's Swedish. Anyone with a drop of Swedish blood celebrates *Midsommardagen*!"

"My father's Swedish. My mother was Norwegian. She used to say that Midsummer was just an excuse for drunken fools to stay drunk all weekend. But I know she loved everything else about it. She used to braid my hair with flowers on Midsummer morning every year...hers too." She paused, then added quietly, "She...she died."

"I'm sorry."

Jenny nodded wordlessly, looking at the river below while he stood beside her in silence. *Where did that come from?* She didn't generally share her private business with strangers. Then again, Sam didn't feel like a stranger to her, which didn't make a whole lot of sense since she had just met him.

"You still have kin?" she asked, eager to change the subject. "In Choteau?"

"Mmmm," he murmured, his breath coming out of his nose like smoke. "Kristian's family. My aunt. She's alone now. My uncle passed away a few years ago. My cousin Katrin still lives up there somewhere too, but I haven't seen her in years. Kristian and I were really close, more like brothers than cousins. Anyway, I am sure there are other cousins up there too; I just don't know any of them anymore."

"It's not *so* far from here," Jenny observed. "Five hours, I guess. Maybe more if there's snow."

"I won't see them this trip."

"Do you wish you were? Seeing them?"

"I don't know," he admitted. "I loved them, you know, when I was a kid. But my life is very far away from here, Jenny. A whole other world."

She held his eyes for an extra beat before dropping them and nodding that she understood. Whatever she was looking for wasn't there, and she bit her lip with a fleeting, inexplicable melancholy as they started walking again.

Five minutes later, they were back at her apartment.

She took Sam's coat and hung it up on a rack by the front door, and he followed her into the kitchen. Casey wiggled her bottom back and forth wildly in her playpen, whining for attention.

"Wow! Look at you!" Sam walked right over to her and picked her up from her nest of shredded newspaper. She licked his nose and whimpered excitedly. "She's beautiful." Then to Casey, he asked, "Who's a good pup? Who's a good puppy?"

Jenny watched Sam with amusement, surprised by him yet again. Puppies were unpredictable and nippy, liable to piddle down your middle or bite your fingers with their razor-sharp baby teeth, but he had picked her up easily, gently, and now stood in her kitchen with Casey cradled in the nook of his elbow, rubbing her bald puppy belly.

Hmmm. There's more to you than meets the eye, Sam—Sam what?

Holy cow! She still didn't even know his last name!

"Sam, I don't know your last name." She glanced at him, putting four scoops of grounds into the coffeemaker and pressing the on button.

He grinned, still rubbing Casey's tummy. "Kelley. Sam Kelley. Can you believe this broad? She's going to marry me, but she doesn't even know my name!"

Jenny instantly gasped in victory and couldn't help the giggle that escaped her as she turned to him, smiling with glee.

He snapped his head up from Casey, and the look on his face said it all, but she couldn't resist declaring a winner.

"You just broke our deal, Mr. Kelley."

Chapter 4

Damn! She was right. He had slipped up and teased her.

"Oh, come on!" His face was a play in indignation. "I was talking to Casey, not you!"

"Fair's fair," Jenny responded in a singsong voice, moving from the kitchen into the living room where her laptop sat on a coffee table in front of a cheery floral loveseat.

"Okay. Fine. You win. What's my punishment?"

Eyes dropping to her rounded butt in tight jeans, Sam's mind briefly fantasized about having his "punishment" in her bedroom, and his heart kicked into a gallop.

Whoa, boy! Whoa. Quit thinking about her that way!

Jenny sat down on the loveseat and curled her legs Indian-style, pulling the laptop onto her lap while Sam told his mind to shut up.

"Did you notice the big sign hanging over town as we *strolled* home?"

Cute. "Yeah. Something about a Christmas *Stroll?* Want me to take you?" he asked hopefully, leaning against the kitchen doorway, still cradling an almost-asleep Casey.

"Why, Sam! That would hardly be a *punishment*," she said, baited eyes daring him to contradict her. "Nope. I want you to help me set up the booth for my school tomorrow."

"Does this require waking up early?"

"I'm afraid so," she responded, grinning wickedly. "And some heavy lifting too. I asked my brothers, but they all work nights, so none of them was very excited to volunteer."

"Wow. You take punishment seriously."

"You said you wouldn't tease me, and you did. About the wedding." She opened her laptop and let it warm up for a moment. "It bothers me."

He placed the sleeping puppy back in her playpen and crossed the room to sit down next to her owner. "Hey...I can't help it. I tease. That's just how I—"

"Not that." She turned to him with serious eyes, and he realized how close they were sitting to each other. "I mean, I don't *love* your teasing, but I'm the youngest of four. I can handle it whether I like it or not." She paused, furrowing her brows in thought, then continued softly, "What bothers me is the wedding—specifically, the vows."

"Saying the vows for Ingrid and Kris?"

"Yes and no. I mean, I want to help Ingrid. I've known her since we were little girls and I love her. It's just...saying *those* words. You know. For the first time with..."

"With me," he supplied, searching her face to understand her better while it dawned on him that what she was saying stung a little, which made no sense at all.

"Yes. But not because you're not perfectly nice—"

"Oh, I'm perfectly nice?"

"No. I mean, *yes*. You're—well, you're fine. That's not the—"

"Jenny?"

"What?"

"Take a breath and just say what you're trying to say."

She did as he suggested, then faced him and met his eyes without blushing for the first time he could remember. "This has nothing to do with you, Sam. I mean, except you *happen* to be the person Kristian asked to be his proxy. Here's the deal: it bothers me to say the words with someone I'm not actually marrying." She stopped and looked down for a moment before meeting his eyes again. "I know *I'm* not actually taking the vows. I know *we're* not getting married, no matter how much you tease. It's just, I always thought that I would only say those words once, you know?"

Actually, he hadn't given it much thought, but he nodded so she'd continue.

"Once," she repeated wistfully. "One time that would last forever, you know? At Grace Church with Pappa and my brothers…and a man I love standing next to me…in front of God and the whole world…with my mom looking down, smiling." She blinked rapidly, and he realized that she was trying not to cry. "Oh, gosh, I'm being silly. I'll still have that moment. I mean, I *hope* I will. Someday. Anyway. It doesn't matter."

"It does," Sam replied quietly, surprised by how much her words affected him. "It matters to you."

She typed in her username and password. Her voice was strong when she responded, brooking no contradiction. "No. It *doesn't* matter, and there's nothing I can do about it now anyway. I promised Ingrid."

There had to be another way. "Hey, maybe we could find someone else to stand in for you? That old bat at the courthouse has to know someone…"

"A proxy for a proxy?" She chuckled ruefully. "No. A promise is a promise. Ingrid's so far away in Germany, and Kristian's in Afghanistan. This is the *least* I can do for them, Sam." She looked up from her computer and gave him another one of those *real* smiles that made his insides run riot. "It's okay. It really is. I feel much better now that I've told you."

That took his breath away.

"Do you want coffee? I'm having a cup." She put her laptop to the side and headed into the kitchen. She turned when she got to the doorway and looked at him quizzically. "Sam? Coffee?"

He shook his head no, offering a weak smile in response. She cocked her head to the side regarding him, then smiled back briefly before turning into the kitchen. He heard her opening cabinets and talking to Casey. He relaxed into the couch, glad she left the room for a few minutes.

He was incredibly touched by her admission, her candor, the depth of her feelings, and her selflessness in light of them. A wave of protectiveness overcame him as he thought about her words—*I feel much better now that I've told you.* He felt unworthy to have inadvertently offered her such comfort.

In a day and age when divorce was rampant, Jenny was so sure that she would say her wedding vows only once, to one man, saying them this extra time by proxy was problematic for her. It made a lump rise up in his throat, made his eyes burn a little.

In an instant, he was irritated with himself, with his visceral reaction to her. *Why should* her *feelings matter so much to me?* He rubbed his jaw between his thumb and forefinger, collecting himself.

She came back into the living room and sat back down next to him, carefully depositing her coffee on the table before them and pulling her laptop back into her lap.

Her blonde head was bent over her computer, but he could see her skin on the graceful curve of her neck where her hair parted in the back, falling forward over each of her shoulders. He stared at the patch of pale skin for a moment, imagining it would be silky and warm to the touch. He breathed in, willing himself to think about baseball or football or something other than kissing her neck. *Pointless.* He was good and distracted by her now.

It didn't help that she had been sitting close to him before, but when she sat back down, she had moved closer to him—no doubt unintentionally—by an inch or so. Cross-legged, her bent knee rested lightly on his thigh, and it was driving him crazy. Every time she typed, her elbow would gently graze his side, which was for some insane, inexplicable reason turning him on: he had a sudden mental image of lifting her face to his and closing the scant distance between their lips. The fantasy was so palpable, he groaned softly.

Jenny looked up at him, brows knitted. "Oh, look at you. You must be tired. Flying to Montana and driving so much today. We can do this tomorrow, Sam."

She was mistaking sexual frustration for weariness. *More's the better*, he thought, glad she couldn't read his mind.

"No, no," he assured her. "Sounds like you're going to keep me plenty busy tomorrow. Let's do this tonight."

"Okay. I'll tell you what I'm typing, and you tell me if you want me to change something, okay?"

Sam nodded and leaned his head on the back of the loveseat, closing his eyes.

Stop thinking about her knee on your thigh. Stop thinking about her knee on your thigh.

Her fingers flew over the keyboard as she read aloud, *"Dear Ingrid and Kristian: Sam and I are here in Gardiner together and are writing to tell you Judge Hanlon was unable to hear the vows today up in Livingston. We are sorry. The judge had weekend plans and left the courthouse a little earlier than expected."*

"So far, so good?" she asked.

"Mm-hm."

"I'm leaving out the part about your wallet," Jenny mumbled.

With his eyes still closed, he listened for her fingers to start typing again, but she didn't make a sound. She hadn't gotten up. He could still feel her beside him on the small loveseat. Perhaps she was figuring out what to type next. Then he felt her position shift slightly, closer to him.

Suddenly her breath dusted his cheek, and his heart started beating faster. He tried to keep his own breathing easy and calm, but his body was becoming increasingly taut with anticipation. *What is she doing?*

He couldn't stand not to know. He opened one of his

eyes slowly, then the other. They widened to find Jenny a hair away from his face, assessing him frankly, and...what was it he read on her face? Tenderness? Wonder? His mind was having trouble processing what was going on.

He blinked twice in surprise, and she jerked back, bowing her head over her computer. "Umm...and then we could say..."

"Jenny!" He leaned his head forward, smiling at her with a dawning realization and growing merriment. "Were you just checking me out?"

She swallowed and looked away, but not before he caught her mortified expression. Staring at the keyboard and refusing to meet his gaze, she answered in a small voice, "Yes. I-I guess I was. I thought maybe you were asleep."

He chuckled at her admission, shaking his head back and forth, marveling at her candor. Then he nudged her gently with his elbow. "Hey. You check me out all you want. It's fine by me, Pretty Girl."

She looked up at him and smiled back tentatively at the endearment, still flushed from being caught. Her blue eyes sparkled. "You think so?"

"I do," he said softly, nodding. He reached up and pushed an errant lock of blonde hair behind her ear, tracing the shell of her ear and tugging on her soft earlobe with his thumb and forefinger, rubbing the soft skin gently between them.

She inhaled sharply and swallowed, holding her breath, unable to look away from him. He stared at her lovely face, flicking his glance to her lips.

"Jenny—" he murmured, leaning intentionally toward her.

For just a moment, he thought she was going to let him kiss her, and his breath caught for a split second in sweet anticipation.

"Wait!" She looked down sharply, and he instantly dropped his hand from her ear to his lap. Her chest was moving up and down, fast and uneven, when she looked back up at him. "I barely know you."

"I know." He clasped his hands in his lap to keep from reaching out to her. "Sorry. I–I got a little carried away."

"Me too," she whispered.

No games. No flirtatious comments laced with innuendo. Just honesty. In an unexpected twist, her frankness kept the ground moving under his feet. Sexy banter was his forte, not simple honesty.

"You keep surprising me, Jenny Lindstrom."

"Me?"

"You."

Her eyes twinkled when she looked up at him shyly from under blonde lashes. She picked up her coffee cup and took a bracing sip. "Back to the task, okay? Let's finish this up."

"Go ahead." Sam spread his arms out on the back of the loveseat but was careful not to touch her—for her sake and his. He needed to cool down and think about what was happening here between them. As much as he wished he could, he couldn't deny his attraction to her. He needed to figure out what he was going to do about it, and with only forty-eight hours between now and Monday morning's appointment, frankly "*nothing*" seemed like the best answer of all.

Jenny kept reading, "*...earlier than expected. However, we were able to make a Monday-morning appointment with Judge Hanlon, so please don't worry. We will let you know as soon as you're married so that you can celebrate. Much love, Jenny & Sam.*"

"Sounds good," he confirmed and stood up abruptly, eager to get going. He needed to get away from her to clear his head.

She seemed taken aback to find him suddenly standing over her in a rush to leave and furrowed her brow briefly like she was trying to figure out if she'd done something wrong. Finally, she shut her laptop with a click and stood up next to him.

"I'll drive you back to the motel."

He followed her to the front hall, and she took his coat out of the closet and handed it to him, regarding him with her head cocked to the side in thought.

"You know, I had a really fun time with you tonight," she said so softly, it was almost like a thought meant to stay inside had stolen her voice.

Immediately, her eyes flew wide open, and she clapped a hand over her mouth in dismay, seemingly stunned that she had actually said the words out loud.

He opened his mouth to say something reassuring, but she looked so adorable, he couldn't resist: whip fast, he placed his palms flat on the wall behind her on either side of her head, leaned forward, and kissed the hand she was holding over her mouth.

That's all he did: Sam touched his lips to the back of Jenny's hand.

But his body registered something else entirely.

Maybe it was being so close to her face, or assuming the position of a passionate kiss, or trapping her smaller, lithe form between his body and the wall, but the jolt he felt was like being zapped by a live wire. He had meant the gesture to be playful, but the sudden urge to haul her up against his body or push her up against the wall behind her was anything but child's play. He leaned back slowly, breathing heavily, unable to release her eyes or calm the fierce intensity in his own as something big and unexpected yet palpable crackled between them. She stared back at him with wide, alert eyes, her face otherwise inscrutable, and he briefly wondered if she might slap him.

"Sorry, Jenny," he said, dropping his hands as he cleared his throat. He buttoned up his jacket. "I think you'd better drive me home."

When he glanced back up, she lowered her hand from over her mouth and nodded once, sidestepping around him to open the door and leaving him, once again, to follow behind.

***

After an awkward drive to his motel, Sam was actually *relieved* to be back at the Lone Wolf Lodge.

He flicked on the light, assessed the dumpy room, kicked off his shoes, and fell onto the squeaky bed, staring up at the ceiling.

What a day. Waking up in Bozeman. Trying to do some work at the hotel before leaving for Livingston. Finally arriving at the courthouse. Seeing Jenny for the first time. Jenny.

He groaned and threw his arm over his eyes. No one— not even Pepper at the very beginning when everything was so damn hot—*no one* had ever gotten under his skin as fast as Jenny did today.

How was it possible he only met her—he checked his watch—*six hours ago?*

It felt like he'd known her far longer. She was totally and completely genuine. You wouldn't feel as though you actually *knew* someone who was less real.

He replayed Jenny moments from today like a slideshow in his mind: angry Jenny click-clacking through the halls at the courthouse, embarrassed Jenny when he took out his wallet, furious Jenny when they learned the wedding couldn't take place, smiling Jenny who rocked his world as they left the courthouse, frightened Jenny gripping the steering wheel of her car, concerned Jenny who apologized to him while still shivering from her spinout, gullible Jenny whose voice was so nervous over the phone, townie Jenny walking through the streets of Gardiner, kind Jenny telling him her church prayed for Kristian every week, righteous Jenny at dinner staring down Missy, giggling Jenny when he lost their deal, poignant Jenny not wanting to take wedding vows more than once, and finally, the Jenny who checked him out as he lay half-asleep on her couch. That was the Jenny whose hand he had kissed. He thought of her trapped between his body and the wall and felt a rush of blood heading to his groin. He groaned again, wishing it away. *At ease, pal. Not happening tonight.*

She was fascinating; he never knew what she would say or do next, and it was drawing him to her like a magnet after years of hearing girls saying what they thought he wanted to hear or what they thought sounded cool or sexy. Jenny was so authentic, it was separating her from the pack, making him want to take a closer look. His smile turned into a chuckle as he thought of her embarrassed face when he caught her checking him out, and then his chest rumbled with laughter remembering her admission of guilt.

They were different, for sure. She was from a small town, a regular churchgoer, a schoolteacher. She was so genuine, so *real*, and she didn't try to hide her emotions behind some aloof veneer. Sam admired those qualities. He had seen her be kind to people today, interested in their lives, and he was sure he'd see more of it tomorrow. She was a good, solid person, and it didn't hurt that she was also so pretty.

She was more pretty than cute, but something about her unaffected wholesomeness made her cute too. It dawned on him that maybe it was her wholesomeness that made him so hungry for her. He was caught off guard by his reaction when he kissed her hand: his blood had heated up in an instant, and his heart had raced because he *wanted* her, and the surprising thing was, cute really wasn't his style. Then again, he thought with growing uncertainty, maybe it was.

Before today, he had been enjoying his post-Pepper

71

freedom. He'd had a few dates, mostly set up by well-meaning friends, and what he had really enjoyed was the thrill of meeting new women. Every pretty girl was a possible "someone," and he found it exciting. In just a few hours, Jenny was redefining everything he thought he was looking for, which was, in a word, disconcerting. It led to a thought that was not only incredibly inconvenient but theoretically distressing: he couldn't possibly be genuinely *interested* in her, could he? Sure, something about her might resonate in him, but he wasn't actually *falling* for her, was he?

He got up and washed his hands and face, looking at his reflection in the bathroom mirror. *No, you're not. You're not, Sam. You could really hurt someone like that if you're not careful.*

He massaged his jaw between his thumb and forefinger. *You don't belong here, and she certainly doesn't belong in Chicago. Two different worlds, brother. Not to mention, this isn't the type of girl you pursue for a weekend of fun, Sammy, and you know it. This is the marrying kind of girl. And if you're not interested in that—and, let's face it,* you're not—*she's not for you.*

He took off his pants, sweat shirt, and T-shirt and slung them over the desk chair, then slipped into bed. He turned the bedside lamp off and settled back on the pillow, lacing his hands under his head as he had at her place. When he closed his tired eyes, he saw her face in his head: those searching blue eyes so close to his face, staring into his eyes when he opened them. His gut constricted for a second with unfamiliar longing, and he threw his pillow across the room in frustration.

She's not for you, man. She's not for you.

***

When she got home, Jenny flopped back on her bed without taking her coat off, her keys still jingling in her hand. She let them fall to the floor with a clunk. Still reeling from her time with Sam, she raised her hand to inspect it, and with her other hand, she gingerly touched the spot where he had kissed her, imagining it still tender from his lips. She circled the area with a feather touch, then closed her eyes and pressed it to her own lips, lingering for a moment before rubbing it gently back and forth against her cheek tenderly. Goose bumps popped up along the back of her arm, and her belly tingled unfamiliarly as she flashed back to his eyes opening under her frank assessment.

Alone in her room, she felt her cheeks burn as she remembered.

She hadn't meant to be so forward. When she had glanced over at him, his eyes were closed, and she had wondered if he was sleeping. He looked so peaceful with his head resting on the back of the loveseat, hands laced under his head, one wing of elbow above her head. It occurred to her in that moment if he had straightened that arm, he'd have it around her. The thought had made her cheeks flush and her heart beat faster, and she had leaned into the fantasy, enjoying the rush of—what? Excitement? Curiosity?

No, she thought simply. *Longing.*

She had leaned closer, pulled to him, drawn inexplicably to his beautiful face—sharply angled cheeks that belied his mother's Scandinavian ancestry, copper-toned blond hair that tousled wildly after their windy walk. A coppery-colored beard shadow came in along his strong jaw after a long day. His lips were full and pink, and she liked how often they tilted up laughing and teasing. Her brothers, "the boys," were a laughing, teasing lot, and she adored them, but their eyes were icy blue, all three, not soft brown like Sam's, which were a dreamy brown, really, with long, dark lashes that—

When his eyes popped open, she wished a crater would open up in the floor of her apartment and swallow her whole.

She was confident she had him all figured out right before they left the courthouse: slick, citified dandy with his expensive wallet and glib sarcasm. She was sure he'd hightail it back to Bozeman for the weekend, or worse, head back to Chicago, leaving her alone to find a proxy for Kristian.

But no. He had surprised her, which had softened her angry feelings. Not only did he stay, he was willing to get a room, near her in Gardiner so she could tend to Casey.

His gentle care of her after she had spun out changed her opinion of him greatly. She thought of him shrugging out of his warm coat and laying it gently over her, and a shiver of pleasure tingled down her arms, making the wrist of the hand he had kissed throb with her beating heart.

Casey yelped from the kitchen, and Jenny sat up, wishing her brain didn't feel so overwhelmed with the events of the day.

"Come on, Little Bit, and let's make it snappy."

She took Casey down the stairs to a small fenced courtyard behind the building and sat on the stoop, waiting for her to do her business.

I love Montana.

When he had said that, her heart just about stopped beating for a second, because she had been thinking the exact same thing before he whispered the words.

And when she'd shared her feelings about taking vows on Ingrid's behalf, his kindness overwhelmed her again. *It matters to you.* She felt, for no good reason but with certainty, that he may as well have said, "It matters to *me*," because he seemed so invested in her feelings. She was so touched by his regard, his careful acceptance of her feelings, which could have been dismissed or ridiculed by a less gracious man.

She made her fingers into fists, pumping them open and closed several times then cupping them around her nose and mouth to warm them up. When had it gotten so cold? *Too distracted to remember your mittens, Jen? Tsk.*

"Hurry up, Casey!"

Jenny's romantic experience was limited: her entire *oeuvre* consisted of some hand-holding on a high school church retreat in Yellowstone and a few kisses with a boy in college who had broken things off when she wouldn't let him touch her breasts.

And let's face it, it's practically impossible to date anyone in Gardiner with three hulking, well-known brothers all living locally.

Anyway, she'd only been working at Gardiner High School for two years, and her job was her first priority. She didn't need any distractions, and if she was honest, well, she knew just about everyone in Gardiner, and there just wasn't anyone to *be* a distraction.

She grinned, shaking her head, bemused. How Sam had

managed to get so close to her in the space of a few hours was a mystery to her, especially in light of the fact that everything between them had gotten off to such a rocky start. She realized, with a little bit of wonder, that when she wasn't *completely* distracted by his good looks, she was comfortable with him. For the first time in a long time— maybe the first time in her *whole life*—she was interested in someone up close, not from a guarded and ultimately futile distance.

"Casey, let's go!"

The puppy came running back over to Jenny, and she swooped her up, paws icy from the cold ground.

Once Casey was settled in her warm crate by Jenny's bed, Jenny changed into her pajamas and washed her face. She scrubbed harder than usual, frustrated by her feelings, unable to create any real order out of them. Her face was red and chafed when she finished, so she applied some cream, looking at herself closely in the mirror.

Pretty Girl, she heard him in her head and smiled at herself, indulging in the warmth of his compliment.

But her smile faded after a second as she imposed a chilly reality on the situation.

Fine. He's funny and beautiful and kind. But, Jenny Lindstrom, get your head out of the clouds and be sensible. He's from a whole different world, and he's going back to it in two days. That's the bottom line. So put him out of your mind, and quit thinking about him with anything but good, old-fashioned hospitality.

She nodded curtly at her reflection, humorless and severe.

Walking back through the living room to her bedroom, she found her laptop was still on, the draft of her unsent email brightening the screen. She reviewed the message quickly for typos and was about to send when she paused at the bottom. Their names were paired at the end of the email with a simple ampersand, "Jenny & Sam."

"Jenny and Sam," she whispered, followed by a small, strangled sound from deep in her throat.

A longing for him, raw and real, bubbled up inside of her.

Oh, no. No, this is no good, she thought, fingers trembling over the mouse. *You don't even know him. You can't possibly be infatuated with him. No. Stop.*

She cringed, knowing protestations were useless. Feelings were feelings, welcome, inconvenient, or otherwise. And Jenny's feelings told her that she was already in the middle of something she never even saw coming.

I didn't mean for this to happen.

Clenching her eyes shut in frustration, she hit Send, powered down, and snapped the laptop closed.

Then she got into bed and turned off her bedside table lamp, lacing her hands under her head and staring at the shadows on her ceiling. Unbidden yet inevitably, her mind turned to Sam's face, his eyes of smiling, teasing, handsome brown. She balled her hands into fists, turning to her side and closing her eyes with determination.

He's not from here, and you're not from Chicago, so let's end this fantasy now, Jenny, and get this straight and fixed in your mind:

He's not for you, Pretty Girl. He's not for you.

Chapter 5

Jenny slept fitfully for the first time in years.

She finally gave up on sleep entirely, got dressed, and took Casey for an early morning walk. The sun wouldn't be up for another hour or so, not until almost 8:00 a.m. The days were as short in December as they were long in June, when even the southern parts of Montana boasted almost sixteen hours of daylight at midsummer. Today was so close to the winter solstice, there would be only eight hours of daylight at best and less each following day. She didn't mind the dark, quiet walk; she relished the time to think about the day before her, to settle her thoughts in the shadows of the early morning.

Sam was just about the first thing on her mind when she woke up, and she wanted to try to make sense of her feelings before he came to pick her up later that morning. She had decided firmly last night before bed that despite her attraction to him, he couldn't be the man for her. Their lives were too substantially different for her to indulge in any real fantasies about him, and she would treat him with nothing more than the same kindness she would extend to any other human being.

I will think of him as I would old Mr. Thornton at church or any of Pappa's friends. His eyes will merely be eyes, not teasing brown under dark lashes. His hands will just be hands, not strong, corded hands that I want to reach out and hold. His lips will only be—

She felt cool resolve melt away into rushing falls of longing and shushed her thoughts with a quick head shake. *This isn't helping. I refuse to give in to this infatuation. There must be another way to shoo you from my mind, Sam Kelley.*

Gardiner was starting to come alive as she crossed the bridge and headed back to her apartment. The lights were on at the Prairie Dawn below Jenny's apartment, and she considered popping in for a latte but had no sensible reason for such an extravagance when there was perfectly good coffee waiting to be brewed at home. Still, it might be nice to sit with Maggie Campbell for a few minutes and get her opinion on things.

Maggie owned the bookstore-cum-coffee shop downstairs and occasionally walked or fed Casey when Jenny couldn't get home from school for her midday walk. She was Jenny's closest friend in town, only a few years older than Jenny and the ongoing secret crush of Jenny's oldest brother, Nils.

No. No, she decided firmly. She didn't need Maggie's opinion or anyone else's: even *addressing* her feelings would just indulge this silly infatuation.

It occurred to her, as she put Casey's leash away and opened her laptop, that there might be another way. Information is power, after all, right? And where better to gather it than on the information superhighway? It wouldn't hurt to know a little bit more about him. Perhaps she would find something so objectionable online, it would immediately reverse her fledgling feelings.

"I'm going to Google you, Sam Kelley."

Sitting Indian-style on her loveseat, she pulled out her laptop, shooing away the voice in her head that chastised her as a voyeuristic busybody. Desperate times called for desperate measures.

She typed "Sam Kelley" into the Google search bar.

Wow. Who knew so many people had that name?

She narrowed it down by typing "Sam Kelley Chicago."

Hmm. LinkedIn. A sportswriter? Probably not. He hadn't mentioned sports once.

Sam Kelley, a banker at Mutual Trust Associates. Maybe. She clicked on the link.

Sam's handsome face stared back at her from the screen in a formal black-and-white photo. He was dressed sharply in a suit jacket and tie over a crisp, light-colored dress shirt. His hair was slicked back like the lead actor from the movie *Wall Street,* and he wore a reserved smile, which was direct yet approachable at once. Under the photo was his title—vice president, Mutual Trust—and a short bio about his education and experience.

Jenny combed over the short paragraph. He had gone to the University of Chicago, where he graduated with a BS in economics in 2004, and it looked like he had worked at Mutual Trust for about seven years; she counted back in her head and guessed his age at twenty-eight or twenty-nine. He had received his last promotion about a year and a half ago, which had made him one of the youngest vice presidents in

MTA's history. It said he had initiated his group's entry into cutting-edge active quantitative strategies and called him "one of the rising stars" at MTA.

Jenny smiled and even felt a little bit proud of him. *He must be pretty smart.*

She stared at his face, feeling her own soften in pleasure, and wondered if she could find more pictures of him. Clicking on the word *Images* on the Google toolbar, she waited until a page of tiny thumbnail photos came up. The first picture was the black-and-white one she had just seen on his company's website. There were several other photos of various unfamiliar faces, and then...

A thumbnail of Sam in a tuxedo, with a stunning woman beside him. Jenny's heart leapt in her chest, and she clicked on the tiny picture. She was redirected to a photographer's website: Joseph Grant Photography—2012 Fall Charity Gala at Navy Pier. She scrolled down until she found the picture again.

It was Sam, all right, looking more handsome than she could have imagined, in a tuxedo with his hair gelled back and a devastatingly beautiful woman by his side. If a picture was worth a thousand words, their body language said it all: he had his arm around her tiny waist, his hand clasping her close. The woman leaned into Sam but offered a dazzling smile to the photographer. She was an inch or two shorter than Sam but still tall. She wore a red silk dress that clung to her perfect body like a slip, ending just above her stylish silver high-heeled shoes. The dress had a plunging neckline and a dramatic slit in the skirt that *almost* went up to her waist, showing a tan, toned leg underneath.

Jenny read the caption under the photo: *Chicago's own Pepper Pettway with her boyfriend, Sam Kelley, attends the Annual Charity Gala at Navy Pier, October 2012*

Pepper Pettway.

Ouch.

Jenny had assumed that Sam's life in Chicago was more glamorous than hers in Gardiner, but she had no idea how incredibly far away their worlds were from one another until she sat staring at his *girlfriend*, Pepper Pettway.

Jenny opened another Google session and typed her name.

Her heart sank.

"Fifty Most Beautiful Chicagoans." Fox Chicago Sunday morning, "What's the Weather? with Pepper." Pepper Pettway and Sam Kelley at the Chicago Museum of Art. Pepper Pettway and Sam Kelley at the Chicago Symphony Orchestra. Pepper and Sam kissing on the huge HD screen at Wrigley Field, wearing matching Cubs caps. Pepper in a bright-yellow skirt suit surrounded by bandaged children, reading stories at the pediatric burn unit of the University of Chicago Medical Center.

Pepper Pettway wasn't a supermodel, she was a television personality. She wore beautiful clothes but still enjoyed a baseball game, and she volunteered her time to read stories to burned children.

She's beautiful and glamorous, and she's a good person too.

Jenny slowly lowered the laptop screen until it snapped shut definitively. Then she leaned her elbow on the side of the loveseat and cradled her cheek in her hand, looking around her plain, old-fashioned living room. She had never looked at her apartment through any eyes but her own, but seeing it through Pepper's eyes made her feel like a guilty Eve in the Garden of Eden with too much knowledge: exposed and embarrassed.

Secondhand furniture, mostly choices her mother made years ago, looked lumpy and worn. Some simple family photos adorned her mantle: Jenny and the boys in the park over the years, Jenny and Ingrid on high school and college graduation days and a copy of her parents' wedding picture. These modest decorations spoke to an unsophisticated life. She swallowed as she looked at the homemade calico curtains she had sewn on her mother's old Singer and cringed at the needlepoint pillow, crafted lovingly by a young student, that read, "A#1 Techer."

She didn't know how long she sat on the loveseat in silence, but by the time she stood up, her confused feelings for Sam were ebbing away with a finality that made her wistful for yesterday. Reading about Pepper was like dousing herself with cold water. Not only was Sam taken, but he was taken by someone as completely amazing as Pepper Pettway.

You can't compete, Jenny. She flinched, then felt her backbone kick in. *Silly girl. You shouldn't have been competing in the first place. A bad night's sleep for nothing. I told you, he's not for you, and now you know it too.*

She jumped up with determination and padded into the kitchen to start her coffeemaker, distractedly scooping too many grounds into the basket. Her mind hummed with some unresolved question, and although she wished she could just stop this merciless focus on Sam Kelley, the question rose up to the surface like bubbles on a pond.

"If he has a girlfriend," she murmured aloud, "then how come he was flirting with me?"

He had touched her finger at dinner, stroked her ear, and—for heaven's sake!—almost kissed her on the loveseat *and* at the door.

She ran back to the living room, grabbed her laptop, and snapped it open on the kitchen counter. *Chicago's own Pepper Pettway with her* boyfriend, *Sam Kelley, attends…*

She checked the date: *October! Just a few weeks ago!*

Her eyes opened wide in indignation, and her mouth shaped itself into an outraged O. Did Sam Kelley set out to philander with her while he was away from Pepper?

"Well!" she hissed. "He's nothing but a smooth, lowlife womanizer!"

Jenny braced her palms on the kitchen counter as the old percolator wheezed and gurgled beside her, coffee spurting into the dome angrily.

With no one else to talk to, she looked down at Casey, whose brown puppy eyes widened at Jenny's upset tone.

"He has someone like Pepper Pettway in his life, but he's trying to make time with me on the side! Probably looking for a weekend fling! Really! Of all the base, disgraceful—"

The phone interrupted her tirade.

Dang it, not now! The machine can answer!

"Jen. Lars here. Heard about you doing pizza with a

dude last night at the Blue Moon. Just wondering about that, little sister…"

She crossed her arms over her chest and looked at Casey, who whined from her play pen. "Guess the Gardiner rumor mill is up and running early today, huh?"

The phone rang again. She knew what was coming. She pulled out a coffee cup and listened to the next message.

"Jenny. It's Erik. Lars called. Who's the guy?"

She counted to ten before the phone rang a final time.

"It's Nils. You didn't pick up for Erik or Lars. I'm coming over to see if you're at your place, Jenny girl, and if you're not, then I'm calling *Pappa*, and you know—"

Jenny snatched the phone off its base and pressed Answer. "Nils! It's Jen."

"Ahhhhh. So you *are* home."

"You three are ridiculous. I'm not a baby. I can take care of myself. For heaven's sake, you made sure of it."

"Well, he's a stranger. No one knows him."

"It's a long story, Nils."

"I'm warm in bed. I could use a story."

Older brothers! "You know Ingrid's fiancé, Kristian? He's Kristian Svenson's cousin. Just visiting."

"Visiting *you*?"

"No. Yes. Sort of, but it's not what you think."

Nils's voice took on an edge. "What do I *think*, Jenny?"

"Gode Gud, Nils, quit it. It's a long, boring story. I'll tell you all about it at Sunday supper." She paused, then added, "Do *not* tell Pappa and worry him."

"Do not tell Pa—sorry, Jen." She heard him chuckle

humorlessly on the other side of the phone. "Now you're digging yourself deeper. Now I want to hear the 'long, boring story.'"

"*Helvete*," she muttered.

"Watch your mouth."

"Fine." She sighed in annoyance. "Ingrid needed some legal work done up in Livingston at the courthouse. Personal legal work, Nils. I had to take care of her part, and Sam had to take care of Kristian's. The judge left early for the park, and we had to reschedule our appointment for Monday. So he's stuck in Gardiner for the weekend, and I had to be hospitable."

"Ahhhh. So that's why you went north yesterday. Wondered why Maggie was walking Casey at midday." Jenny rolled her eyes.

Nils *watching* Maggie but doing nothing *else* about Maggie was old news. She thought about giving him a hard time about it but decided to keep the peace instead. No sense in teasing him and getting him all riled up. Maggie could be a pretty touchy subject with Nils.

"What's his name?" asked her big brother. "The dude?"

"Sam. Sam Kelley. Pretty much kin of Ingrid, so leave it alone, okay? No need to worry Pappa."

"Yeah, okay." He paused. "You still need a hand at school today? With the booth?"

Jenny thought about this for a moment. She *should* accept Nils's help and tell Sam she had no interest in seeing him again until Monday's appointment. She certainly wasn't the sort of girl who went around with taken men. But indignation surged up in her, and she realized she wanted to give him a piece of her mind personally. That meant she couldn't cancel on him yet.

She glanced at her watch: 8:05. Sam would be here in forty minutes. "I think I've got it covered, Nils. You can still stop by and pick up everything later to put it together. I'll call you boys if anything changes. See you later or tomorrow."

She hung up quickly and raced to her room to get dressed; she needed to get to Albertson's Grocery and back before Sam got to her place.

Jenny knew *exactly* what she wanted to offer Cheating Sam for breakfast.

***

Sam slept like a baby.

Maybe it was gulping in all that sweet, clean Montana air or spending time with a sweet, clean Montana miss, but either way, Sam woke up feeling great. He stretched languorously, rotating his neck to get out the morning cricks. He swung his legs over the side of the bed, sitting there for a moment, groggy until he caught sight of the alarm clock out of the corner of his eye.

"No! Crap!" He shot up, eyes wide open, realizing he had to be at Jenny's place in twenty minutes.

After showering and shaving in record time, Sam surveyed his limited options and decided on a pair of jeans, a plaid flannel shirt, and the sweat shirt he'd worn last night. He jumped into his rental car and raced to Jenny's apartment, giving himself a pat on the back as he pulled up in front of her building. *8:44. Not bad, Sammy. Not bad.*

He took the stairs two at a time, excited to see her again. Maybe they weren't *meant* for each other, but they were *stuck* together for a weekend, and she kept him on his toes. Might as well enjoy her company.

His mouth watered as the smells of a good old-fashioned country breakfast wafted out into the hall. *Eggs and bacon, if I'm not mistaken!* He was so impatient to see her, he felt like an eager suitor, like he should have chocolates tucked under his arm or flowers hidden behind his back.

Whoa, boy! Calm down and remember—she's not for you. Just be friendly and nice. Don't make this more complicated. You're leaving the day after tomorrow.

He knocked lightly at her door and heard her call from inside, "It's open, Sam!"

Walking into her bright, cheery apartment felt like coming home.

Sure, he'd been there last night, but it was harder to get a feeling for a place at night. He walked through the short, tidy front hallway, peeking into the living room.

Bright sun shone through two windows that looked out onto Main Street. The overstuffed loveseat and chair looked cozy and inviting, places to really relax with a cup of coffee, as opposed to the stark, modern furniture Pepper had favored. The cheerful curtains reminded him of the handmade ones his mother had made for his room when he was small, only Jenny's had flowers, and his had been patterned with falling leaves. Relieved that there was no fancy, modern artwork to pretend he liked, he glanced briefly at her family photos. Jenny and three blond boys in hiking boots standing from shortest to tallest in front of a massive boulder, and teenage Jenny hugging teenage Ingrid, both wearing black mortarboard caps.

He picked up the picture and looked at her face. Probably ten years ago, but she didn't look so different from now, really. Fresh and unpainted, blonde hair curled around her shoulders in what he guessed was a special hairdo for graduation day.

Pretty Girl. I would have tried to hold your hand.

He didn't want her to catch him snooping, so he returned the frame to its place and headed into the kitchen. Casey wiggled from her playpen in the corner, whining for Sam to come and pick her up. He obliged happily.

"Jenny?"

The table was set simply with two plates, two coffee cups, and two napkins. Just what they needed. No fuss. He could smell the coffee, and his mouth watered, so he poured himself some joe before sitting down at the table with Casey on his lap.

In the middle of the table was a spice wheel like his mother used to have. He put Casey in the nook of one elbow and used his other hand to spin the plate slowly: hot sauce, mustard, black pepper, white pepper, red pepper, salt, red pepper flakes, a wooden pepper mill, a clear plastic pepper mill, cayenne pepper, chili pepper, maple syrup, and some honey.

Wow, he thought. *Someone likes her food spicy!*

He scratched under Casey's neck. "Where's Jenny?

Where's your mama?"

"Jenny?" he called toward the living room.

"I'll be out in a minute," she called. "Help yourself to coffee…and anything else you see."

He glanced at his half-finished cup and winked at Casey. "Good thing she didn't mind!"

Casey bucked up and licked his chin from where she was lying in his elbow. He looked around the kitchen for breakfast, but he didn't see anything else to help himself to, just the spice wheel on the table. He assumed breakfast was warming in the oven and figured he should wait for Jenny before he got started.

Jenny came into the kitchen dressed in jeans and a white, long-sleeved, button-down shirt. Her jeans were belted with some sort of Indian-style beaded belt, and she wore them slung low on her hips, like Sam imagined a cowgirl would wear them. She had on leather boots too—the real deal, not from Bloomingdale's or Saks—and they were well worn and scuffed from years of use.

She smiled at him, but he couldn't read her face and sensed something standoffish in her manner. Maybe she was still upset about him kissing her hand last night. He waited to see what would happen. He was starting to learn that with Jenny, you never knew.

"Morning," she said, not meeting his eyes.

"Morning."

"Hungry?" she asked pleasantly. He caught it again: that smile that didn't reach her eyes.

"Sure."

"What're you in the mood for?"

You. On the table. Shirt optional. "Ummm. I don't know. What're you offering?"

"I made omelets and bacon."

"Sounds great."

She opened the oven and took out a warm platter of omelets and placed it gingerly on the table between the two place settings: four small omelets sat prettily on the platter, with a bunch of bacon on the side. She took Casey from him and sat down across from him, smiling that unpleasant, pleasant smile. It was starting to unsettle him in the same way a man gets unsettled when a woman says she's "fine" but is clearly perturbed about some unknown thing.

"Wow. Four. Is anyone else coming?"

"Nope," she replied. "All for you. The first one is green *pepper*, the second one is red *pepper*, and the third one is yellow *pepper*. Want to know what the fourth one is?"

"I don't know."

"It's an all-*weather* omelet. Has one vegetable in it from every season…spring peas, summer corn, autumn yams, and winter squash." She got up and placed Casey back in her pen, then turned to face Sam, hands on her hips, her eyes boring into his. "Peppers and weather. And a little bit of cheap pig on the side. I wanted you to feel at home."

***

He stared at her, speechless, and Jenny stared right back, daring him to confess everything.

So she wasn't totally sure what to do when his face suddenly contorted with a loud guffaw and he started laughing so hard, his face turned red. In between sob-like chuckles, he grabbed his napkin off the table to dab at his eyes.

Her indignant confidence took a hit from his unexpected reaction. This couldn't be the standard response when a man was caught trying to cheat on his perfect girlfriend!

She crossed her arms over her chest and pursed her lips, watching as he, at long last, collected himself.

"Jenny," he finally said when he could actually speak again, wiping at his eyes.

"Sam," she replied tartly, every bit the aggravated schoolmarm.

He gestured to her laptop and crossed the kitchen to stand beside it. Grazing the space bar with one finger, a picture of Sam and Pepper suddenly sprang to life on Jenny's kitchen counter. "Someone doing a little Googling this morning?"

Conferring her *most* contemptuous look, she knew she should declare, *Yes, that's exactly what I did, bucko, and you've got another thing coming if you think you're going to cheat on Pepper Pettway with me!*

However…a little seed of doubt was taking root in her gut based on his reaction, and she started to worry that she may have jumped to conclusions from looking at a few glamorous pictures on the internet.

"Jenny." An errant chuckle escaped his lips, and it took him a second to straighten his expression to declare, "Pepper and I aren't together anymore. We broke up."

She swallowed and covered her mouth with her hand. Her cheeks were burning, no doubt turning thirty shades of scarlet. She wondered for the second time in twelve hours why the forces of the universe couldn't see fit to open large craters in the floor of one's apartment when a situation clearly called for it. When she looked up at him, he was smiling, and to her relief, he didn't seem angry or upset, just sort of amused, eyebrows raised in quizzical merriment, waiting for her next misguided assumption about him and his life.

"I thought...I mean, last night you...kissed my...hand and..." She let her voice trail off because she could hear how weak and ridiculous she sounded.

Oh, Lord. When you're wrong, Jenny, you're good and wrong.

Ashamed of herself for getting so carried away with her quest for information on Sam and for believing the worst of him, she couldn't meet his eyes. He'd done nothing to deserve her distrust. Though her eyes burned, crying wasn't the prerogative of the transgressor in her family growing up, so she bit her tongue and held her tears. She looked down at her boots instead.

"Jenny, look at me," he said, his rumbly voice gentle and kind. "Please look at me."

She looked up, meeting his eyes sheepishly.

"Listen, I know you don't know me very well, but I need you to know this: when I'm *with* someone, I'm really *with* them. I wouldn't have touched you yesterday if I wasn't free to do so. We may live in different worlds, Jen, but that's just not the kind of man I am, or would be, in *either* world."

He was waiting for an indication that she understood and accepted what he was saying, so she gulped over the lump in her throat and nodded at him.

"Okay!" he said, rubbing his hands together as he sat back down at the table and turned his attention to the omelets. Using a spatula, he slid the all-weather omelet onto his plate with several pieces of bacon. "I'm not actually a big fan of peppers."

"Noted."

"Hey! You didn't *do* anything to these omelets, did you?" His eyes sparkled with laughter. "I'm not going to die from too much cayenne, am I?"

She closed her eyes, breathing in, then opened them, breathing out. It didn't help. She had done it again after she had promised herself she wouldn't: jumped to conclusions. Misjudged him. How in the world could she offer a sufficient apology? *Lord help me to swallow my terrible pride and show him how sorry I am.*

"No, Sam. They're fine. I promise."

"Then come sit with me and have some breakfast." He gestured to the empty seat across from him. "And if you want, I'll tell you all about Pepper."

Burning cheeks. Wounded pride. Repentant heart.

She sat. There was nothing else to do.

***

Jenny, Jenny. He glanced over at her as they shared breakfast, sipping coffee in the silence of her kitchen. She looked young and miserable, occasionally taking a small bite of egg or bacon. He couldn't deny it—he admired both her panache and her chagrin.

"So," he began after polishing off half the omelet and several pieces of crispy ba—cheap pig, "do you want to know about Pepper or not?"

"Sure," she muttered.

She picked at her bacon distractedly, Sam noticed, and she didn't meet his eyes. He wasn't a fan of mopey Jenny. He was eager to dispense with Pepper's story and get on with their day.

"You may already know that I work at an investment firm, and schmoozing is pretty important to my boss."

"Schmoozing?" she asked. "What's that?"

"Uh. You know…taking clients out to over-the-top dinners…going to galas to rub elbows with millionaires…that sort of thing." She nodded and he continued. "So my boss had two tickets to a fundraiser at the Chicago Cultural Center. He couldn't go at the last minute and asked me to go. I didn't have a date, and he suggested that his niece, Pepper, who was supposed to be going with him, could just as well go with me. I didn't put two and two together until she met me there and I realized the girl from 'What's the Weather? with Pepper' and my boss's niece were one and the same. After that, we started dating."

"She's perfect, Sam. Beautiful. And the burned children…" Jenny looked at him so earnestly, *so miserably*, with such vulnerability etched on her face, his heart clenched with tenderness.

"Jenny." He sipped his coffee, pushing his plate away. "Those are just pictures. Pepper Pettway *is* really beautiful.

You're right. She is. But her beauty is skin deep and goes no deeper, I can assure you. Those burned children? She read three sentences of a story while the camera was flashing, then marched out of there to get her nails done a minute after the reporter left. I doubt those poor kids will ever find out what happened to the grumpy puppy."

Jenny seemed unconvinced. "She seems so selfless, helping with so many fundraisers and good causes."

"She was an 'honorary member' on most of those committees." She cocked her head to the side, and he realized she didn't understand. "Someone whose name goes on the invitation because they're a public figure but who does nothing to contribute to the event aside from showing up and having her picture taken for publicity."

"With you."

Ah, Jen. You're killing me with these searching blue eyes. I want to hold you and kiss all that uncertainty away.

"Sure. Sometimes. When we were together. Next week, it'll be someone else."

"Did you love her?" Jenny asked.

"For a while, I thought I did," he said, wishing they could finish this conversation sooner than later. Pepper wasn't one of his favorite conversation topics. "But I'm pretty sure it was something different."

"What?"

Pride. Lust. Stupidity. Take your pick.

"Listen…almost two months ago, a week after that picture was taken, I was in a car accident. A hit-and-run."

"What? No!" Jenny gasped and reached across the table

for his hand.

He was surprised by her impulsive gesture and sensed she was too, but she didn't release his hand immediately. Yes, her cheeks flushed a little, per usual, but instead of drawing back, she allowed him to curl his fingers around her hand and hold it. He stared at their joined hands for a beat before lifting his gaze back to her face.

"Jenny…"

"Go on. Hit-and-run."

"Ummm…so, I was in a hit-and-run, and when the other car left, I was bleeding from my forehead, and it hurt to breathe. The ambulance came, and the EMTs couldn't be sure whether or not I had a concussion, but they were pretty sure I had cracked or bruised a rib, so they took me to the hospital." He cleared his throat. "Anyway, I called Pepper from the ambulance to tell her what had happened. We had plans that night to go to a charity dinner, and I knew she'd be upset to miss it, but I was *sure* she'd come to me. I mean, we'd been dating for more than a year."

Jenny squeezed his hand gently. "So…did she?"

"Not for a while. The hours ticked by, and she didn't show up. I didn't call my folks or my sisters. I didn't want to worry them. I had a concussion and a couple of broken ribs that would heal on their own." He decided not to add that things had been strained with his mother and sisters with Pepper in the picture. They'd never liked her, which should have had more of an impact on him. "I was asleep when she finally got there."

He would never forget her sweeping onto his hospital

floor *after* visiting hours, dressed to the nines, soused from champagne. She had woken him up from a deep sleep as she made a drunken scene with the nurses about how her *future husband* was wounded and needed her.

"Screw visiting hours!" she shrieked. "Don't you know who I am?"

Security had finally made her leave. Truth be told, less of a knockout might have been arrested for such behavior, but Pepper had her charms. He had cringed listening to her from his hospital bed, and his stomach curdled, horrified by the words "future husband."

"I'm so sorry," Jenny murmured.

"She had gone to the benefit with a friend of mine, an associate at work, and came by the hospital when it was over. She explained later that she had a new dress and didn't want it to go to waste. And you know? I just decided then and there: she wasn't the girl for me. So we broke up. It was a few months ago."

He remembered the morning he'd broken up with Pepper.

"You think you're going to find someone better than me?" she'd spat at him with furious green eyes, her perfectly manicured fingernails digging into her slim, taut hips.

He'd stared back her, thinking, *Just because I know what I don't want doesn't mean I know what I do.* It's not like he'd had someone else lined up. All he'd known was that Pepper wasn't right for him.

Now it occurred to Sam…he'd wanted something more, something good, something real in his life. Something more like what his parents had, like the marriages his sisters had.

He rubbed his thumb back and forth lightly across the soft pad of skin at the base of Jenny's thumb, thinking about how much he'd like to pull her into his arms and kiss her. He'd like to watch her eyes close as his lips moved closer to hers, pressing softly on them, running his hands through her silky blonde hair as he held her more intimately against his body.

His eyes flicked to the spice wheel covered with different peppers and the pepper omelets still sitting on a platter. Something sort of amazing occurred to him, and he decided to take a chance, whispering, "You had nothing to be jealous about."

When he looked up, she nodded and smiled at him. To his delight, she didn't turn scarlet or purple or rush to contradict him, and once again he was captivated by the honesty of her reaction. "I see that now."

After a moment, she withdrew her hand gently, squeezing his before she pulled hers away. "How did you stay so calm yesterday? When I spun out? I mean, I would think seeing someone else in an accident so soon after yours would—"

"I was worried about you. I was focused on you."

She smiled at him with such tenderness, his heart leapt in his chest.

"How're your ribs?" she asked.

"Right this minute?" *My heart's hammering the hell out of 'em, Jen.* "Just fine. All healed up."

"I'm glad you're not with her anymore. I'm so sorry she wasn't there for you when you needed her. I'm so sorry you were hurt and alone."

How does she keep doing this? Cradling my heart in her hands?

He knew how much courage it had taken for her to reach out and hold his hand, but she had done it, in spite of her reservations. Comforting him was more important to her than feeling comfortable herself. Once again, he was humbled by her selflessness.

"Sam." She cleared her throat and lifted her chin. "I owe you an apology."

"Nah, I'm flattered. Anyway, you make a mean omelet, Jenny. It's okay."

"No. It's not okay." She held his eyes uncompromisingly. "I owe you an apology, and I'd like to offer it, if that's okay. I thought you were attempting to dally with me while you were away from your girlfriend, but you've done nothing in the short time I've known you to lead me to believe you are the sort of man who would do something like that. And yet I jumped to that conclusion after looking at a few pictures on Google. I do that sometimes, rush to judgment. It's a bad habit of mine, and I am just so sorry and so embarrassed."

"Really," he said, "it's fi—"

"And I—I also just want to say…I've been pretty difficult since you met me. I sure would understand if you'd like to be left alone for the rest of the weekend…to, um, just explore Gardiner on your own. You don't have to help me today. I can get Nils to come help me. He already offered. I don't deserve your help."

She said her piece, then released his eyes with a single nod. Standing up, she gathered the dishes and put them in the sink, giving Casey the solitary piece of leftover bacon.

Man, she is brave.

Most of the men he knew—hell, most of the *people* he knew—wouldn't have offered up an apology that thorough and sincere. She took it on the chin, that's for sure. He suddenly thought of Jenny as a little girl, being raised alongside three older brothers. No doubt she sat in on all the life lessons they would have had about courage and integrity and standing up for themselves throughout childhood. *She's strong like that. She's tough.*

Then again, he thought as he watched her at the sink washing the breakfast dishes, *she's all woman too.*

She had her white shirt rolled up to her elbows, and he could see the skin on her forearms was still holding onto a summer tan against the white of the shirt. He moved his eyes lower to her waist and hips, then lower still, and— *hallelujah!*—her backside was cupped to perfection by the soft, molded denim of her jeans, highlighting every pert curve.

No way she's putting up that booth with Nils today, whoever the hell he is. Screw Nils. No way.

"Hey, Jen."

She turned to face him from the sink where her arms were elbow-deep in suds. "Mmm?"

"I know you may think an urban Chicago playboy isn't fit for hard work, but you're not getting rid of me that easy—"

"No, I just—"

"You just didn't think I could cut the mustard."

"No! I'm sure you can! I just—"

"You just think I'm a man who welches on deals he makes?"

"No! Sam! I just didn't want you to feel like you owed me anything!"

"But I do," he responded, eyes twinkling. "We had a deal, and I broke it. I owe you a booth."

It dawned on her that he had just teased her into accepting his help again, but it still didn't feel right. "Okay. You owe me a booth for too much teasing. I accused you of infidelity. What do I owe you?"

He beamed at her. "I could use a date for the Stroll tonight."

Chapter 6

Sam and Jenny made their way from her apartment to Gardiner High School, which was a short walk down Main Street toward the river, over the bridge, and a right turn onto Stone Street, where they approached the campus through the empty parking lot.

Sam wasn't impressed with the relatively small, squat, brown-brick public building before him, but he stopped walking abruptly, staring gape-mouthed at a herd of about a dozen bison grazing on the football field between two goal posts as they approached.

"Are…are those…"

Jenny stopped walking and nodded, smiling at Sam. "Bison. They wreak havoc on that field every year, but it gets fixed in the spring."

"How often does this happen?"

"Bison coming to town?" She shrugged. "Couple times a week. Especially when it's cold. The building throws off heat. Not that they need it, but it melts the fields faster around here, and they can graze." She tugged on his coat sleeve. "Come on, Greenhorn, we've got work to do."

She unlocked the front door of the school, and he stepped inside behind her, the familiar smell common to every high school in America surrounding him.

"This takes me back. I feel like I'm fifteen again."

"The smell, right? Everyone says that."

"You forget it over time, but wow! It's really evocative."

"Good or bad?"

"Mmm. Good, I guess. I liked high school well enough."

She started down the corridor, and he followed.

"Did you do any sports?" she asked over her shoulder.

"Yeah. Lacrosse in the spring. I played a little hockey but mostly sat on the bench."

She looked back at him, raising an eyebrow, and he sensed she was trying not to smile. "That must have hurt."

"Frankly, it would have hurt a lot more to be smashed into the boards on the ice. Is hockey big here?"

"Not as big as it is in Minnesota, but all the kids skate. You know, on lakes and ponds and such. You can't grow up in Montana without learning how."

He nodded. "I believe that."

They passed the main office, and Jenny paused, glancing in. "There's a light on. I wonder if Paul's here."

"Paul?" he asked, following her into the office.

"The principal."

The main office was quiet, and they passed a long counter covered with piles of paper and two empty desks, where two secretaries would probably sit. Jenny knocked softly at a door that had light pouring out of the bottom. The sign on the door read, "Your Principal is your Pal." Sam rolled his eyes.

A cheerful voice boomed from behind the door. "Come on in!"

Jenny pushed open the door, and a young man stood up from his seat behind the desk, his handsome face breaking into a beaming smile. Tall and blond, with an athletic, well-built body and a stupid grin totally directed at Jenny, he was dressed sharply in light khakis and a crisp blue-and-white gingham dress shirt, which was rolled up casually midforearm to reveal a light smattering of blond hair on a muscular arm.

"Jenny!"

"Good morning!" she answered.

His eyes met Jenny's easily and held them for a longer-than-necessary second before noticing Sam behind her.

"Who's this with you, Jen?" he asked, his face cooling a touch as he flicked his eyes to Sam.

"Paul, this is Sam. Sam, this is our principal, Paul."

Your Principal is your Pal, indeed.

A sick feeling started fanning out from Sam's gut. It got incrementally worse when he turned to Jenny, who was smiling at the attractive, young principal with an easy grin.

"Good to know you," said Paul, offering his hand.

"You too." Sam returned the strength of Paul's grip, pumping his hand twice before dropping it.

Paul turned to Jenny with that dopey grin back in place. "How're you today, Jenny? Always good to see my favorite science teacher!"

His favorite *science teacher?* Sam found it hard to believe

105

there was more than one science teacher in such a small school anyway, which meant Paul's comment was a corny joke too.

"Oh, you!" she said, shaking her finger at the principal like she'd heard that one before. That said, she was still smiling at him.

Sam felt a sheen of sweat break out on his forehead. "Warm in here, right?"

Jenny turned to him. "N-Not really."

Paul pushed his preppy tortoise-shell glasses up on his nose to stare at Sam intently.

He looks like a J. Crew model, Sam thought with derision. *What principal in the middle of Nowhere, Montana, is thirty years old and looks like a J. Crew model? And what's he doing* here *when he should be sailing regattas in Connecticut?*

"So, Sam…you visiting family? Passing through?"

Sam smiled at him tightly.

"Sam's cousin is marrying my best friend Ingrid," Jenny offered.

Paul nodded. "In town for the wedding then?"

"Something like that," Jenny replied. She turned her eyes to Sam, and her expression, caught between tenderness and laughter, like she was holding on to an inside joke that only they knew, made his heart skip a beat.

"Where's home?" asked Paul.

"Chicago."

"Ah-ha. Great place, Chi-Town." Paul's shoulders relaxed perceptibly then, and the next smile he offered Sam was a hell of a lot more genuine. That's when Sam's suspicions were confirmed. Paul's interest in Jenny was not just professional. "When do you head back?"

"Next week," Sam answered, purposely vague. "Looking forward to helping out Jenny today, though."

Paul turned to Jenny, eyebrows raised in question.

"The booth," she confirmed. "For the Stroll tonight. Sam's going to help me bring the pieces up from the basement."

Paul thumped his forehead with the heel of his palm then nodded at her, smiling. "What would I do without you, Jenny Lindstrom? I totally forgot that needed to be done. Let me help you two get the basement unlocked, and we'll find those pieces."

Paul rushed to the door, practically side-checking Sam out of the way, then put his hand on the small of Jenny's back to usher her through the office.

"Why aren't the boys giving you a hand?" Paul asked, keeping his shoulder next to hers as they strolled down the hallway with Sam following behind.

"They bartend until late on Friday nights...may as well let them sleep. Sam and I can bring up the pieces, and they can pick them up later."

They descended the stairs, and Paul led them to the caged room that held the twenty large, unwieldy plywood pieces. He unlocked an exterior door that opened with a view onto the bison still grazing on the football field.

Sam turned to Jenny, ignoring Paul. "So we'll just bring them out here? Stack them against the wall?"

She nodded. "Perfect."

"Can I help you two?" Paul stood tense beside Jenny, watching Sam with cool, irritated eyes.

No thanks, chum. You scurry back upstairs to your office and leave us alone now.

"No, thanks." Sam shook his head, smirking. "I'll handle it from here."

"Sam!" Paul clapped him on the back. "That is so terrific, because I could sure use Jenny's help in my office collating the newsletters in time for tonight."

Crap on a cracker. I've been outmaneuvered.

Jenny flicked her glance to Sam. "Are you sure you'll be okay?"

"He'll be fine!" Paul chirped, shepherding Jenny toward the stairs before she could change her mind.

***

When Jenny looked back, Sam was staring at her and Paul without any trace of his usual teasing smile. He didn't seem like himself at all.

"I can stay and help yo—"

"It's fine, Jen," said Sam, stepping into the cage to get started on the heavy lifting.

She didn't sense it was fine, but what else could she do? When your boss needed help, you helped, that was all there was to it.

The countertop in the main office was covered with ten piles of paper that needed to be collated and stapled. About fifty newsletters had already been put together, so she got started collating the next 150. She walked down the length of the counter, grabbing one of each sheet and then handing them to Paul in neat piles. He sat at the end of the counter ready to staple.

"So," he started, "Sam."

Jenny nodded and smiled. "He's nice to help, isn't he?"

"Umm. Yeah. Real nice." Paul stapled a packet, then cleared his throat. "Now, how is it that he's visiting you again, Jenny?"

"Oh, he's not really visiting *me*. We're doing some, er, legal work for Kristian and Ingrid."

"I thought you said Ingrid was getting married. What kind of legal work?"

Jenny flicked a glance at him without stopping her workflow. She really wasn't sure what to say. She hadn't anticipated having to tell anyone about taking marriage vows on Ingrid's behalf, so she didn't have some smooth way to explain. *The less said, the better.*

She stopped what she was doing and gave him a direct look. "It's complicated, Paul. Personal."

He held her eyes for a moment, his expression surprised. "Okay. I know when I shouldn't pry."

Eager to change the subject, Jenny asked, "Are you and Lars fishing on Sunday?"

Paul was the best friend of Jenny's middle brother, Lars, and looked so much like Lars, it was almost impossible to tell the two apart from a distance. In fact, folks in Gardiner called Principal Paul the "fourth Lindstrom" because he was tall, blond, and ice-blue-eyed like her brothers…which was oddly comforting to Jenny. It made Paul seem familial to her and eliminated the uneasiness she generally felt around young, single men.

"Fishing. Hmm. Good question," Paul said. "Lower Slide already had a good six inches of ice last weekend."

Lower Slide Lake was about twenty minutes from Gardiner and a popular spot for ice fishing. Paul and Lars headed down there just about every Sunday afternoon or evening from December to February.

"Lars got that fourteen-inch cutthroat last year," she reminded him in a teasing voice. That particular trout had almost been big enough to feed all six of them and had started a wicked rivalry between Lars and Paul.

"Dang fish! Don't remind me!"

Jenny giggled as she handed him another packet.

He looked at her thoughtfully, intently, holding her eyes. "You have the best laugh, Jenny."

Heat poured into her cheeks.

"Thank you," she said, dropping his fawning gaze.

"So how long is Sam staying?"

"Just until Monday."

"I think he likes you."

She shrugged. "Oh, I don't know."

"Another man can tell," said Paul.

Shoot, shoot, shoot. No, Paul. I don't see you like that, she thought, her heart beating faster with the sudden, unwanted realization that Paul might be interested in her.

He stopped what he was doing and stood up, closing the short distance between them, and Jenny swallowed uncomfortably, dreading what she knew was coming next. He stood before her, hands by his sides, and spoke plainly.

"I have to admit, I was a little surprised to see you with Sam this morning. Surprised by how it made me feel." He paused, scanning her face. "You must know how I feel about you, Jenny. And I…well, I probably should have spoken sooner, but I've—I've tried to give you space and time to heal. I know your mother's passing took a toll, and I just always thought—or hoped—the perfect moment would present itself." He reached out to touch her arm. "For a long time, I've wanted—"

"Paul, stop! Please stop. Please don't do this."

"Jenny, just let me tell you how I feel—"

"I don't see you like that!" she blurted out, stepping back from him, her heart about to beat through the wall of her chest. She looked down at her shoes, overwhelmed by the sheer awkwardness of the situation.

Oh, she had noticed Paul's eyes hold hers a beat longer than necessary from time to time. Or that when he came to dinner, he always sat next to her and always insisted they hold hands for grace instead of folding their hands as they did when he didn't join them. He often stopped to chat with her in the halls or at school functions. But she had chalked up all of this, naïvely or not, to the close relationship he shared with her family through his friendship with Lars and the boys.

To be careful, though, she had also kept Paul at a brotherly distance to repel any possible romantic expectation, and she assumed whatever rogue feelings he occasionally felt for her weren't substantial enough for him to pursue: just a symptom of an available young man in a town without a lot of options. She had figured that the occasional romantic interest she felt from him was fleeting, not fixed, and that was exactly the way she wanted it.

"You see *him* like that?"

Her head snapped up, effectively ending her musings. "Not that it's any of your business, but I barely *know* him! I met him yesterday."

He nodded at her, his expression closing up. "You seemed pretty chummy."

Jenny didn't want to talk about Sam. "Paul, you're important to me. You're my boss, my coworker. You're my friend. You're Lars's…"

"I'm Lars's friend." He sat back down and smiled at her ruefully, shaking his head back and forth. "I thought—"

"No." Jenny's voice was firm, brooking no further argument. "You're my boss. And—and like a brother to me, if anything. I just can't see you that way…" He winced, and Jenny cringed, sorry that she was hurting him. "I'm sorry."

Paul stapled the pile of papers in front of him and spoke softly. "You're special, Jenny. Always have been. Can't blame a man for trying."

"Be my friend?" *Please be my friend and don't turn this into something awkward.*

"Sure, Jen." He looked up and smiled at her, but it didn't reach his eyes, and sadness lingered on his face.

They worked quietly for several uncomfortable minutes before Paul spoke up again. "But, Jenny…feelings don't just…disappear. So if things don't work out with Sam, I'm still here, okay?"

What in the world was he talking about? There's nothing spoken between Sam and me! Things weren't going to work out or not work out—there wasn't even anything to work out, for heaven's sake!

"There's nothing between me and Sam," she said, but that tone of finality that came so easily in rejecting Paul's feelings didn't resonate in her voice…and she knew it.

So did Paul, apparently. "That's not what I saw. But I could be wrong, I guess. I'm just saying, I'm here for you, Jenny."

That's not what I saw. The words turned around in her head as they worked in awkward silence. She thought of Sam's life in Chicago. Hair slicked back, wearing a tuxedo. Cubs games. Pepper. He wasn't with Pepper anymore, true, but she was someone Sam had chosen for himself.

That's not what I saw. She was Jenny Lindstrom. Simple Jenny. A schoolteacher from a tiny town in Montana, with a shabby little apartment and an uncomplicated life.

That's not what I saw.

What did Paul see? Jenny wondered. *And why do I wish I could see it too?*

***

It took fifteen trips back and forth, but Sam had stacked all twenty pieces of the booth in a tidy pile, leaning up against the brick wall of the school building so Jenny's brothers could pick them up later if the building was locked. He was sweaty and dusty when he walked back into the school to find Jenny. When he heard voices coming from the office, he couldn't help himself and tiptoed closer to listen.

"There's nothing between me and Sam." Jenny's voice.

He stopped in his tracks, his heart thumping in his chest at the sound of her voice and his name.

"That's not what I saw…I'm here for you, Jenny." Sam couldn't hear the middle of Paul's comments. His voice was farther away than hers and muffled.

Sam backed up against the wall outside of the office door and stayed as still as he could. He didn't want them to think he'd been eavesdropping, plus he was bothered by this exchange, especially the last part: "I'm here for you, Jenny." *Oh, I just bet you are, buddy.*

Sam tiptoed back down the hallway as quietly as he could and out the front door, finally sitting down on a bench facing the bison on the football field.

He breathed in, savoring the shock of the cold air to his lungs. She was very clear nothing was going on between her and Sam, and her "pal" Paul was very clear he was *there* for her.

It stung a little to admit it, but it made perfect sense, actually, that Jenny and Principal Paul would be a couple-in-the-making. She deserved someone good-looking and kind, with his act together, who lived somewhere she lived, worked where she worked, and loved it as she did. What better match for Jenny than a young principal in the school where she worked? *Certainly not you, Sam.*

He shook his head, wishing it didn't bother him. He knew he had a connection with Jenny. She was kind and strong, spirited and beautiful. As much as he hadn't really entertained the possibility of being with Jenny, the reality that she wasn't interested felt pretty bad.

It also meant his feelings for her had grown beyond a connection or impression. It meant that Sam was falling for her.

"*Here* you are!" Jenny plopped down on the bench next to Sam. "How long have you been done?"

"A little while. I didn't want to disturb you and Principal Paul."

"Disturb us?" She made a face. "We were just collating newsletters."

"Mmm," Sam demurred.

"Sam!" She elbowed him lightly, and he looked at her face, her lovely face that had him all turned around in such a short amount of time. "Paul's my boss. He's just a friend."

Sam nodded vaguely and looked at the bison with fascination. "Yup. He seems very friendly."

"Stop. He's my brother's best friend. Folks around here call him the 'fourth Lindstrom.' He may as well be, as far as I'm concerned."

"I overheard you two talking."

"Oh." Her shoulders slumped, and she sighed. "What did you hear?"

"That there's nothing between you and me."

"Well, there…isn't. Is there?"

"I don't know," he said, facing her. He shook his head, then shrugged. "I just know how I feel. I hated the way he took you away from me to go upstairs. I wanted to punch him in the nose, Jenny. I don't know where that came from."

She smiled at him, cocking her head to the side. "Sam? I don't want to be with Paul. I told him so."

Sam's forehead wrinkled in confusion. "What do you mean?"

"Well, Mr. Eavesdropper, I guess you missed the part where he confessed he had feelings for me, and I told him I didn't see him like that." She paused for a second, still grinning at him. "You had nothing to be jealous about."

He wanted to deny he'd ever been jealous, but it would have been a lie. Instead, he reached for her hand and took it in his, lacing his fingers through hers before she could pull away. And sitting there in the wintery sunshine, the tension he'd been holding onto for the past hour slowly left his muscles, and he relaxed with Jenny beside him.

It was a peaceful few minutes too...until Sam's stomach gurgled with hunger, which make them both laugh with surprise.

"Want to get some lunch?" he asked.

She glanced at her watch. "It's only eleven."

He dropped her hand and stood up. "So says the person who dawdled in the principal's office with a stapler while someone else lifted twenty heavy pieces of plywood across the length of a high school basement."

"If only you hadn't teased me," she taunted in a singsong voice.

He beamed at her. "Brash words from the woman who cooked...what was it? *Cheap pig* for breakfast this morning?"

She half cringed, half smiled up at him from her seat on the bench. "That was pretty bad, eh?"

"You're pretty cute when you're mad, Jen."

"You think so?"

"I do."

Sam offered her his hands, which she took so he could pull her up. He might have stood there holding her hands all day if he hadn't heard an approaching voice ask, "Since when can't you stand up by yourself, little sister?"

"Oh, Nils!" Jenny leaned her head around Sam and stuck out her tongue toward the sound of the voice.

Sam looked over his shoulder to find three blond giants heading over to them from the nearby parking lot, eyes trained on Sam.

***

It should have surprised Sam to be having lunch alone with three hulking Swedes, but he was becoming accustomed to a different rhythm of life with Jenny around. And it didn't include a ho-hum, predictable sort of sequence of events.

Turns out Paul had called Lars, Lars had called Erik, and Erik had called Nils. And all three of Jenny's brothers had decided it was time to meet this Sam, kin of Ingrid or not, before he spent too much more time with Jenny.

Jenny invited her brothers to join them for lunch but insisted on the Prairie Dawn so she could run upstairs and grab Casey for a quick walk, leaving Sam alone with "the boys," a moniker so singularly ridiculous, he wondered how she'd gotten away with it for so long. Then again, judging from the protective way the boys felt about Jenny, he imagined she could get away with just about anything.

They could almost have been triplets, they looked so alike. All were taller than six feet, surpassing Sam's six foot one easily. All had light-blond hair and ice-blue eyes. Their chests were broad and filled out from hard work or active lives, and they all had the rugged coloring of men who spent a good portion of their lives outdoors.

Erik, the youngest and closest to Jenny in age, had a rounder face than his older brothers and was the shortest of the three by a hair.

The middle brother, Lars, was the tallest and most built of the three. Sam guessed from looking at him that free weights were part of his regular routine; no way he looked like that just from bartending and hiking.

And Nils, the oldest, had a cleft in his chin and looked the most like he wanted to punch Sam in the nose.

When they all sat down in the small booth, Jenny had taken the seat beside Sam, leaving Erik, Nils, and Lars to squish together onto the bench across from them, which essentially left Nils facing Sam head-on and his brothers bookending him with their backs, their legs hanging over the sides of the small bench.

Since Jenny had left with a promise to return—a promise Sam was frankly clinging to—the Lindstrom brothers effectively sat in judgment of Sam across a picnic table, with interest in him anchored somewhere between curiosity and whoop-ass. *Protective* actually seemed a hopelessly weak word as he smiled engagingly at them across the table. He tried the smile he used with especially difficult clients, but the Lindstroms weren't a real smiley bunch in return.

"So, Sam," Nils began, putting his paws flat on the table, "what are you doing here?"

"Didn't Jenny tell you?" He didn't know how much she'd told her brothers about Ingrid and Kristian's unconventional nuptials.

"She said he's giving some kind of legal help to Ingrid," Lars piped up, speaking to Erik.

"We like Ingrid," Erik offered.

"Yep. Ingrid and Kristian needed help with some legal work and asked me and Jenny to lend a hand."

"Where you from? Up north? Billings? Missoula?" Nils named the two largest cities in Montana.

"Chicago," Sam answered.

Erik whistled low. "The city."

Lars's brow furrowed much like Jenny's. "Chicago!"

Now Erik again: "Awful long way to come for *legal work*. Hard to get here from there."

"That's true," Sam agreed. "I flew into Billings and had a long drive after that."

Nils nodded. "Must be a serious *legal issue* to make a trip like that."

Sam was getting sick and tired of the cat-and-mouse-style questions and comments. He folded his hands in front of him on the table and spoke directly, adding some steel to his tone.

"You know what, guys? It's this simple: Kristian's my cousin. He's like a brother to me. If he asked me to jump out of a plane, I wouldn't ask too many questions before jumping. That's just how it is. So, yes, when he and his fiancée asked for my help, I flew here from Chicago, and yes, I'm going to handle his legal business for him because he's in

Afghanistan and he can't handle it for himself." He paused for a second, then asked, "Any more questions about Kristian, or are we good now?"

Nils eyed him back, then nodded in approval, suddenly showing a mouthful of the whitest teeth Sam had ever seen. "You *sure* you're not from Montana?"

"Spent a good bit of time north of Great Falls growing up."

"Jenny-girl loved it up there in Great Falls," Erik stated.

This was new information to Sam, and it surprised him. "Jenny lived in Great Falls?"

"Went to college there," said Erik.

Nils nudged his middle brother. "Couldn't get her to come home, remember, Lars?"

Lars nodded. "Me and Nils didn't like her living alone up there, so far away from us. We tried to get her to come home, but she wouldn't budge. Loved it there. Took that job and everything."

"What job?" Sam asked, fascinated that small-town Jenny had once settled down in Great Falls, a small city with more than fifty thousand residents, an international airport, a symphony orchestra, and several semiprofessional sports teams.

"Teaching. At one of the schools there. Private one," said Erik.

"She was teaching science to the little kids," Nils clarified. "Jenny always loved the little ones. She didn't really want to work with the teenagers."

"But the little kids didn't need a science teacher here,"

Lars finished.

Sam leaned forward. "Why didn't it work out? What made her—"

"Come home?" Nils cocked his head to the side as Sam had seen Jenny do many times. "Because our mamma got sick."

"Jenny came home to tend to her," added Erik.

Sam didn't realize he had been holding his breath until it came out in a sudden rush of sympathy. "Sh-she came home to take care of your mother? I'm sorry. Jenny only mentioned her once, and I—"

"Mamma got sick three years back, and it went quick after. Jenny came home to be with Mamma, and then she stayed on even after she passed. To be near Pappa. And us, I think." Nils finished and folded his hands on the table.

"Had to be hard for her to come back here after liking it so much up there in Great Falls," Erik said, frowning. "Maybe you two should have left things alone like Mamma wanted."

Nils elbowed his younger brother in the side. "What's right is right. Jenny would agree with me and Lars if you asked her, *little* brother. She needed to come home."

Erik pursed his lips but said no more.

"I'm sorry about your mother," said Sam.

Lars nodded. "She was a good lady. Jenny-girl's a lot like her."

"Jen got back here and found the apartment upstairs there and got the job at the high school. She has a good life," said Nils. "Never talked much about Great Falls again."

They were all silent for a moment. Sam couldn't stop thinking about Jenny living in Great Falls. She seemed so at home in Gardiner, he just assumed returning home after college had been her first choice. What a revelation that she would have made a different choice if fate hadn't intervened.

He thought of young Jenny losing her mother and her dream at the same time. Life was incredibly unfair.

A petite redheaded waitress stopped by their table and smiled at all four of them, her warm brown eyes finally resting on Nils. "Jenny comin' back?"

Erik and Lars suddenly busied themselves with the menus. Nils cleared his throat and nodded at the young woman, his voice suddenly deeper than it had been a moment ago. "She'll be back, Maggie."

Sam glanced up at Maggie and smiled politely, then caught a glimpse of Nils's face and did a double take, realizing the telltale scarlet flush was not singular to Jenny. It must be a Lindstrom thing because Nils was turning an interesting shade of salmon as he faced Maggie.

Now that Sam was clued in, he realized Maggie had offered a polite greeting to the rest of them, but the way she looked at Nils was eons away from mere politeness.

When she spoke again, Sam noticed her soft Scottish burr. "Then I'll hold yer food 'til she gets back."

Sam watched her go, then turned back to Nils, grinning at Jenny's oldest brother. "Maggie, huh?"

Jenny plopped back down next to Sam, winking at Lars. "It's *always* been Maggie for Nils, right Lars? Not that he's done much about it."

"*Gode Gud.* Shut up, Jen," Nils snarled, frowning at her and elbowing Lars in the side roughly. Erik tried to hide a grin behind a menu.

"Oh, for heaven's sake, Nils. Ask her out already. Everyone in town knows you're sweet on her." Jenny whispered this across the table, and Sam sensed she was enjoying herself immensely.

"When I want to ask someone out, Jen, I'll good and darn well ask them out. Until then, it's exactly none of your business, *lillesøster.*"

Jenny burst into barely stifled giggles and was quickly joined by Erik and Lars, whose shuddering shoulders gave away their amusement. Nils crossed his arms over his chest and rolled his eyes at his younger siblings, no doubt wishing he was anywhere but trapped on a bench between them.

The lady of the moment returned with their sandwiches and asked if she could bring them anything else. Four sets of eyes turned to Nils, but he stammered out that they had everything they needed.

"Thanks, Mags," said Jenny. From the way Maggie smiled back at Jenny, Sam got the feeling the two women were pretty good friends.

Erik pushed the salt and pepper to the center of the table. "Salt, pepper, Sam?"

"Sam's had enough pepper for today," said Jenny, winking at Sam.

Erik nodded in understanding. "Allergic?"

"Umm." Sam could feel Jenny's shoulders shaking with mirth beside him. "Something like that." Finally, he shrugged, letting the Lindstrom brothers in on the joke. "My ex-girlfriend's name was Pepper."

"How's that?" Erik furrowed his brows in the Lindstrom family trademark way. "Pepper's a condiment."

Already giddy, Jenny lost it, laughing until tears slid down her cheeks.

"Long weekend ahead for you, Sam," offered Erik with feeling, gesturing toward Jenny by jerking his head and cringing. Lars and Nils nodded earnestly, full of sympathy for Sam. "He broke the mold after He made Jenny."

Yes, He did, thought Sam, looking at her, feeling his heart fill. *Indeed He did.*

Chapter 7

What a day.

Jenny flopped down on the loveseat in her living room, leaning her head back and closing her eyes.

Lars and Erik would pick up the booth pieces and assemble them at the high school's designated spot in front of the Tackle Shop, and Sam left Jenny at her apartment with a promise to pick her up at five that afternoon. She glanced at her watch; she had a few hours.

Her head ached from all the developments of the day: so much to think about and process. Sam, Pepper, Paul. She turned her mind to Paul first and thought about writing him a quick email to clear the air but then thought better of it. His feelings were bound to be tender, and she didn't want to pour salt on the wound. She was still flustered by his near declaration; for as much of her life she had spent in the company of men, she still didn't understand them.

Paul had been like a brother to her for years, for as long as she had known him, comforting her after her mother's passing, joining her family for Sunday supper more times than she could count, leading the PTA meetings that she attended faithfully. For heaven's sake, how long had he harbored romantic feelings for her?

She pictured him in her mind. He was handsome, yes, but not her type at all. *Kissing Paul would be like kissing my brothers. Now, kissing Sam would be a different thing—*

Whoa, Jenny! Her eyes flew opened as she halted her thoughts midstream. *Where did that come from? Kissing Sam? That is* not *something that should be on your mind.*

She walked into her bedroom, determined to distract herself from such bold ideas, but she couldn't banish the fantasy of Sam's mouth lightly touching hers, feather soft, searching. Her pulse sped up, and she gave up the fight, sitting on her bed, touching her lips softly with her fingers, succumbing to the dream in her head. *What would it feel like to kiss Sam?*

The boy she had kissed in college was eager but impatient. He had pressed his lips to hers gently several times on their third and fourth dates, which felt exciting and interesting. On their fifth date, however, out of nowhere, he had shoved his tongue between her lips and snatched one of her breasts in a way that had frightened her. She'd pushed him away and told him to cut it out, but he'd moved in on her, meaning to touch her again. So Jenny had done what her brothers taught her: she'd placed her hands firmly on his shoulders and brought her knee up sharply to his groin with a swift, incapacitating thrust. He'd fallen to the floor, clutching at his man-parts, cursing her every which way from last Sunday.

That had been quite enough for Jenny. She was only too glad not to pursue another romance and had kept men at a careful distance ever since.

Yet here was Sam, making her mind whirl unexpectedly with ideas of romance.

The heart wants what the heart wants. Beyond common sense. Beyond higher reason. Beyond all material and emotional considerations that should make the heart give up its longing. The heart *still* wants what the heart wants, in spite of everything.

And Jenny's heart wanted Sam.

***

Jenny checked herself out in the mirror and grinned.

Yep. She was ready.

Sam asked her to be his "date" for the Stroll, and that's exactly what Jenny intended to be. Not a companion or a tour guide, but a date.

She decided to leave her practical jeans and boots at home and put on her black velvet jeans, a luxury she had purchased at the mall in Great Falls long ago. She paired these pants with a cream-colored silk blouse she had worn on her job interviews three years ago and a cream-colored angora cardigan sweater with tiny cubic zirconia buttons. She dug through her closet until she found the pair of black velvet ballet flats she had purchased to wear with the pants. Dusty from years of neglect, she swatted them against each other until the dust settled elsewhere. She knew they were a silly choice for cold, possibly icy streets. But she didn't care. It was only one night, and she wanted it to be special.

In her modest jewelry box, she found her mother's crystal earbobs and decided to wear them. She had never worn them before, but the crystal in the earrings would match the crystal buttons on the sweater. Besides, it was Christmastime. Why not sparkle a little?

She laid her clothes out on her bed, smiling at them with anticipation, and took a long, hot shower. She washed and blow-dried her hair until it was straight and shiny, then searched her bathroom cupboard for her makeup case. Once she had blown off two years of dust from the zipper, she opened it up and applied a bit of mascara, a hint of eye shadow, and some pale-pink lip gloss. She put on her clothes, brushed her hair, and added the earrings last. Then she looked in the mirror.

A whole new Jenny stared back at her.

The jeans had always looked good, but she had lost a few pounds between the years she spent in college and the years she lived in Gardiner, so the waist fit perfectly now. The cream of the blouse and sweater matched her hair, and she was right about the crystals—the buttons on the sweater caught her eyes, and she followed them all the way up to her ears.

Her reflection was a revelation. She still looked like herself, only better, sleeker, more sophisticated. She could definitely pass for a girl from Great Falls tonight, if not somewhere even more cosmopolitan. She blushed at her conceited thoughts and remembered Pepper in her gowns and designer labels.

No need for a swollen head, Jen. You look good. Good, and that's it.

She was holding Casey at the kitchen table when Sam knocked on the door. Her tummy leapt, and she couldn't stop the spreading smile on her face. After putting Casey back in her playpen, she took one last look at her face in the hallway mirror before she answered the door.

He had his hands braced on the doorframe and was looking down when she opened the door. He looked up slowly, from her little shoes, to her velvet pants, to her soft cream sweater. His eyes lingered on her blouse, and Jenny stood frozen, waiting. She swallowed nervously and bit the inside of her lower lip, waiting for his eyes to meet hers.

And then they did.

Surprise on Sam's face was nothing new to Jenny. She'd even seen admiration before now, but this expression was entirely different. Inexperience notwithstanding, she knew instinctively that she was looking at *want*.

Focused. Carnal. Want.

He swallowed, his body tense and almost completely motionless except for his eyes, which lowered again in languid approval from her eyes to her toes. His breath exited his lungs until they were empty, and the end sound was ragged, labored. As he breathed in deeply, he raised his eyes again, and his gaze shifted then, tenderness phasing out want. He searched her face, and she recognized hope dawn in his eyes, which were vulnerable and unguarded. His lips turned up in a slight, impish smile, which suddenly made him seem very much himself again—the Sam she recognized.

Watching these feelings play out on his face, an awesome joy exploded like fireworks in her head. She started laughing softly with satisfaction and pleasure.

I've never felt this beautiful in all my life.

"Hi," she offered shyly.

"I can't speak."

"You just did," she teased, flicking her own eyes up and down to check him out too.

Was it effortless for him to look as good as he did?

Casually handsome, he was what Jenny would special order if she wanted her heart to skip a beat and her throat to go dry with wanting. He still had on his jeans from earlier, but he had swapped out his flannel shirt and sweat shirt for the crisp white shirt he had been wearing with his suit yesterday, and added a black belt. His black coat was long and sleek, and she knew it would be soft if she ran her fingers over the sleeve or along the collar—soft and maybe warm from his skin. She noticed the pulse in his neck, beating like a beacon.

Warm, for sure.

Sam cleared his throat, staring at her, watching her with a quiet intensity. "I've never seen anything as pretty as you."

A flush of heat colored her cheeks, and she looked down, overwhelmed by such flattery. "Even in Chicago?"

"Nowhere. Never."

He took a step toward her, and Jenny backed up so he could come inside, though she felt a little nervous to be alone in her apartment with him. The attraction between them was like a tight guitar string attached from his heart to hers; it was as though someone had just plucked it, and it hummed and vibrated between them like a current, like something alive. It was too much, too intimate, like something irrevocable or life changing was about to happen.

"I have to get my bag," she said. "Give me a sec."

She turned and headed for her room, shutting the door quietly behind her and sitting on her bed to collect herself.

His reaction was everything she had hoped for, and from the look on his face, she guessed that he was falling for her as hard as she was falling for him. The comfort in knowing her longing for him was mutual wasn't exactly comfort*able*. It frightened her too. This wasn't a man who lived in Gardiner, to whom she could willingly and safely give her heart. While Sam might be *technically* available, the differences in their lives also made him *unavailable,* and if she wanted to protect her heart, she needed to remember that.

Be careful, Jenny. You're playing with fire here. Be careful of your heart.

How she wished she could talk to her mother. Ask her how she knew she was falling in love with Pappa. How it made her feel and if she was frightened and unsure and excited all at once. She closed her eyes, breathing in, and opened them, breathing out.

Noen elsket meg en gang. Jeg er velsignet.

Like an answer to her prayer, she heard her mother's loving voice in her head: *Make memories tonight, Jenny-girl. Just be sure they're memories you want to keep.*

"*Ja, Mamma*," she whispered.

Then she grabbed her bag and left the quiet of her room behind.

***

Sam hadn't moved since she left the room.

He was trying to breathe normally.

131

He was trying to assuage the effect she had just had on his body *before* she came back.

He was trying to remember he was leaving on Monday.

He was losing the first two battles. His pulse was so fast and his blood was rushing so hard to one specific place, he was feeling light-headed. Finally sitting down on the little loveseat, he put his head between his knees. He concentrated on slowing down his heart, breathing in and then out. In, then out. His head started to clear, and he felt other areas of his body relaxing too, thank God. He sat back, shaking his head, at a loss.

He was telling the truth when he said he'd never seen anything as pretty as her. Just as he had expected a chubby Brunhilde at the courthouse, tonight he had expected the same Jenny from today in her old jeans and beat-up boots. The most he had hoped for was that she might leave her hair down for an evening out. The Jenny that had materialized at her apartment door was a revelation. She was a stunner, a knockout, a beauty in any context, in any city, in any town, anywhere.

And she offered this gift to him.

Every moment he spent with her was making him dread Monday. He moved toward it like a condemned man, wanting to grasp and claw at the clock, turn back the hands and slow down time so he had more moments with her, more memories, more warmth to take with him when he returned to his cool, slick life in Chicago.

Why couldn't he have met her there? Why couldn't she have been in Chicago for some reason, any reason, and they could have met and had a chance with each other? The unfairness of finding her and not being able to have her frustrated him. His forehead creased in thought. *But, wait, Sam. Wait.* A small kernel of hope materialized in his head, and he couldn't shake it. *You don't know if she'd consider coming to Chicago. Maybe to visit. Maybe to just visit and see what happens. And maybe she'd like it. Maybe she'd give it a chance.*

Could he ask that of her? A small-town girl, living a perfectly contented life? Sure, he could. He could ask her to visit. He wouldn't pressure her, but if she said yes, he'd show her the best of Chicago and see what she thought. And sure, maybe it was unlikely that she'd agree, but he couldn't shake the possibility. Besides, he'd never know unless he asked. He would just have to wait for the right moment.

She came back out of her room with a bright smile, and he stood up.

"Thanks for this," he said. "For your beautiful outfit, and…" He gestured at her helplessly, unaccustomed to feeling so clumsy around a woman.

"Thank you. It was fun to dress up. I don't get the chance very often. The last time I wore this was at UGF."

She moved to the front closet and took out her parka, struggling to put it on while holding her purse.

"Let me help you," he said.

"Thanks."

As she zipped up, he lifted her hair off her neck where it was trapped under the collar, just as he had at the courthouse. He gently laid her hair back against the open parka hood, watching it mix effortlessly with the white fur of the hood, then put his hands on her shoulders, turning her to face him.

She looked up at him, searching his face, then flicked her glance quickly to his lips before finding his eyes again. And it was that gesture—that tiny gesture—that gave him the courage to do something he'd wanted to do since the moment he arrived tonight.

Later, he would have sworn his heart stopped beating as he bent his head toward her, touching his lips to hers for the first time.

Her breath released in a soft sigh against his mouth as she moved her hands up, flattening them on his chest. Leaning into her, he moved his hands down her back slowly, over her shoulder blades, following her spine to the small of her back, where they rested against the shell of her down parka. He ran his tongue lightly along her lips, eliciting a small moan from deep in her throat and making his fingers curl in excitement and pleasure. Her mouth parted slightly in invitation, and he touched his tongue to hers, sucking it gently into his mouth.

Sam had kissed a lot of girls in his life. A lot. So the fact that this girl—this sweet, beautiful country girl who tasted like fresh air and sunshine—could make shivers run down his arms told him something. If he hadn't been sure before, he was sure now: he was *definitely* falling for Jenny Lindstrom.

Her knees must have buckled a little because he felt her lean into him, and he wondered if she could feel his hardness against the soft cradle of her hips.

She turned her head away and broke off the fledgling

kiss before he could deepen it any further, stepping back and looking up at his face. He stared back at her lips in amazement. He noted no difference in them, and yet they were permanently changed for Sam. He had touched them, tasted them, and staring at them now—for one brief, desperate moment—he wished they belonged to him.

She smiled at him, tentatively at first, then with more confidence as she closed her eyes and breathed in deeply.

"Jenny, I—"

"Me too, Sam." She opened her eyes, and his breath caught.

Is the tenderness in her eyes just a mirror of my own?

"Jenny…"

He was lost in her eyes. The same bright eyes he'd seen flash with spirit and kindness were now heavy with passion. If he kept staring, he'd kiss her again. He'd kiss her senseless. He'd kiss her until tomorrow morning if she let him. But he didn't want to scare her. He didn't want to ruin anything as amazing as the kiss they'd just shared.

She didn't resist him as he pulled her against his body and put his arms around her, closing his eyes as he held her. She smelled of shampoo and wind and the outdoors. He waited, breathlessly, to see if she would pull away, but after a moment, he felt her arms encircle him, her palms flat against his shoulder blades. She gently leaned her head sideways, resting it on his shoulder.

Wild promises and impetuous declarations flooded his mind at the threshold of such sweetness, but one prevailing thought stilled them all: *Holding her is the best feeling in the whole world.*

He felt her lift her head and start to pull away, so he leaned back, looking at her face, smiling into her eyes. She wriggled away from him and unlocked the door, then turned to face him, offering him her hand. "Come stroll with me?"

He took her hand and let himself be led out the door.

***

Gardiner loved Christmastime.

The street was festooned with sparkling red-and-white lights like blinking candy canes, zigzagging across the small Main Street. Hundreds of people walked in and out of stores, restaurants, and boutiques, greeting one another cheerfully with "Merry Christmas!"

A musical system piped jolly carols through Main Street, and as the strains of "All I Want for Christmas Is You" filled the air, a smile spread across Sam's face. He squeezed Jenny's hand, feeling happiness bubble up inside of him, caught up in the festive fun of a country Christmas Stroll. Not that he would admit it to anyone, even under torture, but the sweet, sexy Christmas song was actually one of his favorites, and he knew the words by heart. *'Cause I just want you here tonight / holding on to me so tight. / What more can I do? / Oh, baby all I want for Christmas is you...*

It was nothing like Chicago, which also bustled at Christmastime in a teeming, moving mass of people who moved anonymously, consumed with their own lives, shopping, pleasure. It had been a long time since Sam had been surrounded by such a genuine sense of community, and he realized how terribly he must have been missing the wholesome cheerfulness of Montana at Christmastime. The engaging familiarity of attending Jenny's Christmas Stroll was like not only restoring a forgotten memory but reviving it totally, to see it bright and blazing before his eyes.

Sam kept Jenny's fingers tightly laced with his as she directed their course.

Their plan was to walk all the way down Main Street, to enjoy the decorations and lights and then have dinner at the Grizzly Guzzle Grill across the bridge, where Lars worked as a bartender. And lastly, they'd catch the tree lighting at Arch Park near the Yellowstone entrance.

"Heya, Jenny."

"Hi, Miss Lindstrom."

"Hello, Jenny!"

It seemed everyone who passed them knew Jenny, and she received more than a few curious looks just as she had the night before.

Sam also noticed, with narrowing eyes, that every man in Gardiner suddenly seemed to have the pretty schoolteacher on his radar. More than one did a double take as they walked by, nodding appreciatively as they took a second look, then grimacing when they realized she was holding hands with someone else.

With a bit of bemusement, Sam realized it wasn't totally unlike walking into a club with Pepper, except Jenny seemed completely oblivious to the attention, smiling and greeting people as kindly as she had the evening before.

What a difference in these two women. Both beautiful, but one knows it and one doesn't.

They peeked in windows, pointing out decorations to each other. Jenny indicated her favorite shops and boutiques, and they grabbed gingerbread cookies from a little booth outside of the saddler's shop.

Nothing tasted quite like fresh gingerbread.

The warm, fresh-baked cookies immediately conjured up memories of Sam's childhood kitchen. Arriving home after school at Christmastime, the smell of his mother's baking would make his mouth water before he even had time to shuck off his backpack in the front hallway. And there she'd be in the kitchen, taking batches of gingerbread out of the oven to be cooled and decorated later. There was always enough for him and his sisters, and there was cold milk too. She'd tell him to wait for it to cool down, but he'd bite too soon in anticipation and not even feel the sting of the burn on his tongue, savoring the spicy sweetness of her Christmas cookies.

"These taste like my childhood," he said with a sigh.

"Good, right?" She reached up a finger to gently brush off a lingering crumb at the corner of Sam's mouth. Currents zapped between them like electricity, and Sam's tongue darted out to lick where her finger had touched.

He cleared his throat. "Any more?"

She smiled like a minx and shook her head slowly, raising her eyebrows at him knowingly. "Nope. No more."

"Tease," he whispered.

"Look who's talking."

He grinned at her, taking her hand again as they continued walking.

Their walk took them to the Gardiner Tackle Shop at the end of the street, and beside it, Sam noticed a white structure that resembled a small country schoolhouse. It only took him a moment to realize it was the constructed Gardiner High School booth, all twenty pieces fit together by Erik and Lars that afternoon. He smiled at how merry it looked, roped with evergreen and white lights.

The booth had open windows on all four sides, and a large shelf in the front of the booth offered hot apple cider and cider donuts. A cluster of senior girls sang Christmas carols *a capella* from inside. Beside them was Principal Paul, looking dapper in a navy suit and Santa hat, greeting his students and their parents and exchanging holiday cheer.

Paul's face brightened as they approached, focusing tenderly on Jenny. But when his eyes followed her arm down to her hand, securely attached to Sam's, he cringed briefly, shifting his eyes up to Sam with disapproval.

Sam followed as Jenny dropped his hand and crossed the sidewalk to talk to Paul.

"Hey, Paul," she said. "Booth looks good."

"Evening, Jen," said Paul. "Sam."

Sam had it in him to feel sorry for the guy. "Good to see you again, Paul."

"Jenny!" She turned and hugged an older woman and young girl beside her, effectively leaving Sam and Paul staring at one another across the booth's cider shelf. Paul gestured for Sam to follow him to the back of the structure, where they couldn't be overheard by the cider-and-donut crowd.

"Don't hurt her," said Paul, flicking his eyes to Jenny.

Sam didn't have a ready answer to this command. He wished he could say he would never hurt her, but their growing feelings and imminent separation would make such a declaration foolish. Pulling two connected things apart always left a mark, which meant that saying good-bye on Monday would hurt. If it were any consolation, she wouldn't be the only one in pain. Sam was sure of that.

Paul read his rival's face like a book, then shook his head in disgusted resignation. "Okay. Then I'll help her pick up the pieces when you go."

Sam clenched his teeth together, tightening his jaw. "We'll figure it out. Jenny and me."

"*Jenny and I*," Paul muttered, shaking his head at Sam. "If she were mine—"

"She's not."

Paul inhaled sharply and stared at Sam with searing blue eyes, hurt and angry at once.

"It won't end well, Sam. She's a small-town girl."

"It's none of your business, Paul." He was about to turn away when he felt he owed Paul some small conciliation. "We didn't know this would happen. We didn't plan it."

Paul sighed, and his face softened. He nodded at Sam as he might to a student who was trying to own up to wrongdoing.

"You don't know her like I do," Paul whispered, agony clear in his voice.

"It doesn't matter," Sam replied, soft and level.

He felt sorry for his rival. He might feel the same way very soon when he watches Jenny walk out of the Livingston Courthouse, out of his life.

Paul held Sam's eyes for a serious moment, his shoulders finally slumping in defeat as he headed back to the cider, leaving Sam alone.

***

Jenny noticed Sam and Paul talking in the corner but decided not to interfere. Whatever they had to say to each other was best left between them. Still, she couldn't help but notice Sam's previous cheerfulness had taken a dip when they headed down Main Street toward the Guzzle to grab some dinner. He didn't try to take her hand, brooding in silence beside her.

"Okay, Sam," she finally said. "Let's have it."

"What do you mean?"

"What was up between you and Paul?"

"Nothing."

She took his arm and pulled him back against the corner of a building, forcing him to meet her eyes. "Tell me."

"He's worried I'm going to hurt you." He met her eyes and then looked down, kicking at a lump of ice on the sidewalk with the toe of his shoe.

Oh, she thought. *Me too.*

But she mustered her courage to respond to him. "That's silly."

Sam's head whipped up to face her.

"I'm not a child, Sam." She smiled at him. "You're here

for a weekend. We head back to Livingston on Monday, and then it's Chicago for you and back to Gardiner for me. You haven't made any promises, nor have I."

The tension in his faced eased a little as he listened to her words. "I would *never* want to hurt you, Jenny. Never."

She smiled at him, cocking her head to the side. "Sam, the only thing that's hurting me is my belly because I'm hungry. Can you please cheer up a little so we can go have supper?"

The worry on his face scattered. "Sassy little thing when dinner's late."

"You bet," she replied, taking his proffered arm and resuming their course.

Well, Jen, hope you don't need any more bravado tonight, because you just used up your whole reserve. She sighed, trying not to think about Monday when it was only Saturday. *Live in the moment. Make this a memory you want to keep.*

They stopped in front of the picture window at the saddler's shop. Sam asked her which of the gingerbread houses on display was her favorite. She grinned and tapped the glass in front of one completely covered in white frosting, messy and haphazard.

"Looks like something my niece would make," said Sam. "I think you're a soft touch, Miss Lindstrom."

"I love the little ones," she conceded, smiling up at him.

"Your brother mentioned that. He said you wanted to work with little children, but Gardiner didn't need an elementary school teacher, so you took a job at the high school instead."

She nodded, waving to familiar faces here and there as they walked on. "That's true."

"Your brothers said you wanted to stay in Great Falls."

"Did they?"

"I mentioned that Kristian was from Great Falls. Lars mentioned how much you loved it up there."

"I did. I loved going to school there. I thought I would stay after I graduated, but…"

"Your mom got sick."

She flinched, dropping her hand from his arm and shoving her hands in her parka pockets. "Yes. She got sick. So I came home."

"I'm sorry it worked out that way, Jenny. I'm sorry about your mom."

"Me too. She was too young, you know?"

They found themselves at the bridge again.

Jenny held onto the railing, staring out toward the sound of the black, rushing water in the darkness. "She didn't want to worry me. When they came for graduation, she told me she was recovering from a bad bout of the flu. She was much thinner and looked frail. I should have asked more questions, but I was so wrapped up in my own life, I couldn't see what was right in front of me. I believed her, and she had sworn the boys to secrecy. I was the only one to go to college, and she told them, 'My Jenny-girl's going to follow her dreams.' Lars and Nils went against her when they came to get me a few months later." She paused, running her hand back and forth across the railing. "I'll owe them for the rest of my life for making that decision. I wouldn't have ever

143

forgiven myself if I'd missed those last few weeks with her."

Sam stepped up beside her at the railing, covering her mittened hand with his own. "Cancer?"

She nodded, biting her lower lip. "It went fast." She swallowed back her tears, which reminded her of a favorite quote. "C. S. Lewis wrote, 'CRYING is all right in its own way while it lasts. But you have to stop sooner or later, and then you still have to decide what to do.' I cried for a long time, Sam. And then the decision came easily. I needed to stay in Gardiner, to tend to the boys and my pappa and to be with my family. There's nothing more important than family."

"Family's important." He nodded beside her. "But what about *you*?"

"What *about* me?"

"You loved Great Falls. Are you happy here? Is Gardiner enough? Is this what *you* want?"

"I love Gardiner. It's small and safe, and all the people I love are here."

She wasn't being honest with him, though, and she knew it. Gardiner was a long way from perfect as far as Jenny was concerned. A little too small. A little too safe. The truth was, she missed Great Falls terribly. *The symphony, the lectures, the shopping mall.* Not that she could ever be comfortable in a huge city like Chicago, but a small city like Great Falls was her idea of heaven.

She looked up at the sky.

"Look. Cassiopeia. The vain queen." She pointed. "See it? The *W*."

He didn't answer, so she turned to look at him standing beside her.

"I want to kiss you again," he murmured simply, gazing down at her.

She wanted to melt into him, to find comfort and warmth in his arms. To repeat the mind-blowing, toe-curling piece of perfect that had been his lips on hers, his tongue gently sucking on hers. To assuage her terrible, unfulfilled longing for him. To know what it felt like for him to want her as much as she wanted him.

A memory you want to keep. Would she want the memory of so many perfect, passionate, heart-stopping kisses once he was gone?

She straightened her spine and looked around, gesturing to the people coming and going around them.

"Not now," she whispered, "where anyone could see us."

He nudged her in the side gently with his mittened hand. "Then how about dinner?"

She smiled at him, hating that confusion that made her feel disappointed and relieved at the same time.

"Dinner it is."

***

The Grizzly Guzzle Grill was hopping with diners taking a break from the cold of the Stroll. Jenny and Sam sat at a table by the windows, and after a moment, two Cokes appeared, courtesy of Lars at the bar.

"I suppose you want a beer?" Jenny asked.

Sam shrugged. "I like pop too."

"Sam, an occasional beer is a vice I can handle."

He grinned at her, appreciating the way she seemed to loosen up the longer he knew her. "Well, in that case, I'd love a beer." He glanced at Lars. "I assume Lars doesn't disapprove, considering his vocation?"

"The boys aren't big drinkers," Jenny shared, "but they are known to partake from time to time. They have woken up the day after many a Midsummer in pain."

They placed their order, which included two burgers and a beer. The latter part of the order prompted a whooping laugh from Lars at the bar when the waitress headed over to collect the beer, gesturing to Jenny and Sam. Jenny looked over at him, and he pantomimed doing a shot, looking at her expectantly, palms raised in question. She held up her glass of Coke and took a nice, long sip, then smacked her lips in satisfaction, sticking her tongue out at her brother.

"Hey," said Jenny, "did you mention a niece before? When we were looking at the gingerbread?"

"Yeah. My sister Colleen has two little girls: Heidi and Greta. Heidi's five now. Greta's only two." Jenny's face was animated and focused, encouraging him to continue. "And my other sister, Muirin, has a little boy, Colin. He's new."

"New?" Her eyes were bright with interest.

"He was born a few weeks ago. Colleen lives north of Chicago in Milwaukee." He gestured to his left with his left hand. "Muirin lives across the lake in Kalamazoo." He gestured to the right with his right hand. "We were all in Kalamazoo for Thanksgiving at Muirin's place." He fished in his pocket for his iPhone and clicked on the photo app, choosing a picture and handing the phone to Jenny. "Uncle Sammy and baby Colin."

Jenny looked at the picture, and Sam watched her face, picturing her with a ginger-haired, brown-eyed baby on her lap. Knowing what he knew of her, she would make a wonderful mother someday. Warm, loving, honest. And they'd be good kids with a mother like Jenny. His gut twisted as he thought about the lucky man who'd make Jenny his wife. Paul's handsome face entered Sam's mind, and he swallowed against the physical discomfort he felt imagining Jenny with Paul instead of him. He thought back to Paul's words: *I'll help her pick up the pieces.*

Like hell you will. I will figure this out. I will.

She handed the phone back to Sam, beaming. "He's lovely."

Sam nodded, forcing thoughts of Jenny with Paul out of his mind. "You want kids?"

"Someday." She looked down, and a pretty blush colored her cheeks. "Of course I do. What would be better than that? A husband who loves me and a baby or two?" She smiled at him. "Someday."

"And in the meantime?"

"Work. Casey. Getting married to handsome strangers. You know, the usual."

He chuckled, raising his eyebrows. "*Handsome?*"

She shrugged, and the blush deepened, but she faced him with a shy smile, biting her lower lip. Damn, he wanted to kiss her again. "Yes. Handsome."

She looked away, then stood up and excused herself to

go to the restroom, stopping to chat with Lars on her way.

Jenny, Jenny, Jenny, you have no idea what you're doing to me.

He thought about their conversation on the bridge when his hopes for her to come to Chicago had taken a hit. She had been very clear. Her life was in Gardiner, and that's where she wanted to stay. He breathed deeply and sighed, because he couldn't possibly consider Gardiner for himself. There simply wasn't any opportunity for him here. Frankly, Gardiner was charming for a weekend stopover, but that was about all. He would still ask her about visiting Chicago, but not tonight. He didn't want to spoil tonight. It could wait.

The waitress came by with their burgers, and Sam sat back, waiting for Jenny. He took a big sip of beer.

He had wanted to kiss her so badly on the bridge, hold her and comfort her after she told him about her mother. But it was a stupid thing to suggest. Jenny was no Pepper, who used any public opportunity to make out, more for her image than because she genuinely cared for Sam. "Hot Pepper" was one of her favorite magazine captions, and faking surprise when the cameras caught her with her tongue in Sam's mouth was a favorite play of hers. Going back to Chicago, back to girls like Pepper, sat like lead in his stomach.

His mind wandered to what Jenny had said about kids, how she wanted a husband who loved her and kids of her own someday. All the time he'd been with Pepper, any dreams of marriage and kids had been strictly kept at bay— he couldn't imagine himself married to Pepper. And yet after knowing Jenny for only two days, he couldn't help but think of her holding a brown-eyed baby in her arms. Brown-eyed like him.

Jenny returned, smiling at him as she sat down.

Sam took a shaky breath, concealing his internal dialogue behind a big gulp of beer.

"Tree lighting in an hour," she said, taking a big bite of burger.

"Near the arch, right?"

"Uh-huh. There's a big old evergreen there that they keep roped with lights all year. Lights go on during the Christmas Stroll and off on New Year's Day. Then Christmas is over."

"What do you do for Christmas?" Sam asked. They'd be far away from each other by then, but he could think of her, imagine her Christmas Day.

"We'll have a *Julebord* at church, a pre-Christmas party. Usually it's the second or third Sunday of Advent, and it's great. We have a big potluck dinner, make Christmas wreaths, the children sing carols, and we bring toys to donate to needy kids. I love it. I help with the Christmas pageant too. I used to love the symphony in Great Falls. They always had some special concert at Christmastime. Maybe I'll head up there for one of their concerts too. Sometimes I can get Erik to go with me, or Maggie from the Prairie Dawn." She shrugged. "Paul asked me to help with…"

She bit her bottom lip, flicking her glance at Sam and then down at her burger.

If she keeps biting her bottom lip, I'm kissing it in front of her brother, and I don't care if he leaps over the bar and slams his fist in my face. It'll be worth it.

"Go on," Sam encouraged her. At the mention of Paul, something uncomfortable and sharp stabbed at him, but he smiled at Jenny.

"Well, he asked me to help with the Christmas concert this year. It's very good. The senior girls often do a special choral piece, and the orchestra plays selections from Handel's *Messiah*. I'm helping put together special freshman and sophomore choruses this year. If there are any students who excel at an instrument, they're invited to participate."

"What about your family?" he asked.

"Well, we still get our tree on Christmas Eve and decorate it after church. The traditional way. Pappa, Nils, Lars, Erik, and me. Paul sometimes joins us too if he doesn't go back east for the holidays. And we have *glögg*, and *lutefisk*, of course." Sam cringed, and she grinned at him. "It's not that bad!"

"It's worse than 'that bad'!" exclaimed Sam, thinking of the salted fish, cured in lye.

"Well, it's *tradition*. We have it. And then we—"

"Wait just a minute, Jen. Back up. *Glögg*?" He raised his eyebrows teasingly. *Glögg* was a hot mulled wine, made sweet with spices and dried fruit.

"*Glögg* for Christmas Eve only!" She looked sheepish, popping a fry in her mouth. "It wouldn't be Christmas Eve without *glögg*."

"Women will have their vices." He chuckled, surprised by her again, loving the gray areas that made Jenny...well, Jenny. "Then what?"

"We all sleep at Pappa's. On the couch, under the tree, or in one of the spare rooms, and then we exchange gifts on Christmas morning."

"Paul too? The foundling principal?"

"The fourth Lindstrom." She paused, her forehead creased in thought. "He's like a brother to me, Sam. He came here five or six years ago from New England. We were lucky to get him. I mean, he went to all these fancy schools, and he only chose Montana because he vacationed here as a child, and he loves having summers off to explore the parks. Working at a school is the perfect job."

Perfect Paul. Perfect job.

Jenny continued, "Really, he's too young and too dynamic for such a small school in the middle of nowhere. He should be the headmaster of a private school in Boston or New York. Did you know that Gardiner High School is ranked number one in the state of Montana? It is, and it's all because of his ideas and programs. I know he's been made offers, but he chooses to stay here in Gardiner. Anyway, his family's in Maine. He goes to see them Christmas week, usually, but it depends on when Christmas falls. If school goes right up to Christmas Eve, it's almost impossible for him to get home. He'd be stuck in Chicago or Minneapolis for Christmas morning, which means he's sort of stuck here without family. Of course we welcome him into ours."

Of course. And of course he wants to make that family connection official. Sam put his burger down, his appetite fading fast. He finished off his beer.

"And then we go to Christmas-morning services. After

that, we drive up to Bozeman to my aunt's house, my mother's sister, and spend the day with family and cousins. Come home late at night or stay up there if the weather's bad. My aunt does a huge Norwegian Christmas meal and...and...that's it, I guess. I'm off from Christmas Eve until New Year's Day, so I get a nice long break."

"What do you do with all that time? Travel?" he suggested hopefully.

"Travel! What...like to Hawaii? Ha! No. Nothing so fancy. Sometimes I do go up and spend a day or two in Great Falls. Once I even stayed overnight in a hotel and treated myself to shopping and a concert. That's when Ingrid still lived there, though, and so I had a partner in crime." She winked merrily. "Otherwise, I read. Spend time with my pappa. Go ice fishing with Lars until Paul gets home. Visit neighbors. Take walks in the park. Volunteer at church if they need painting or a closet reorganized or something like that. Just a quiet week off."

Ask her! Ask her to come to Chicago for Christmas break! It's the perfect time!

"How about you?" she asked, finishing her Coke and sitting back in her chair. "What's your Christmas like?"

He sighed. The moment was gone.

"Well, my office has a huge Christmas party, generally at a nightclub or other cool spot. Loud music, cocktails. I get invited to a lot of Christmas parties."

"That's fun," Jenny commented.

He thought of the one last year that included a jolly Santa Claus, surrounded by beautiful women dressed as elves, handing out kisses and vodka shots. "Mmm. They're okay."

"What else?"

"Um…well, they decorate Chicago. There's Christmas music everywhere and decorations. The big department stores have great decorations, so I try to walk by to check them out. My office has a Christmas tree in the lobby." Everything he was offering sounded so pathetic compared to the traditional warmth of Jenny's Christmas plans.

She nodded. "Do *you* get a tree?"

"Pepper didn't like the needles, so we didn't…"

"You *lived* together?" She spoke quickly, and Sam could hear the surprise in her voice, and something else. Disappointment. *Damn it.*

"Not technically. I kept my apartment."

"But you *mostly* lived with her." Her voice was soft and unsure, like she was realizing something unpleasant. "You stayed over at her place regularly."

He scoffed and licked his lips. He didn't know what to say. Yes, when they were together, he had slept at Pepper's place three or four nights a week. *It's just what people do when they're together. It doesn't mean anything.* But it did mean something to Jenny, and he hated the thought that he was letting her down.

"I had a key to her place," he admitted, looking her in the eyes, deciding that honesty was the best course of action. "Yes. I spent a lot of time there."

"Oh." Jenny looked down.

Sam didn't know what to say, so he was quiet. Was he

153

proud of his shallow relationship with Pepper? No. But at a certain time and place in Sam's life, she must have been what he needed. He felt an almost overwhelming urge to comfort Jenny, to reassure her, but he didn't want to apologize for his life either.

Finally, he reached his hand toward her, tapping the table in front of her to get her attention. When she looked up, he caught the uncertainty in her glance, so he cocked his head to the side like all the Lindstroms did and offered gently, "It's in the past, Jen. Feels like a lifetime ago. Who I was with Pepper isn't who I want to be…that's why I'm not with her anymore."

He watched with wonder as Jenny's eyes softened and her lips tilted up in a small smile; he knew he'd managed to redeem himself. He also realized, quietly, to himself, that he meant what he said. He wanted to be better than the man who had settled for Pepper Pettway. Sam wanted to be a man worthy of—

"What about your family?" Jenny asked. "Don't you see them at Christmas?"

His heart thumped as he realized where his thoughts were going and felt relieved for the distraction her question offered. He grinned at Jenny, picturing of his family, thinking he'd like to spend more time with them this year, maybe.

"Sure. I head up to my mom and dad's on Christmas morning, usually. Sometimes on Christmas Eve. My sister and her husband come with the girls. Muirin and my other brother-in-law will come with Colin this year. The kids make it really fun. Heidi's a pip, begging for her presents on Christmas Eve—the ones my mom puts under the Christmas tree from her and my dad before Santa comes. But Colleen stays firm. We all have to wait until Christmas morning. Sometimes I try to sneak her one behind Coll's back, but Heidi cackles with laughter, and I shove it back under the tree before Coll or Mom catch us."

"You sound like a great uncle." She drew circles on the table with her finger. She whispered her next question without looking up. "Do you want kids, Sam?"

"Someday. With you." He heard the words come out of his mouth before he could stop them, and his eyes flew open in horror.

Her head snapped up and her mouth dropped open in a shocked *O*.

"Wait. No. I mean…" He rushed to fix his error, tripping over his words. "*Like* you. Like how you said 'someday.' When I asked if you wanted kids, you said 'someday,' right? Like that. Like. *Like* you."

He couldn't tell if she was offended or amused. Her face was impossible to read one way or the other but turning pinker by the second, her blue eyes wider than dinner plates. He could not believe those words had come out of his mouth.

First the Pepper cohabitation stuff and then this? He could work a whole room in Chicago, leaving with millions of dollars for investments after a slick, witty pitch, every word like a perfectly positioned missile.

Where exactly was that verbal precision now, Sammy? He knew where. Gone. Somehow stolen by the fresh-faced, blonde, blue-eyed beauty who sat across from him.

"I-I'm going to go ask Lars about, um, tomorrow's supper." She hopped up, leaving him alone to berate himself in blessed peace.

He stared at the table, shaking his head in disbelief, and only looked up again when the waitress asked what else she could bring.

The last five minutes of my life back?

"The check. Now. Please."

Chapter 8

With you.

With you.

Jenny wasn't about to bring it up or ask him about that slip, but she was still reeling from the words: *Someday. With you.*

She believed one hundred percent that he had misspoken. His eyes couldn't have been more horrified and shocked when the words popped out of his mouth. But once they were out, they were out. He couldn't *unsay* them, and she couldn't get them out of her head. She couldn't stop wondering if there might be a grain of truth to them.

As they walked in awkward silence toward Arch Park, Jenny couldn't help but think about what their children might look like. *Blond hair like me, or with red highlights like him. They could have blue eyes, or brown...They'd have his long lashes, and they'd be tall, for sure, and maybe—*

"This way, Jen?"

"Um...yes."

She nodded, gesturing to the small park down the street to the right and forcing the lovely, dreamy thoughts from her mind.

He didn't mean it, for heaven's sake! Get a hold of yourself!

But try as she might, the images were already there. Sam with a redheaded toddler on his shoulders as she walked beside him, holding his hand.

Dangerous territory, Jen. Don't forget he's leaving on Monday.

She squeezed her eyes shut, wishing away the yearning that threatened to make her eyes water. Thankfully, when she opened them again, they were almost at the park, and she distracted herself with the annual festivities.

Most of Gardiner turned out for the tree lighting, so the community park was full of holiday cheer. Christmas carols played over a loudspeaker at the bandstand. Red-cheeked children, ready for the "official" start of the Gardiner Christmas season, scurried around merrily, turning their eyes up toward the top of the giant Christmas tree, where a gray star was about to light up their world. A bonfire behind the bandstand scented the air with the smell of burning logs and created a nice spot for hand warming while waiting for the thousands of rainbow-colored twinkle lights to brighten the small park.

The music suddenly stopped, and the head of the Chamber of Commerce stood up in the little bandstand, which was dwarfed beside the enormous tree. In one hand he held the plug for the lights and in the other a massive extension cord. He welcomed everyone to the Annual Gardiner Tree Lighting and started the countdown.

"Ten…nine…eight…seven…"

Jenny stood beside Sam, smiling like a six-year-old, bunching up her shoulders and biting her bottom lip as she kept her gaze fixed on the star at the top of the tree. She felt

Sam's warm, bare hand take hers, and her tummy leapt with a flurry of happiness: for Christmas, for the tree lighting, for the magic of him standing next to her holding her hand.

"Three…two…one!"

In an instant, the entire park was twinkling. The music started up again, and the entire crowd broke into a chorus of "We Wish You a Merry Christmas." Parents held up small children to take in the full length of the tree, old sweethearts pecked, and new sweethearts…*Well,* Jenny thought, *new sweethearts held hands shyly, looking up at the tree and then at each other with wonder.*

"Merry Christmas, Sam," she mouthed, smiling up at him, feeling like they were the only two people in the world.

"Merry Christmas, Jen," he answered, squeezing her hand and lacing his fingers through hers. They stayed for a few more minutes to enjoy the merriment before Sam asked, "Should I walk you home?"

With most of the townsfolk still enjoying the caroling, the streets leading back to town were quiet. They were well away from the cacophony of the crowded park when Jenny spoke, holding Sam's hand tightly as she walked the balance beam of the curb.

"I'm thinking pajamas, hot chocolate, and a Christmas movie with Casey."

"Sounds cozy," he said, tugging her hand to pull her closer to him as they walked.

"I don't suppose you'd like to…"

"To what?"

"Would you like to…um…"

"Would I like to come over and watch a movie with you?"

"I mean, if you're not busy…"

He chuckled merrily. "I'm not sure I can clear my calendar at this late notice."

"You're a tease."

"I can't help it. I *love* it. I love teasing you." He brought their hands to his lips and kissed hers as they walked along.

A wave of pleasure rippled through her. *A memory I want to keep.*

"So that's a yes?" she asked.

"I don't know, Jen. Just you and me in your apartment? Alone? I'm not sure about your intentions. You're not going to…to take advantage of me, are you? I wouldn't want the other girls in town to think I go gallivanting around, watching movies willy-nilly with just anyone. Is my virtue safe?"

"Safer than it was in Chicago."

"Phew! Okay. That's a relief," he said, swiping at his forehead. "Yes, I will come watch a Christmas movie with you. But you better keep your hands to yourself, Jenny. I mean it."

She shook her head back and forth and smiled as they made their way across the bridge. "Sam Kelley…you are an ass."

He gasped in mock indignation. "*Jenny Lindstrom!* A swear word!"

She giggled beside him. "An animal."

"The back end of one."

160

"As you said."

"Do you kiss your father with that mouth?"

"I kissed *you* with that mouth."

He stopped walking beside her, but their hands connected them, and she had to drop his hand or stop and turn back to him. She stopped and turned. He was standing beside the last lamppost on the bridge, leaning against it with his arm outstretched to her. As she approached him in the dim light, she could see his eyes sparkling.

"No, Jen. *I* kissed *you*." He pulled her closer. "But I'm open to a do-over if you'd like to make good on that claim."

He tugged her toward him and pinned the hand he was holding behind her back, eliminating any real distance between them. With her arm held behind her back, her chest was forced forward, and she gasped lightly when his other arm snaked around her waist, pulling her flush against his chest. Trapped in his arms, she tilted her head back to see him. She raised her free hand and waggled it at him, smiling. "What was that about keeping my hands to myself?"

He grabbed it and pinned it with the other behind her back. His voice was thick and soft. "You won't need your hands."

He leaned his head down toward her, then stopped deliberately, his lips a breath away from hers, closing his eyes, waiting. Her heart was racing, and her breathing was so fast and so ragged, she knew he could feel it hot on his lips every time she exhaled. She could feel his too, see the puffs of white between them as he exhaled.

Her heart drummed in her chest, making her breathless

and hot as she stared at his face. There was nothing she wanted more in the world than to kiss him, but she was scared too. She felt herself falling for him, unable to keep herself from thinking about him, fantasizing about him. She worried about her heart when he was finally gone—for how much she would miss him.

"Jenny," he whispered.

She was so deep in thought, she was almost startled to hear his voice. His eyes were still closed, and she twisted her neck slightly so that her ear was beside his lips, to better hear him.

"Y-Yes?"

"Stop thinking," he said, his warmth breath on her ear making her shudder in his arms.

She couldn't have stopped herself even if she wanted to. She closed her eyes and faced him, her lips brushing against his as her neck turned up toward him. Soft and pliant, she nipped his lower lip between hers, kissing it, loving the feeling of being in his arms, of being in control of what was happening between them. He released her hands, moving his to the small of her back, and she raised hers to the nape of his neck, where her cold fingers ran gingerly through the short hairs that curled behind his ears. He groaned, and his lips finally moved, like he couldn't help himself anymore. He intensified their kiss, his hands on her lower back pushing her closer to his body.

His tongue pushed gently between her lips, and she sighed into his mouth, touching her tongue to his and marveling at the heat, the satiny heat, of his tongue stroking hers. His hands slid from her back to her hips, his fingers pressing through her coat, and she wished there weren't so many layers between them. She wished his hands were pulling and pushing her clothes away, finding the soft, untouched skin of her belly. A warm, welcome burst of sensation fanned out from her chest, making her breathless, making her want more of Sam.

More, more, more…

She ran her fingers through his hair with more pressure, and he pulled her closer, until the hardness of his body pressed intimately against the softness of hers. Her mind exploded with a hundred wanton wishes, and she instinctively stepped closer to him this time, wanting him to know that despite her innocence, her body was feeling things she'd never felt before.

But he pulled back from her, whispering her name, a note of warning in his tone. "Jenny."

She dropped her hands and turned her head away gently, resting her forehead on his shoulder, feeling relieved and deprived at once. She knew she wasn't ready for more, but kissing Sam felt so good, so right, she was confused and overwhelmed by feelings and sensations she'd never experienced before. She kept her eyes closed, savoring the shivers of pleasure along her spine. Her insides were in riot; her whole body was electric, like it was suddenly wired for touch, and every nerve ending begged for more.

She gathered her wits, coming out of the fog of passion, feeling grateful to Sam for stopping their steamy kiss when he did.

Steady now, Jenny.

Sam slid his hands back to her lower back and pulled her closer, and she could feel his chest move up and down roughly; she knew if she moved her ear to his heart, the thumping would be deafening. He held her for a while until she felt his hands slacken and his arms loosen around her. She lifted her head to look at him, and he smiled at her, shaking his head in wonder.

"*Now* you've kissed me with that mouth."

She chuckled quietly, surprised by his words, nodding. "So I have."

He pulled away from her but reached for her hand as they started walking again. "I can't believe I'm about to say this…but I think I should go back to my hotel."

"Oh." She felt deflated and confused. She hadn't seen this coming. Had she done something wrong? Was it possible in her inexperience that she'd misunderstood what was happening between them?

"Jenny? To be clear, there is *nothing* I would like more than to come up to your apartment with you. But another kiss like that, and…well, I just don't trust myself."

"Oh!" She understood, and it made her smile. He wasn't leaving her because he didn't like her. He was leaving her because he did like her, and—more importantly— because he respected her. It made her heart burst with relief and tenderness.

"What are you doing tomorrow?" he asked in a soft, heavy voice, drawing her knuckles to his lips to press a kiss against them.

"Church in the morning. Then…"

"Then spending the day with me?"

"Okay."

They stopped in a dark corner by her apartment door, and he smiled, leaning forward to kiss her cheek. He took his time pressing his hot lips against her cold skin, leaning into her. She rotated slightly so that her body was flush against his. She felt the rough stubble of his beard on her cheek, the warmth of his skin near her face. She closed her eyes, heart-stirring sensations rising up from her belly, making her want to melt into him and never let go. Her hands were trapped between them, and she flattered them on his chest, marveling at the hard muscles she could feel through his clothes, wondering if she should throw caution to the wind and insist he join her up upstairs, despite his warning.

"What time should I be at church?" he whispered into her ear, putting his hands on her hips.

"Nine," she murmured, feeling her knees weaken.

"Nine is good." He found her earlobe with his teeth, teasing it gently and sending surges of tingly pleasure down her neck. She sighed and tilted her head to give him better access to the warm skin of her throat, to be closer to him, closer to the source of her pleasure.

Oh, my God, this feels good. This feels amazing. More. Please, more.

"Where's your church?" he whispered.

"It's near…the high school…" She sighed, eyes closed, barely able to concentrate on anything but the touch of his lips trailing fire down her neck.

"I remember." He brushed his lips across her skin, his face next to hers, his hands softly molding her hips into him.

She lifted her face to smile at him, feeling dreamy and needy and still wanting more but knowing it was time to say good night. He took a long look at her face and chuckled softly, dropping his hands from her trembling body. "'Night, Pretty Girl. See you tomorrow."

"'Night, Sam." She turned, walking through the door to her apartment, and when she looked back once more, he was gone.

***

Casey was quick to do her business, thank goodness, and Jenny was glad to change out of her fancy clothes and into her comfy pajamas, warm inside for the night. She sat on the loveseat with a sleeping Casey curled up in her lap, her body and mind a jumble of sweet confusion.

On the one hand, her body felt taut, like that humming guitar string she imagined connecting her to Sam. She had never felt so desired, so wanted, so alive. But she also felt frustrated, unrequited, hot in places she barely allowed herself to think about. She touched her lips with her fingers, searching for the imprint of Sam's lips on hers. In twenty-four years, she had never felt anything close to the awakening she felt tonight. It was exciting and terrifying all at once, and she yearned for more.

On the other hand, her mind—her poor, sensible head—was trying so hard to maintain some semblance of order, and it was losing the battle wildly, going down in flames and smoke. She hadn't even tried to control her thoughts tonight. If anything, she had flat-out ignored all the reasonable, sober advice she'd given herself about restraint. But ignoring it didn't change the truth: Sam was still leaving on Monday. He would return to Chicago to resume his life there, and she'd be left alone in Gardiner with a handful of beautiful memories.

She flicked on the TV and surfed the channels but found she didn't have the heart for a Christmas movie after all. She turned it off, staring blankly at the dark-gray screen.

How can I bear to say good-bye? To live with excitement and attraction and the possibility of love one day only to have it ripped away the next?

The possibility of love.

She couldn't be falling in love with Sam—she had barely known him for more than a day. The *possibility* of love, though, was real and felt imminent and far safer than love itself.

How will I bear saying good-bye?

She swallowed, running her hand absentmindedly over Casey's soft fur, deep in thought. And then she knew. The answer came to her.

Without flowery words or comforting explanations, she heard the words in her head: *I will bear it. I will. Because the alternative*—not making the most of these precious days with Sam—*is impossible.*

"I will say good-bye, and I will bear it," she whispered.

Throwing caution to the wind wasn't a familiar path for Jenny, though, and in spite of her determination to enjoy every minute until they parted on the steps of the old

Livingston Courthouse, a creeping melancholy began its assault on her unprotected heart.

***

Sam wasn't ready to go inside his dreary room. His body was revved up and humming, and he needed to clear his head before he was trapped in that tiny hotel room for the night. He parked his car and walked around the hotel grounds. There wasn't much to see—a covered swimming pool and basketball courts, surrounded by a few well-worn picnic tables. He sat up on top of one of the ice-covered picnic tables, buttoning up his coat and hugging himself against the cold.

He'd never get used to winter night skies in Montana and never stop longing for them when he was far away. They were as much a part of him as being half-Swedish or half-Irish or having two sisters—simply but irrevocably a part of who he was. He found Cassiopeia easily, remembering Jenny pointing it out to him earlier. What had she called it? "The vain queen." He ruefully wondered why they hadn't named it "Pepper" instead.

Pepper. Chicago. He breathed in deeply, the cold air stinging the inside of his nose and making his eyes water. After the homey, small-town charm of Gardiner, he wasn't feeling excited about going home.

A custom-designed silver-and-turquoise Christmas tree in his building's lobby?

Parties with models dressed in skimpy elf outfits offering high-end vodka shots?

Sam's Christmas season was mostly about wild parties,

an excuse to let loose and get drunk, and annoying crowds of bustling people on the streets making his commute fifteen minutes longer. The real meaning of Christmas—the real *reason*—was totally forgotten by him until Christmas Eve, when he went to church with his folks and gave the Christmas story his brief and passing attention.

He wished Jenny could be there with him, to ground him with her no-nonsense reason, to bring her warmth and homespun goodness, to give significance to a place fast losing all meaning to him.

I need Jenny in Chicago.

He thought of her face before they had parted tonight. She had no idea she had been looking at him with the most mind-blowing bedroom eyes he had ever seen, and it had made every cell in his body fight against his decision to leave. He had never been with anyone so unpracticed and genuine; she was just Jenny opening herself to romantic love, he believed, for the first time in her life. That she chose to open herself to Sam was intoxicating and humbling at once, and he couldn't let go of her now.

I want Jenny in Chicago.

Suddenly, he had an idea. It burst into his mind fully formed, and he jumped off the picnic table and strode quickly into the main lobby. He approached the girl at the front desk.

"Hey, if I needed to print something out, could you do that for me?"

"Of course, sir," she said. "And what are we printing tonight?"

"Airline tickets," he responded, running to his room to grab his iPad.

***

Sam set his alarm for eight o'clock just to be safe.

He knew good and well how Jenny felt about tardiness, and with only one more day together, he wanted it to be perfect.

Walking to the little church, not two miles from his hotel, he passed by Jenny's apartment, over the bridge and down past the park. He was amazed by how good it felt, after years of eschewing church for hangover-relieving brunches, to shower, shave, put on his suit and coat, and walk to church.

He walked up the steps of the church jauntily and scanned the small sanctuary for Jenny. Standing in the back vestibule, he looked for her amid the bustling congregation of parishioners visiting with one another before the service started. It didn't take long for him to find her. It would have been impossible to miss the five blond heads lined up in the second pew.

Lindstrom, party of five?

Sam grinned as he headed up the aisle.

Jenny had saved him an aisle seat and turned to catch his eye as he was about halfway down the aisle, her face registering surprise followed by a beaming smile.

"Bet you thought I'd be late," he whispered, sliding down beside her.

"You don't have the most punctual track record."

"Morning, Pretty Girl," he murmured. "I missed you."

170

She shook her head lightly and looked down at her folded hands, but he could tell she was pleased.

He glanced beyond her to their left and saw her brothers and Mr. Lindstrom in a straight line, all four heads craning for a look at Sam. He offered them a reserved smile and a small wave. The boys smiled and waved back in greeting. Mr. Lindstrom's blue eyes held Sam's unwaveringly for a moment, then he nodded curtly before turning his attention ahead.

The pastor entered from a side door, wearing his robe and vestments, and the congregation chitchat hushed to a murmur as he lit the Advent wreath candles and welcomed everyone to the service. They opened their hymnals to a Christmas carol, and Sam smiled, glad to be sitting next to Jenny in church at Christmastime.

***

After the service, Jenny guided Sam to the fellowship hour where she poured them each a cup of coffee, waiting for her family to join them. Her father and brothers had gotten tied up in a conversation about ice fishing with the folks in the pew behind them, and she had gestured to them to come find her at the coffee social when they were finished.

"Jenny," Sam whispered, catching her eyes over the rim of the paper cup he held, "what do you want to do today?"

She smiled at him, delighted. "I don't know. What do *you* have in mind?"

He raised his eyebrows, teasing her, making her remember his knee-buckling kisses from last night. "We can figure it out after."

"Sam!" Nils was suddenly at Sam's shoulder, slapping his back in hello.

Lars, Erik, and her father approached from a distance, and Jenny breathed deeply. It was one thing for Sam to meet the boys; meeting her father was another. They formed an awkward semicircle around Jenny and Sam, eyes—mostly—on Sam.

"Sam," she said, "I didn't get to properly introduce you before. This is my father, Carl. Pappa, this is Sam. He's kin of Kristian, who's marrying Ingrid."

Sam offered Carl his hand. "Mr. Lindstrom. It's a pleasure, sir."

"Heard about a fella you were keeping company with at the Stroll," said Mr. Lindstrom, ignoring Sam's hand, eyes on his daughter, blue eyes to blue eyes.

"Oh, Pappa. We're not…keeping company. Sam's just visiting until Monday." She studied her toes, embarrassed. *Who said things like "keeping company" anymore?* Her father was hopelessly old-fashioned. "The boys met him yesterday."

Her father nodded sternly and turned back to Sam, finally taking his hand. "Ingrid's your cousin, Sam?"

"No sir," he replied, his shoulders square and sure. "Ingrid's fiancé, Kristian, is my cousin."

"Uh-huh. One over in Afghanistan, eh?"

"Yes, sir."

"Did military time myself," he said, dropping Sam's hand. "You?"

"No, sir."

"Uh-huh. My boys didn't neither." Her father nodded

172

again, then cocked his head to the side and narrowed his eyes, putting his hands on his hips and leaning toward Sam with purpose. "Your intentions toward my daughter…are they pure, Sam?"

"Pappa!" Jenny exclaimed in a shocked gasp. *Where, oh, where were those caverns of the universe when you needed one to open at your father's feet?* "Sam is just a *friend*—"

"Yes," said Sam, firmly and without hesitation.

She turned her glance from her father and looked at Sam, as if in slow motion, as if seeing him for the first time. He stood planted on the ground, holding her father's eyes without excuse or explanation, without pause or any trace of intimidation. He was surefooted, tall, and proud, and a smile spread across her face as her heart burst with pleasure. She was sure Sam didn't realize the nuances of this exchange, but she was touched beyond words that he would stand up for her with such a confident declaration.

Her father nodded at Sam slowly, his face unreadable. Then out of nowhere, he flashed Sam a wide smile as his weathered face relaxed, showing six decades of laugh lines. "You sure you're not from Montana?"

Sam chuckled then, sharing that his mother had grown up in Choteau, and he had spent a good bit of time up there throughout his childhood. Her father pumped Sam for information about his folks in Choteau; every Swede was always convinced they could figure out they were sixth cousins thrice removed to another Swede if they were just given enough time.

Lars clapped Sam on the back and kissed Jenny's cheek,

leaving for Upper Slide, where he and Paul would be putting up their fishing shack on the lake. Erik said he'd give them a hand and followed him out. Nils and her father needed to iron out some details for a group of tourists arriving tomorrow. Her father's eyes twinkled.

"We run tours up there in the park. This one's a wildlife group. You like wildlife, Sam?"

"Sure, Mr. Lindstrom. Can you see a lot in winter?"

"Oh, yah. Best time to see 'em. Nowhere for 'em to hide. Clean white backdrop. If you have some time today, Jenny could take you for a walk out there. See a bit. She knows all the right places." He winked at his daughter. "See you for supper later, Jenny-girl?"

"Four o'clock, Pappa," she responded, waving as he and the boys exited out a side door.

Once they were out of sight, Jenny turned to Sam, eager to be alone with him for whatever time they had left together. "Ready to go?"

He nodded, taking her hand in his.

"Sam...you, um, you didn't have to say that," she said as they walked through the front courtyard, onto the street, and back toward the bridge.

"Say what?"

"You know, the whole 'pure intentions' thing. He's just really old-fashioned."

"I meant it."

She whipped her head up to meet his eyes, confused. "You *couldn't* have meant it."

"Of course I did, Jen."

Her heart started beating like crazy. He *couldn't* have meant it. He couldn't have fully formed intentions for her. He couldn't possibly mean he was ready to court her. She stared at him hard, wondering if those words meant the same thing to him as they did to her.

"Sam, I don't know if we're talking about the same thing here."

He shrugged. "Well…I can only speak for myself, but I meant I would treat you with respect. I wouldn't dishonor you. I wouldn't do anything to compromise your reputation."

"Oh," she answered, a little bit relieved and a little bit sad at the same time.

"What did you think I meant?"

She stopped at the railing, looking out over the white water. Bright sunshine made the water sparkle, and melted small bits of ice wept into the river, becoming part of the rush of sound and fury.

She sighed loudly, blowing the air out of her lips in big white puffs and resting her mittened hands on the railing.

"My father's old-fashioned. He uses old-fashioned words and phrases sometimes. It's just his way. 'Pure intentions' isn't about you seducing me." She bit her bottom lip, feeling beyond embarrassed. "You…You…" She groaned, meeting his eyes, then finishing in a rush, "You essentially just assured him you're courting me with an eye to marriage."

His eyes widened, and his mouth fell open. She almost started giggling, but thinking about the conversation she was going to have to have with her father to clear up this misunderstanding sobered her up a little.

"Well then it's a good thing we're getting married tomorrow," he quipped.

"It's not funny, Sam. He takes these things seriously."

"I'm sorry, Jenny. I just—I don't know what to say. Who uses phrases like that anymore? It's the twenty-first century."

That got her back up. She could say her pappa was old-fashioned. Even the boys could say their pappa was old-fashioned. But that's where the list ended, and Sam's name wasn't on it.

"Oh, no, Sam, *I'm* sorry. I guess we're just a little too provincial for sophisticated you. My father cares about my reputation and—you know? Forget it. Don't trouble yourself, Sam. You're from a big city. He'll understand."

She turned from the railing and started walking briskly again. He quickened his pace to keep up, finally putting his hand on her arm.

"Jenny. Wait. Slow down. I feel like you're picking a fight with me. We're not on opposite sides here." She stopped walking and faced him as he continued. "I didn't mean to put you in an awkward spot. And I didn't mean to mislead your father. And you, yourself, said he was old-fashioned. I don't know why you're getting so mad at me."

He was right.

She *was* picking a fight.

She was angry that he was leaving tomorrow. She was angry that she cared about him so much. She was angry that his "pure intentions" weren't the ones her father meant, even though that would have been crazy. She hadn't known him long enough to consider courting, let alone marriage. It was ridiculous. But he hadn't done anything wrong.

"You're right. I'm sorry, Sam." She closed her eyes, breathing deeply, then exhaled and opened them, murmuring, *"Noen elsket meg en gang. Jeg er velsignet"* as quietly as she could.

"Hey, what is that? That meditation thing you do. That's Swedish, right? You're saying something about love?"

She started walking again, but slower this time. He reached for her hand, and she let him take it.

"It's Norwegian. From my mom." She took a deep breath. "When she was dying, we were all brave. Upbeat, you know? But one afternoon, she caught me crying. I started crying because I knew how much I was going to miss her." She felt a fat, hot tear roll down her cheek. "And she said when I missed her so much, it was hurting—h-hurting my h-heart—I should close my eyes and picture her face. And I should say, *Noen elsket meg en gang. Jeg er velsignet* to myself, which means, 'S-Someone loved me once. I-I am blessed.'" Tears were streaming down her face as she finished speaking, but she made no move to swipe at them. They stayed where they fell. She bit her lip and inhaled through her nose, sniffling. "Sometimes it makes me feel better. Sometimes it makes me feel worse. But it always makes me remember her, and then I feel closer to her."

"I bet she's very proud of you," he said gently.

"I doubt it. I haven't done anything very special with

my life."

"That's not true. You teach kids. You impact every one of their lives. You're very kind. Everyone in this town knows you and loves you. Any fool walking next to you at a Christmas Stroll could see that. *Nothing special?* Everything, Jenny, *everything* about you is special. I can't believe you can't see that."

You don't know, she thought to herself. *She wanted more than this for me.*

C. S. Lewis had written at the time of his wife's death, "I never knew that grief felt so much like fear." As Jenny emerged from the cocoon of grief following her mother's death, she had clutched onto her family more strongly than ever. The ultimate question was childish but haunting: *If I lost my mother when I left for Great Falls, what would happen if I left again?*

So even though her mother had wanted more than a life in Gardiner for Jenny, her mother's wishes for her had taken a backseat to the gripping fear that demanded she stay close to her father and brothers. If her mother was watching, Jenny was certain she was disappointed.

Still, she wanted to weep from the beauty of his words, from his kindness, his reassurance, the way he saw her.

How will I bear to say good-bye?

They stopped in front of the Prairie Dawn. His black-gloved finger swiped gently under each of her eyes in turn, then he touched her nose with a tap, smiling tenderly at her. "Are you going to be okay?"

She nodded, smiling for him, grateful for him.

"Now…no more crying or fighting, Pretty Girl. It's our last day. We have a whole afternoon, and I was thinking…"

She looked up at him with anticipation, sniffling for the last time and giving him a fresh, hopeful smile. "Mmm?"

"I heard tell about some wildlife in these hills, and I am a pretty wild guy…"

"For Chicago." She teased with good-humored sarcasm.

"For Chicago. That's right. And I think I need to see if the wildlife in Yeller can hold a candle to the wildlife in the big city."

"No contest," she challenged, hands on her hips.

"So you say. Think you can take down a city mouse? Bold words, kitty-cat."

"Time for *you* to see some of the park."

"Pick you up here in an hour?"

She smiled at him, wishing she never had to say good-bye. "In *half* an hour."

***

Sam was driving, but Jenny was in charge.

They entered the park via the Roosevelt Arch, and Jenny told Sam just to keep going straight on I-89 into Wyoming. Her plan was for them to drive the Grand Loop Road, a 140-mile tour, past Mt. Washburn and back to Gardiner. It would take them around the Rim of the Caldera, and they should be able to see a fair smattering of animals: bear, deer, bison, bighorn sheep, elk. She crossed her fingers. With wildlife, there were no guarantees.

Jenny knew this part of the park like the back of her

hand, and the Grand Loop was the best way to get an overview of the northern park when you only had half a day to spare. It wasn't more than a three- or four-hour drive at most, even if they stopped once or twice, so they should be back in time for her to make it to Sunday supper at her father's house at four.

She had packed sandwiches, chips, and apples for their lunch, and Sam had some soft country music playing. Jenny kicked off her boots, relaxing in the passenger seat, trying to savor these last few hours with Sam.

Enjoy yourself. You can be sad tomorrow after you've said good-bye. Don't let it ruin today.

"Some folks say the Grand Loop is like a safari. You're definitely going to see some wildlife, Sam. It's just a matter of what and how much." She glanced over at him. He'd changed back into jeans and looked casually powerful in the small bucket seat of his rental car. He belonged in a truck or an SUV, she decided, not a little sedan. "Just keep your eyes open. We'll stop in a little bit to check out Mammoth Springs. It's coming up soon."

"Mammoth Springs?"

"Hot springs. They're really interesting, I promise. We can park and walk around on the boardwalk a little bit. The springs are especially beautiful in the winter because you can barely tell where the white calcium deposits end and the snow begins. And it's going to be all misty with the fog. You'd think with all the salt and heat, the snow wouldn't have a chance, but it somehow manages to stay cold."

He glanced over at her and smiled. "Your dad brought

you to the park a lot growing up?"

"Dad's an expert on northern Yellowstone, and all of the boys help with the business. Nils is good with the business side, and the ladies love Erik, but when it comes to Yellowstone, I think Lars knows the most."

"And you?"

"I only lead private tours," she said, winking at him playfully.

"Oh, I see. Lots of private tours?"

"Nope. I have a client list of one."

"Any chance it could stay that way?"

"You'll have to let me know how I do."

"So far? *Awful.* You should never give another private tour again."

She burst into giggles and hit him lightly on the shoulder. "What do *you* know, city slicker?"

"If you want to sharpen your skills," he offered, "I'd be glad to be a repeat customer."

"Hard to make that promise from Chicago," she observed. She had meant the comment to be light, but it fell with a thud, and she cringed at her clumsiness.

Quit it, Jen. Today is supposed to be fun, not sad!

"Never say never." Sam turned into the parking lot for the springs and winked at her. "Life can be surprising."

***

They stopped at the Norris Geyser Basin, where Sam took pictures of Jenny with his iPhone. They skipped Old Faithful—Jenny declared it was overrated and not as "faithful" as it used to be, sometimes making the tourists wait almost two hours for an eruption—and drove in companionable silence for a while beside the Yellowstone River, taking in amazing views of the Teton and Absaroka Mountains.

At one point, a herd of four bison crossed the road in front of them, and Sam watched them in amazement as Jenny rattled off fun and interesting facts about Yellowstone's bison population.

No, he didn't know that a bison's winter coat is so thick and well insulated that snow can cover their backs without melting. One of the few new fun facts he had at his disposal, he thought with a smile.

He was blown away by her breadth of knowledge and how handy it was for her, pulling fascinating facts out of her head and sharing just the right amount of information to keep her dialogues captivating, not boring. No wonder her father's tours were in year-round demand. If Jenny was any indication, he was well worth the cost, whatever he charged.

They headed back up north toward Gardiner and had been driving for a while in the quiet of the car when she said, "Tell me about your mom. How'd a nice Swedish girl from Choteau end up in Chicago?"

He smiled at her sideways, then turned his gaze back to the road. "My mom, Margaret, and her sister, Lisabet, were small-town girls. Churchgoers. Potluck dinners and summer picnics on the green. Long braids woven with flowers at Midsummer. A lot like someone else I know, Jenny."

He flicked his gaze to her, smiling, thinking about how much his mother and aunt would approve of Jenny if they ever got the chance to meet her.

"Go on," she urged him.

"My grandparents owned a bed-and-breakfast-style lodge up there in Choteau. Mostly for hikers headed to the Rockies or people from Great Falls looking for an overnight getaway. That sort of thing. My mother and aunt worked at the lodge, which, by the way, is not in my family anymore but is a pretty swanky vacation spot, if you're ever looking for a place to stay north of Great Falls. Indoor pool, spa, wrap-around porch, helipad, amazing views, gourmet restaurant. You'd like it."

"Maybe I'll check it out sometime."

"My dad, who was born and bred in Chicago, was—and still is, actually—a curator at the Field Museum in Chicago, with a specialty in paleontology. I don't know if you know this, Miss Montana, but Choteau is near one of the most important paleontology sites in the world: Egg Mountain. Egg Mountain was discovered in 1977, and my father was sent west in 1978 to collect various specimens to be put on display in the Field Museum. He was sent up there for a week, and of course…"

"He needed a place to stay!" she finished for him, her voice conveying how engaged she was in the story.

"Bingo!"

"So how did it happen?"

"Well, there he was every night at dinner, dusty and tired. He wears glasses, my dad. One night he was sitting quietly by himself eating dinner, and my mom came over to him, and without saying a word, she gently took his glasses off and cleaned them with her breath and her apron before she put them back on his face. When she did, she said, 'Now I can see your eyes, Sean.' After that, he couldn't take *his* eyes off *her*." He was thoughtful for a moment, thinking of his parents, how in sync they were, how loving, such good friends. Out of the blue, he realized how much he wanted a marriage like that for himself one day. Someone who loved him, someone who set his heart on fire but was still his best friend.

"They're a love match," he blurted out, an extension of his thoughts. "They're best friends. Everything they do is better or more fun if they do it together. You can tell that about them. He told me one time that after he found her, he couldn't imagine his life without her."

Jenny sighed beside him and cocked her head to the side. "Why didn't they stay in Choteau near her folks?"

"Because she was a maid in her parent's lodge, and he was a rising, young curator of a world-famous museum. It wouldn't have made sense for him to stay in Choteau."

"But her family—"

"She missed them, of course, but where there's a will, there's a way. She figured out how to stay close to her sister and parents." Sam sensed they weren't talking about his parents anymore and wanted to tread very softly, choosing his words carefully. "She lived in the Chicago suburbs and raised her family near her husband's work. But we were here in Montana a lot, Jenny. It took some planning and driving and commitment, but we were here regularly. I told you, I love Montana. That's all because of my mom." He paused, then added, "Going to Chicago with my dad didn't mean abandoning her childhood home or her family. She *married* my dad—"

"And *left* her family."

Sam took a deep breath and held it, trying to figure out what to say next. If he was trying to use his parents as a model for his and Jenny's future, it wasn't going well. She was getting upset, and she wasn't hearing what he was trying to say.

"Yes," he said, keeping his voice level and soft. "But they were still her family, and she still made time for them. Look how close I am to Kris. Isn't that evidence that it all worked out?"

She didn't say anything, and a tentative silence filled the car as he continued driving. When he looked over at her, she was chewing her bottom lip, brow furrowed.

"Looks like waterfalls up ahead, Jen. Great Falls. Fitting last stop, huh?"

"Sure," she said uncertainly. "It's worth a look."

***

As they approached Gardiner, Jenny checked her watch. She had to be at her dad's house in thirty minutes. Their drive was almost over, which meant their time together was almost over…and her resolve to be cheerful was starting to crumble.

"What time is it?" asked Sam.

"I have half an hour."

"Today went fast," he noted.

"We should stop so you can check out the arch," she

said softly. "It's the major attraction of Gardiner. Who knows when you'll be back?"

He nodded and parked on a snowy patch of grass in an adjacent parking lot. Neither of them made a move to get out of the car, each feeling the emotional impact of Jenny's words. She stared down at her hands, willing back the tears that threatened to gather in her eyes. Sam shifted in his seat to face her and reached over to take her hand in his. She looked up, and the tenderness in his eyes was her undoing. The first tear made its lazy way down her cheek, past her nose to rest on her lip.

"Jenny," he murmured, searching her eyes, "we need to talk."

He got out of the car and perched on top of a picnic table, looking out at the mountains, waiting for her. She opened her door and walked the few steps to sit beside him.

***

Sam took her hand in his, rubbing his fingers over her palm and stroking it with the pad of his thumb, his head down, trying to figure out how to begin.

Finally, he turned to her.

"Jenny, I've never met anyone like you, ever. I know we're still getting to know each other, so this might seem kind of crazy…but I just know for sure I'm not ready to say good-bye to you tomorrow. I know it should be impossible for me to have feelings this strong after only three days, but…" He shook his head, looking down at their hands, then back up at her face, seizing her eyes with a fierce longing. "I do. I am falling for you so hard, and you're here, and I have to go home, and it feels *awful* to think of being so far away from you."

Jenny's eyes filled with more tears as he spoke to her, and they rolled freely down her face. He reached up and held her face between his hands, dipping his head toward her, placing his lips on each errant drop until her face was covered with kisses instead of tears. Then he reached around to his hip pocket and pulled out an envelope. Her eyebrows creased with questions, looking up at him as he offered it to her.

She opened the envelope and unfolded the papers inside as he explained.

"They're tickets for Christmas break. I thought maybe you'd consider coming to see me. You could see what Chicago's like, and we could give *this* a chance, whatever's between us." He smiled at her hopefully when she lifted her eyes. "It's not as bad as you think. Maybe you'd even like it there—"

"Oh, Sam. I can't go to Chicago."

"Why not?"

"Because my family's *here*. My father and my brothers are *here*. My life is *here*." Wide, watery eyes regarded him. She held the papers in her hand, and they fluttered in the cold afternoon wind. "I can't just leave them."

"I'm not asking you to leave them forever..." *yet.* "Just come to visit. Just a visit."

"Sam...I'm...I can't." She sniffled. "I don't want to give you the wrong idea or send you the wrong message, and that's what I would be doing by visiting. I'd be telling you

Chicago's possible for me."

"Because it's a city?" The sting of his disappointed hopes made him grimace. "You wanted to live in Great Falls."

"You can't compare the two! Great Falls is in Montana. It's only five hours away from here. Chicago's a plane ride away. There are over two million people in Chicago. I'd be lost. I'd be swallowed up. The littlest fish in the biggest pond." Jenny closed her eyes tightly, shaking her head. She whispered, "I can't go. I'd be giving you false hope."

As she folded up the papers, putting them carefully back into the envelope, he gulped over the growing lump in his throat.

"Sam," she said, her voice thready with emotion, "I'm not ready to say good-bye either. I've never felt like this. Never in my life. You know I have feelings for you, don't you?"

He nodded once, feeling a small flicker of hope, but it was quickly replaced by the realization that while she cared for him, she didn't care enough to come to visit. When he didn't cover her hand with his, she reached out farther and placed her hand over his heart. "You know I care for you, Sam. You know I do."

He grabbed her hand and kissed her palm, lovingly, longingly. When he looked up, his eyes besieged her. "Then *please*, Jenny. Come and visit me."

"I can't." Her eyes shone brightly with unshed tears.

"You won't."

He kissed her palm again then folded it closed and

placed it back on her lap.

She stuffed her hands into her pockets. "Sam, think of it the other way around. Could you ever live here? In Gardiner? Be happy here?"

He was shocked to hear a glimmer of hope in her voice. Had she hoped he could *possibly* make Gardiner his home? *Unthinkable.* He had a position with a major bank in Chicago. Her suggestion was absurd.

He turned to face her, his face hardened, his mouth a tight line. "No. Absolutely not."

She nodded slowly, as if figuring something out for the first time, and her voice was cooler when she spoke. "So there it is. I can't be there, and you can't be here."

"You *could* be," he said. "You choose not to be."

"So do you. I'm sorry," she said, taking the envelope from the table beside her and giving it back to Sam.

"Me too."

He took the envelope and pushed it back into his pocket, hopping down from the table, kicking the dirt angrily as he headed back to the car.

Without looking at her, he sat down, slamming the door closed loudly behind him. The engine turned over, and Jenny came to his window, tapping softly. He pushed the button to roll it down but didn't look at her.

"I'm going to walk home," she said. "I think that's best."

"Whatever," he muttered.

"Please, Sam. Please say you understand."

"It doesn't matter, Jen." He *couldn't* look at her. He

couldn't bear for her to see how much he wanted her, how much he needed her.

"I-I'll see you t-tomorrow?" she asked between soft sobs. "In Livingston?"

"I'll be there. I promised Kris."

Then he rolled up the window and drove away from her without looking back, banging on the steering wheel twice in frustrated sorrow, unfamiliar tears stinging his eyes.

Chapter 9

Today I say "I do."

It was Jenny's first thought when she opened her puffy eyes, still raw from crying last night. Somehow, probably because the Lindstrom kids were encouraged to "tough it out" in lieu of tears, she had made it through Sunday supper at her father's house without breaking down. But holding in her feelings for those two hours made the tears flow all the more freely—all the angrier and more frustrated—when she got back to her lonely apartment.

Casey stirred in the kitchen, and Jenny checked her clock: 6:45 a.m. She didn't have to leave for Livingston for an hour and a half.

Thoughts of their final conversation at the arch yesterday made her heart clench. She turned onto her side in bed, drawing her knees up and hugging herself. *It wouldn't be so bad if I didn't have to take those vows today. It wouldn't be so bad if we had just said good-bye yesterday once and for all.*

She knew that wasn't completely true. The vows were only incidental to her pain. Yes, the memory of saying the words to Sam would compound her sorrow once he was gone. But it was his absence from her that would be at the crux of her regret. Their heartbreaking exchange didn't change Jenny's feelings for him. If anything, she cared for him more after hearing him share his feelings and voicing her own at the arch. She *wanted* to see Sam today; she just wished they didn't have to say good-bye.

She was honest with Sam when she said she had never felt anything like this in her life. The closest word she could think of was *love*, and yet any rational person knew you couldn't fall in love with someone over the course of a long weekend. Love took months, years even, to develop properly: Meeting each other and moving from acquaintance to friendship to courtship. Building a relationship over a series of dates and meetings. Introducing each other to friends and family over time. Seeing each other through some of life's challenges and overcoming them together. Then finally, finally knowing with certainty there is love between you and committing to a marriage. She had only known Sam for three days; it couldn't possibly be love.

And yet it *felt* the way Jenny always imagined love would feel.

Every free moment from Friday afternoon to now, her mind had been consumed with Sam. When she was without him, she longed to be with him. When she was with him, she yearned for more from him than his presence. She battled a constant, unrequited hunger for more dialogue, more discussion, a return of her increasingly passionate feelings. It felt impossible that he would care for her when Jenny had seen the women who populated his life in Chicago. He could have a supermodel by his side, but he wanted Jenny. It made her feel special and cherished, like she was something precious to someone who had his pick of beautiful things, and gave him a depth and authenticity that captivated her heart. It was as if he saw through the outward layers of her plainness, beelining with meticulous precision to her heart, which he seemed to see with clarity and regard with...*with what, Jenny? Love?*

He hadn't used the word *love* yesterday. He said he had "strong feelings" for her and was "falling hard" for her, but *love* wasn't a word he had used to characterize his feelings.

He barely knows you, Jenny. He can't possibly be in love with you.

And of course, when it all boiled down, neither of them was prepared to budge for the other. She sat up and swung her legs over the side of the bed, hanging her head in confusion.

This can't be love I'm feeling. It must be something else.

She padded into the bathroom and looked at her face in the mirror, touching her lips lightly where he had kissed her on Saturday night. She cocked her head to the side, considering her attraction to him. For the first time in Jenny's life, her body had come alive, responding eagerly to Sam's tender touch. Even now, she craved the touch of his hands laced through hers, the gentle swiping away of a tear with his knuckle, or the cradling of her face in his hands, as he had yesterday. She burned even more for the heat of his lips on hers, for the touch of his breath on her skin, and simply—*pathetically, Jenny*—for the comforting warmth of his arms around her.

She stepped into the shower, the hot water soothing

and restorative. She breathed in, leaning her head back, closing her eyes.

Was that it, then, this terrible, wonderful feeling?

Not love, just an intense physical attraction; in your inexperience, you are mixing up the two. Because love would make you trade Gardiner for Chicago, love would make you willingly leave your home as his mother had, love would conquer all your fears. Wouldn't it? This can't be love. Love would leave you irrevocably changed.

She hadn't changed; she was still sensible, grounded Jenny. She had told him no. She wasn't the sort of girl who went running away with the first man who asked.

Toweling off, she felt more confident and secure. She would take Ingrid's vows, return to Gardiner, and resume her life.

This was all probably just an infatuation. Yes, that was it.

Once he was gone, her life would go back to normal, and she would know for sure Sam had just been a short, sweet infatuation. She would think back on their weekend together as she did on any pleasant memory.

Later, as she left her apartment for Livingston, Jenny caught her reflection in the hallway mirror and paused to look at herself. She examined the face that stared back, and an unexpected realization rocked her, upsetting her careful logic about love versus infatuation. She was dressed exactly the same as she had been last Friday morning: blonde hair brushed shiny, loose and long down her back, and a simple gray sweater-dress from Sears.

Outwardly, she looked the same, yet the girl looking back at her was a totally different person, fundamentally and irrevocably changed from the person she had been on Friday. She gasped softly and touched her fingers to her earlobes, her cheeks, her lips, her waist, her hips—all places conquered and claimed by Sam.

Love would leave you irrevocably changed.

The thought was uncomfortable, so she ignored it, grabbing her bag and keys and sailing out the door.

But as she left, one last thought formed in her head:

Before Friday, life had been pleasant, content, even fulfilling in its own way. Now she knew that her world had been a dull gray in contrast to the blinding, vibrant color that had painted her world the last few days.

She swallowed, biting her upper lip in defeat.

How do you go back to gray when you've seen your life in Technicolor?

***

Sam waited in the chair at the top of the stairs.

He glanced at his watch, then at the double doors in the lobby below. They still had twenty minutes before their appointment. He had no doubt she'd be on time.

After a terrible night's sleep, he conceded defeat at 7:00 a.m., got showered, got dressed, and got the hell out of Gardiner.

He wished someone else could stand in for him as proxy today so he could just leave Montana and never look back, try to forget ever meeting Jenny, ever wanting her, ever feeling the intense ache of longing he had never felt for another person in all his life.

Alas, a promise was a promise.

195

He brushed some lint off the sleeve of his cashmere coat, wondering if she'd be wearing that ridiculous-looking puffy parka when she arrived. He wanted to stay focused on his anger toward her to ward off the confused sadness that kept threatening a hostile take-over, but her face invaded his mind, and he lost the battle, softening as he pictured her laughing, smiling, leaning forward to press her lips against his.

Damn it, Jenny. Why won't you come to me?

He knew, of course, why she had refused him.

After losing her mother, she held onto her family with an unwavering devotion, setting aside her dreams for them. Part of the reason he cared for her so much was her traditional values, which included a deep commitment to her family, so how could he ask her to break it? Then again, how could she ask him to move to Gardiner? It was impossible for him. He had a plan for his life—get a good education, find a job in finance, choose smart investments, show better and better returns, impress the powers that be, move up in his company, make bigger and bigger deals, live in a big house, marry a beautiful woman, have a few kids, and live happily ever after.

What the heck was he supposed to do in Gardiner? Help her dad lead wilderness tours? Run a restaurant for tourists? Be a teller in a local bank? He grimaced in distaste. He'd be giving up on *his* dreams, just as she had.

In his heart, he knew her feelings for him were genuine, which roiled his stomach until he thought he might be sick. It made the situation so much worse to know for sure that she cared for him. He stood up and shrugged out of his coat, taking a deep breath of cold air as the double doors opened and an older lady made her way to the information desk, nodding and smiling her hellos. He folded his coat and placed it on top of the chair, straightening out his suit jacket and tie. He looked at his watch again. Ten more minutes.

If she didn't care for him, he knew he would be able to leave without looking back; he was sure his infatuation would have faded quickly if it had been one sided. He'd find some cute thing in Chicago and take her out a few times, down peppermint schnapps shots with her at a holiday party, and smile as she licked the candy cane garnish suggestively. He'd take her home for hot, forgettable sex and do it all over again the following weekend. If Jenny didn't have feelings for him, he'd have a better chance of moving on, and she'd eventually settle in the back of his mind as a passing infatuation, a quaint interlude, a sweet memory.

He thought of her placing her hand over his heart and closed his eyes. He remembered her blue eyes, brightened with unshed tears, besieging him to understand. How long would those eyes haunt him? And how could he resume his old ways when his heart knew somewhere in Montana, there lived someone infinitely better, sweeter, deeper, and more worth having than the parade of meaningless relationships that, he was sure, waited for him?

I will conquer this. I will eventually banish you from my head, Jenny Lindstrom. I will be free of you one day…

The double doors whooshed open, and suddenly Jenny stood on the threshold. As if she knew where he'd be, she raised her head, and her eyes captured his with an intensity that made him gasp quietly. His languishing heart danced when he saw her face, and in spite of himself, he smiled at her, lifting his hand in greeting.

…but, today is not that day.

***

Seeing him at the top of the stairs was like turning her face to the full light of the sun after living in darkness since yesterday afternoon. She moved toward him with an unhesitating certainty, holding his eyes intently as she made her way up the stairs. When she got to the top, he opened his arms, and she fell into them wordlessly, gratefully, as an exhausted person falls into bed at the end of a terrible day. Tears welled up in her eyes as she laid her forehead in the crook of his neck, but she blinked the tears away, closing her eyes and breathing deeply. She lost herself in the strength of his embrace, his familiar scent, the way his chest rose and fell with the force of his breathing. His arms enveloped her completely, and he rested his chin on her head, letting his breath out in a forceful sigh. She felt him swallow hard and leaned back to look up at his face.

He was smiling at her in a sad, resigned way. His eyes weren't laughing or teasing; they were tired and defeated.

I know, she thought. *Me too.*

He released her gently and cocked his head to the side. "Ready?"

She nodded, swallowing down the lump in her own throat, returning his sad, resigned smile. *Oh, Sam, I wish things could be different.*

He put out his hand, and she searched his eyes before taking it. She didn't see hope there; she didn't see much of anything. He was protecting himself. She looked back at his hand. It might be her last chance to hold it, so she took it in hers, savoring the muscled warmth, allowing him to lead her down the hallway to the clerk's office.

He released her hand to hold the door for her, and she stepped through and made her way to the same secretary who had been there on Friday. Sam stood next to her. She felt his fingers lace through hers under the counter as the woman looked up at them.

The secretary adjusted her glasses and sniffed with annoyance. "So you got alarm clocks."

Jenny nodded. "We're here for the—"

"Double proxy wedding. Nordstrom-Svenson. I know." She looked up at them over her glasses, her gaze shifting back and forth between them quizzically. She raised her eyebrows and cleared her throat before looking back down at her keyboard. "Humph."

"Ma'am?" Jenny asked.

She didn't look up from her keyboard. "You look different. That's all."

Jenny glanced up at Sam in confusion, and he squeezed her hand reassuringly. "We're the same."

"If you say so." The secretary cleared her throat again and wheeled her stool a short distance to a printer, waited a moment, then scooted back to them, handing Jenny the printout. She gestured back to the door. "Go back out, down the hallway. Third door, room 303. Judge Hanlon and the witnesses should already be there waiting. If not, take a seat, and they'll be there directly."

Jenny swallowed. This was really about to happen. She was going to take vows with Sam. She knew they were for Ingrid, but it was all very real to Jenny, who would hear the words come out of her own mouth, and her misgivings made her tremble with the gravity of what she was about to do.

Sam squeezed her hand again, pulling her away from the counter toward the door. "Thank you, ma'am."

"I was right, you know." They turned their heads back in unison to look at her. "Didn't hurt you a bit to stick around for a few days. Did you some good." She nodded once at Sam humorlessly, then resumed her typing.

Jenny locked her eyes with Sam's for a moment, and she could see the pain there. She knew differently.

It had hurt him to stay.

***

The witnesses were already seated in room 303 when Jenny and Sam entered. It was a very small room sparsely furnished with a rectangular conference table and six chairs. No artwork adorned the walls; they were blank except for a functional black-and-white clock fastened to the wall above the doorway.

Sam sat down in an open seat on one side of the table, and Jenny took the seat opposite him. The female witness sat beside Jenny and the male witness beside Sam. They exchanged handshakes in greeting, then the witnesses resumed their quiet conversation while Jenny stared down at her hands on the table, the seriousness of this ceremony and her part in it turning doubt into panic.

Wedding vows should only be said once to one person. You have no business doing this.

Her heart started pounding, and she couldn't seem to take a good, deep breath. She breathed in, closing her eyes, and then opened them while she breathed out, but it didn't help. Still staring down, she saw Sam's hand move toward her before she felt it take hers.

"*Jenny!*" he whispered sharply. When she looked up, she saw tender concern etched on his handsome face. "Just look at me, okay? Just look at me."

She swallowed and nodded at him once, holding his warm, confident eyes in her nervous, frightened ones. She breathed in slowly until her diaphragm was finally full and let out her breath slowly. He mouthed it again slowly, with a calming intensity, releasing her hand. "*Just look at me.*"

The door opened, and a white-haired man in his seventies entered, sorting through papers. He took the chair at the head of the table between Sam and Jenny.

"Thanks for being on time, folks." He rifled through the papers, and Jenny handed him the sheet the secretary had given to her. "Ah, yes. Okay. Here it is." He put on glasses, reading the paper briefly, then turned his glance up to greet the witnesses.

"Mary, John, good to see you both. Thanks for witnessing today. Ummm. Sam?" He turned to Sam, absentmindedly scanning the paper before him. "And Jenny?" She nodded once, still holding Sam's eyes. "Have you folks ever stood proxy before?"

"No," Sam answered for them.

"Okay, well, it's painless and quick. Jenny, I'm going to ask you Ingrid's vows, and you will simply answer twice with the words 'I will.' Sam, then I'll turn to you on behalf of Kristian, and you'll do the same. I'll declare them husband and wife, and you'll be free to go." He signed something on the bottom of the paper, scooting it to Mary, who signed it and scooted it to John. John scooted it back to the judge with practiced efficiency.

"Shall we get started?"

***

"We are gathered here today in the presence of these witnesses to join in holy matrimony Ingrid Nordstrom and Kristian Svenson, who have applied for and received a marriage license from this state.

"Jenny, first to you. On behalf of Ingrid Nordstrom, will you have this man by proxy to be your lawful wedded husband, and with him to live together in holy matrimony pursuant to the laws of God and this state?"

Jenny heard the judge say her name, but otherwise his voice was a faraway baritone of sound. Sam held her eyes fiercely, and she stayed focused on his beautiful face. His reddish-blond hair was tousled and wavy, and his brown eyes held her blue ones with unwavering care.

"I will," she whispered, and the corners of his mouth twitched up for the barest moment.

"Will you love him, comfort him, honor and keep him both in sickness and in health, and forsaking all others, keep you only unto him, so long as you both shall live?"

Her heart pounded as she really listened to the words, glancing down at the table in a moment of pure panic. A short tap-tap on the table in front of her made her look up into Sam's eyes again, which reached out to her, his lips turning up in an encouraging smile. She lost herself in his eyes, allowing him to hold her up above the water line so she could breathe, so she wouldn't drown. He mouthed the words, and she said them aloud:

"I will."

He smiled at her then, and she knew her part was finished. She broke their eye contact and stared down at the table before her, exhaling raggedly, shoulders rolled forward in defeat.

"Now, Sam. Will you, on behalf of Kristian Svenson, have this woman by proxy to be your lawful wedded wife, and with her to live together in holy matrimony pursuant to the laws of God and this state?"

"I will."

His voice was breathy and emotional, and Jenny couldn't help but look up. He must have been staring intently at her bowed head because her lifted eyes slammed into his. He swallowed, and his shoulders relaxed in relief, his eyes devouring hers, not letting her leave him again.

"Will you love her, comfort her, honor and keep her both in sickness and in health, and forsaking all others, keep you only unto her, so long as you both shall live?"

As Sam nodded slowly at Jenny with a heartbreaking tenderness, his lips tilted up in a sad, tender smile.

"I will," he answered, with eyes only for Jenny.

"By the virtue of the authority vested in me by the state of Montana, I now pronounce Ingrid Nordstrom and Kristian Svenson husband and wife by double proxy marriage."

The judge scribbled on his notes as the witnesses filed out of the room. If Jenny or Sam had looked up, they would have noticed the judge pause at the door, looking back and forth between the young couple before smiling knowingly and closing the door silently behind him.

They stared at each other across the table until Jenny finally stood up slowly, unable to look away from Sam, holding his eyes wildly, as though she might die if she let them go.

He stood up too, moving around the head of the table with urgent purpose to stand before her.

Reaching out to cup her face in his hands, his lips came down on hers in a hungry kiss. Tears flooded Jenny's eyes, and they fluttered closed as she surrendered to him for the last time.

***

Jenny's heart was breaking.

Sam held her to him like she was about to be ripped away by some evil force, besieging her, "*Please* come to Chicago."

She rested her cheek on his shoulder, her lips raw from kissing him, her hands flattened against his back. "I can't, Sam. I'm just Jenny in western boots teaching kids, helping out at church, spending time with my dad and my brothers. I can't just leave them in any real way. There's no use in me visiting." She leaned back and looked into his face. The words rushed out of her mouth: "Why do you *have* to be in Chicago?"

"Jenny, my *life* is there. My job, my contacts, my clients, my apartment—*everything*. You can't possibly think I could actually *live* in Gardiner!"

Her face flushed hot, and she pulled back from his arms abruptly, crossing hers over her chest protectively. "I'd never *dream* of it, Sam. I'd never want you to *lower* yourself to living somewhere as *beneath* you as Gardiner."

"That's not true—"

"*True?* You want *truth?* Your life in Chicago is about as deep as a puddle. Your money, your *schmoozing*, your parties, your plastic Christmas trees, your bimbos—"

"That's not fair—"

"Surrounded by shallow, selfish people who couldn't care less if you died in a car crash, but you'd choose them over—"

"Ha! How about you, Jenny, Miss High-and-Mighty-Know-It-All? Want some *truth?* How about you giving up on your dream in Great Falls and coming home to Gardiner to hide your head in the sand?"

"How *dare* you! I came back to take care of my mother, and—"

"And you *stayed*. This wasn't your dream for yourself, and it sure as hell wasn't *her* dream for you. This wasn't where you wanted to be. This is where you *gave up*. Where you *sold out*. Don't lecture me about the life *I* have, you coward!"

Her chest rose and fell with the painful force of her breathing, and she stared at him like she didn't know him. Shivering, she took in the hard anger of his face. She whispered more to herself than to him, "This *never* would have worked out."

"*Clearly.*" His voice was angry but ragged and out of control, like she imagined it would be before tears.

"Well, then it's good it didn't," she whispered, still looking down.

He struggled into his coat, punching his hands down through the sleeves. "Know what, Jen? You can always go running to Principal Paul. Sell out on love the way you did on life and make sure *all* your dreams *don't* come true."

Her face snapped up to meet his, an ocean of unshed tears brightening her furious eyes. She grabbed her coat and slapped her bag over her shoulder in a hurried, angry motion. "And I am sure *you* can find another beautiful, self-centered Pepper Pettway to entertain you and never have anything *close* to the marriage your parents had. So *goody* for *you!*"

"*Great!*" he shouted, face red and furious. "I guess we'll *both* be very happy."

"I guess so!" Her heart was racing, and she knew she was on the brink of violent, relentless tears. She couldn't hold them back much longer.

He shook his head back and forth like someone in shock and rubbed his jaw between his thumb and forefinger before he put out his hand.

"Well, good-bye, Jenny. It's been—"

"Good-bye, Sam."

She didn't touch his hand.

She turned and rushed out of the room, through the corridor, down the stairs, across the lobby, and through the double doors into the cold Montana air. It hit her face like needles, making tears spill down her face in torrents. She rushed to her car and finally surrendered completely to her sorrow, wrenching sobs filling the otherwise quiet of her car all the way back to Gardiner.

Chapter 10

"Sammy!" Ron Johnson knocked lightly on the door to his office. "Good weekend?"

Sam looked up from the documents he'd been reviewing.

"It was fine."

"Where were you again? Minnesota?"

"Montana."

"Ouch! The boonies! Kill me now!" Ron said, inviting himself to sit in one of Sam's guest chairs. "You missed an awesome time at the Spy Bar on Saturday. Remember that cute Asian chick? *She. Was. On.* Seriously, I was fighting her off, man. And tell me this, Sammy, are you ready to par-tay next Friday?" Sam raised his eyebrows in question. "*The Christmas party*, man!"

"Oh, yeah. Yeah, right. Well, you know me…"

"Another year to remember, eh?" Ron winked. "You old dog!"

Sam scoffed uncomfortably, looking down at his desk, rapping his pen on the desk softly, distractedly. "Yeah, well…"

Ron popped up and headed for the door, pausing to leer at Sam before leaving. "And no girlfriend this year,

Sammy. You're a free agent! Some lucky lady's gonna get it!"

"Yeah. A free agent." He smiled and saluted a departing Ron, then threw his pen across his desk where it hit his stapler with a loud clatter.

"A free agent," he muttered, clenching his jaw until it ached, seeing Jenny's pretty face in his mind and using all his energy to push it away.

She doesn't want to be with you, Sam. Let her go.

He turned his attention back to the spreadsheets, determined to overcome this infatuation.

Hours later, after work, Sam started his Christmas shopping, hoping that being out and about among his fellow Chicagoans would give his spirits a lift.

Colleen had sent him a list of books for the girls, and in lieu of five minutes online at Amazon, he decided to go to Barnes & Noble on the way home and buy the books himself.

He admired the huge Christmas wreaths on the windows of the store as he approached the front door, noticing the gingerbread village on display in the front picture window.

See, Jenny? he thought. *Christmas cheer, right here in terrible, awful Chicago!*

It wasn't real gingerbread, of course, but it was still festive, a gingerbread mountain village covered with precise white glitter, a working train at the base of the mountain, and a tiny chairlift that magically transported tiny gingerbread men and women to the plastic brown gingerbread chalet at the top of the mountain. Once there, they skied down the glittery slope on plastic licorice-looking skis and were picked up by the tiny chairlift once again. Several young children crowded around the window, watching the scene with wonder.

Sam smiled too, but his cheer faded a little as he recalled the messy white gingerbread house he and Jenny had seen in the window of the saddler's shop during the Christmas Stroll. She had named the messy confection her favorite, and he had called her a "soft touch." Then she had smiled at him, sharing, "I love the little ones." He could see her blue eyes sparkling before him, the gentle curve of her lips, the sweet—

"Excuse me! It's for the kids! Can my daughter take a peek now?"

A woman behind him tapped him on his shoulder, pushing her chubby daughter forward. The girl's red lollipop snagged on his cashmere coat, sticking there and drooping sadly as he stepped out of her way, stumbling backward, moving away from the crowd of children.

He'd only left Jenny two days ago, but it felt so much longer. He couldn't stop thinking about the way they'd said good-bye—or *hadn't* said good-bye. It hurt him to remember her face as she'd run from the room where, just moments before, they'd shared the most soul-shattering kiss of his life. The same room where she'd declared, *This never would have worked out.*

He clenched his jaw with regret and frustration, dodging around people until he found some open sidewalk where he walked at a fast, angry clip. Taking a deep breath of cold air that burned his lungs, he scolded himself: *Stop thinking about her! It's over. Let it go.*

The doorman opened the bronze-and-glass door of his apartment building, and he stepped inside the warm, chic lobby, surprised to find himself home, his plans for Christmas shopping ambushed by ceaseless thoughts of Jenny Lindstrom.

***

When Sam's business school friend, Joe, had texted him to meet at Club Blue, it had seemed like a good idea: get out and about, see some friends, and remember how great the nightlife was that Chicago had to offer. He put on some jeans, a while button-down shirt, and a navy blazer, slicking his hair back and dousing his cheeks with aftershave.

Looking good, he thought, glancing in the lobby mirror before hailing a cab in a ritual as familiar as breathing. *You've got this. This is just what you need!*

The music seemed louder and more grating than usual, but he tried to maintain an open mind as he pushed his way through a throng of people to get closer to the bar. Slogging sideways through the wall of hot, sweaty humanity, he finally made his way to Joe.

"Sammy-boy! Merry Christmas, man!" Joe shouted from where he leaned against the bar. "What're you drinking?"

"Scotch, rocks!" he yelled over the thumping house music: Lady Gaga was singing her newest Christmas anthem: *The only place you wanna be / is underneath my Christmas tree… / Light you up, put you on top, let's falalalala…*

As the Lady Gaga song phased out, a new beat thumped into place, and Sam was surprised to hear the xylophone chords that opened the remixed version of "All I Want for Christmas Is You." And just like that, he was back in Gardiner. Sure, his body may still have been standing in the sweaty, cacophonous throng of Club Blue in downtown Chicago, but suddenly his heart and head were a thousand miles away as memories of the Gardiner Christmas Stroll came into sharp focus. He swallowed the lump in his throat as he remembered the feeling of Jenny's hand laced through his while they walked up and down Main Street, eating gingerbread, sipping cider, looking in shop windows—

"You said Scotch?"

"Make it a double!" he shouted back as the beat picked up, Mariah's voice singing the familiar words over the dance beat.

"Wait! What?"

I just want you for my own, / more than you could ever know. / Make my wish come true. / Baby, all I want for Christmas is you.

Sam held up two fingers, thrusting them at Joe. "A DOUBLE!"

"Oh! Yeah! Sure!"

Sam gave his friend a tight smile, reaching across two seated heads to take the drink Joe passed to him. A big plop of liquid sloshed from the rim of the glass onto one of the heads, drawing Sam's attention down to a blonde woman sitting on a barstool between him and Joe, with her back to him. And for a second—a *split second* of crazy, totally irrational thought—he wondered if it was Jenny.

She turned around, frowning at Sam over her shoulder. "Hey! Watch it!"

Irrationally disappointed, he said "Sorry" as he took a bracing sip of scotch.

Joe backed away from the bar and maneuvered through the tightly packed bodies to stand next to Sam. It was too loud to talk without shouting, so they stood there side by side, looking out at the packed club.

Royal blue lights painted everyone blue. Women danced in skimpy metallic dresses, businessmen pursued scantily clad girls who looked half their age, bodies gyrated on a packed dance floor, couples made out in dark corners, small clusters of people sat around bottles of expensive champagne in the velvet booths of the roped-off VIP area. *Thump, thump, thump* went the music and the floor and Sam's head.

'Cause I just want you here tonight / holding on to me so tight. / What more can I do? / Oh, baby, all I want for Christmas is you.

He took another swig of Scotch, wishing Mariah would just finish up her goddamned song so that he could try to enjoy his evening without constant memories of Jenny.

"Sam!"

Sam leaned his head down to Joe, who was a few inches shorter.

"Max and the guys have a table over there!" Joe gestured to a space way up near the dance floor and to the left the way an army scout would indicate friendlies hidden in the jungle.

Sam nodded, taking another sip of his drink. Before he could lower his glass, however, someone bumped him forcefully from behind, and more than half the drink splashed onto his shirt. He turned to find the blonde girl from the bar checking out his shirt, smirking at the wet spot. She yelled over the thumping noise, "How do *you* like it?"

"Thanks! Are you for *real?*" he yelled at her sharply.

"All's fair," she shouted with a sexy shrug.

Edgy. Interesting. Okay, I'll play.

"Is this love or war?" he asked.

She moved in closer and yelled back, her warm breath tickling his ear, "Ask me again tomorrow morning."

So here it is, Sammy. She's amusing, good-looking, blonde, and blue-eyed. Yours for the taking. What's your move?

He stared at her, working his jaw. The answer was quick and clean, like an arrow to the heart:

I don't want her. I want Jenny.

"Sorry. I'm taken."

All I want for Christmas is you, baby. / All I want for Christmas is you, baby…

She feigned disappointment, snapping her fingers. "The one that got away."

He smiled his first genuine grin of the evening and winked at her before she moved on, giving him one last come-hither look over her shoulder.

"All I Want for Christmas Is You" faded out, and another, more raucous song started thumping.

His head pounded from the music and the scotch, and if a hot blonde couldn't persuade him to stay, it was unlikely any other girl could either. He pushed his way out of the club onto the sidewalk, where he filled his lungs with icy cold air and walked home.

***

Without a hangover to deal with, getting up early the next morning to attend church services at St. James wasn't physically painful, but comparisons were inevitable, and the cavernous sanctuary and enormous congregation made the service feel impersonal to Sam after the intimate warmth he had found at Grace Church in Gardiner. He knew he was trying to comfort himself, but without Jenny beside him, the service felt cold, and he felt empty. He left halfway through and walked home in disappointment, lonelier for her than ever.

It wasn't just at the club or at church either. He was looking for her everywhere.

After a week, he realized his search stemmed from the outlandishly ridiculous hope she would suddenly arrive in Chicago to find him, tell him she'd been just as miserable as he, declare her feelings for him, and they would finally be together.

His heart leapt whenever his answering machine blinked with messages or when he checked his personal email account to find a message waiting, which was ridiculous. He'd never had a chance to give her his contact information, so unless she'd tracked him down through Ingrid, it was unlikely he'd hear from her. Even so, he couldn't seem to stop hoping—couldn't seem to accept the fact that the feelings he had for her should be truncated. His heart simply wouldn't move on.

Another problem, though, was Chicago didn't feel

comfortable to him anymore. It didn't feel like home. It wasn't Chicago's fault, but everything about the city he used to love felt different since he got back from Montana. What used to be chic felt fake. What used to be cool felt cold. What used to be fun felt...empty.

Not to mention, he saw everything filtered through Jenny's eyes now, and it was maddening and funny and heartbreaking to have her constantly in his head and not in his arms. With every passing day, he longed for the wholesome Christmas fun of familiar carols; homemade gingerbread and Christmas movies in pajamas; Christmas tree lightings and a Christmas pageant followed by hot, spicy glögg. Quite simply, he longed for Christmas Jenny-style.

He wished he could stop looking for her.

He wished he could stop missing her.

He wished he could forget every moment he had spent with her and—mercifully—let her go.

He thought of her in the courthouse whispering, *This never could have worked out,* and it made him wince with regret, but the refrain in his head was the same:

She didn't want you, Sam. She didn't want you enough. Let her go.

***

He got up for a run the next morning, dark and early, even though the wind off the lake would be brutally cold. He put on long underwear and sweat pants, then layered on top with a thermal long-sleeved T-shirt, sweat shirt, and his North Face wind jacket. The key was to keep moving at a decent clip, and the wind wouldn't be so bad. He put on some shearling gloves and a black wool cap before heading out the door.

From his apartment in posh Streeterville, it was only two short blocks across Lake Shore Drive to the Lakefront Trail, a decent stretch of paved path perfect for joggers, cyclists, and walkers who wanted to enjoy the views of the lake as they exercised. Living in Streeterville was a huge status symbol, and when Sam had purchased his apartment, he was chuffed to officially be a part of the exclusive area where he could claim celebrities like Oprah Winfrey as a neighbor. With views of Navy Pier and the lake beyond, Sam's neighborhood was a glamorous world of nightclubs, museums, parks, skyscrapers, and some of Chicago's finest restaurants.

But it was his building's proximity to the Lakefront Trail that had been the clincher for Sam when he purchased the modest—though exorbitantly priced—studio. The lake was hands-down Sam's favorite part of living in Chicago. No challenge was so insurmountable, it couldn't be solved by spending some time jogging, walking, or thinking by Lake Michigan. He had, in fact, spent a good deal of time on the Lakefront Trail after his concussion, walking slowly first, then briskly as he worked back up to his usual two- to three-mile daily run. It was on that very trail he had decided to break up with Pepper. It seemed every important life decision Sam had made in the past five or six years had originated with a run along the lake.

More than ever, he needed to remember why he loved Chicago and why staying here was so important to him. How better to reaffirm his allegiance to his hometown than by enjoying the very best it had to offer?

Dawn fought its way through the clouds that covered the somber sky until the city glowed with a hazy light. There was a dusting of snow on the ground—it was December, after all, and this was Chicago—but that didn't slow Sam down, and after a good stretch in the lobby of his building, he found his way to the path.

In May, the blue of the sky and lake would contrast against the crisp gray of the paved trail and the bright-green grassy patches of the park. Budding trees in cheery shades of lime green and yellow and flowering trees with bursts of pink or white would paint the landscape with vibrant color.

Today, of course, the scene was bleak and colorless. City buildings created a cold, steel-gray basin that held the austerity of the winter scene. The gray path was dusted white, and the lake was colorless and hazy. Dark-brown leafless trees and bare, wiry branches were stark against the muddled morning sky.

He didn't love the trail any less for the severity of its cold, ashen palette. The trail was his friend in any season—in *all* seasons—and he valued it as much for its spare, quiet beauty now as he did for its vibrant cheerfulness in spring and summer.

Few people passed him: one on a bike and later two joggers. It wasn't an ideal day for exercise—the sun hid behind murky, undecided clouds, and until it made a solid appearance warming the air, only the most intrepid athletes—or confused insomniacs—would venture out. He kept his pace up, and his body felt warm despite the unforgiving wind. At some point, Sam realized his brain was keeping rhythm with his pace by verbalizing the beat in his head, and it frustrated him when he acknowledged the sound his brain had chosen, like a pulse with each stride:

Jen-ny. Jen-ny. Jen-ny. Jen-ny.

Jenny. He slowed down until he stopped, staring out at the lake, lacing his hands behind his neck, as the wind scraped and buffed his cheeks until his eyes shone.

Here, in his sacred place, in his favorite place, his mind could not turn away from her. And suddenly, it occurred to him that the trail—where every important decision of his early adulthood had been made, where every problem found a solution, where every trouble was soothed—was part of his past. His weekend in Gardiner was acting as a cornerstone, and his life now existed in two parts: an older, outdated part that included everything he loved about Chicago on one side, and a newer, more vibrant, more visceral part that included Jenny on the other.

It wasn't that the Lakefront Trail was any less beautiful or meaningful to Sam, but in the blink of an eye, its meaning went from actual to sentimental. The soothing place where he had solved his life's conundrums was nothing more than a picturesque snow-covered trail beside a cold, gray lake where a man could run and run and run, but couldn't run away.

He turned his eyes to the sky.

Make. It. Stop. Or tell me how to make it stop! How do I get over her? How do I move on? Tell me, because I don't want to feel like this anymore! I don't want to miss her like this every second of the day! Please!

His answer was the muffled sound of cold winter waves and the crackle of wind in his ears.

He closed his eyes and let his head drop to his chest. The place that always held neat and tidy answers to tough questions had none to offer today. He shook his head in heavy-hearted frustration before starting back to his apartment.

***

Ron stuck his head in Sam's office, rapping lightly on the door. "Sammy-boy!"

"Hey, Ron." Sam squinted and rubbed his eyes. He'd been working for eight or nine straight hours, only breaking for a bag of chips and bottle of water from the vending machine.

Ron plopped down in one of the guest chairs. "Heading to the old family homestead for Christmas?"

"Yep. Thinking about leaving tomorrow."

He was hoping that his suburban childhood home and the company of his family would give him some clarity and help him not feel so lonesome.

"So, duuuude…you were missed at the Christmas party! What *happened?*"

"Yeah, I heard. Sounded out of control."

Instead of heading to the annual party, Sam had opted, instead, to stay at the office and work late. Work was the only thing left that seemed to distract him from Jenny, so he had been burning the midnight oil lately. Although he was efficient and thorough, the usual satisfaction he derived from working hard was absent, unbalanced as it was by the missing "playing hard" component. It was more like drudgery, but at least it kept him busy until his feelings for Jenny faded.

Please fade soon. I can't take much more of this.

"Oh brother, you have no idea. Sandra from accounting brought a friend, and afterward, we went to her place. Suffice it to say, the party continued." He raised his eyebrows suggestively, putting his palm up. "High five, man!"

Sam sighed, gesturing to his computer, leaving Ron hanging. "Ron, I've got a lot of work to do. Do you *need* something?"

"Just came to say hey," he said dejectedly, lowering his abandoned hand. "So, listen, Sandra and her friend Kiki wanted to get some drinks tonight, and I know you and Pepper are ancient history, so I thought you might want to…"

Sam shook his head. "Buried in work."

Ron sighed. "Dude, what *happened* to you? You used to be party central. You're turning down drinks and a sure thing for…for *work?* Did I mention the friend is suh-mokin'?"

Sam looked up at Ron and cocked his head to the side.

He was sick and tired of missing Jenny.

Give it a try, man. You're not with Jenny; you're here. You've got to move on. Maybe you'll like this girl. Anyway, you've got nothing to lose, Sammy.

He forced himself to smile at his friend, reaching for his

mouse to shut down his computer. "You know what, Ron? Sure. Count me in. I'll meet you in the lobby in ten."

Ron jumped up and drummed his hands on Sam's desk. "And he's baaaaaaaack!"

Sam watched Ron go, then turned in his chair to look out the window at Chicago. *I never got back*, he thought ruefully.

***

Ron had chosen a small, classy bistro, but the girls were running late, so Sam sat at the small table with Ron, knocking back a scotch, hoping it would numb him into a pleasant state before Sandra and Kiki arrived.

Ron was yammering on about how much easier girls were during the holidays.

"It's a smorgasbord out there, man, and I'm not kidding. They all want some chump lined up for the New Year's kiss. So it's all low-hanging fruit. Some rotten, some luscious, but all easy picking." He downed his beer and signaled to the waitress to bring another, drumming on the table in his version of holiday cheer. "Sammy, Sammy, Sammy! What *happened* to you?!"

Sam looked up from his drink and smirked. "What do you mean?"

"So serious. So brooding. Where's the funeral, dude?"

Sam leaned his head to the side, regarding his friend. Ron was a pig, yes, but it had never really bothered Sam before. They'd partied hard, met some pretty cute girls, and had a good time together. So it wasn't necessarily fair that Sam felt a quick spike of disgust for his friend. Ron hadn't changed, just like Chicago hadn't changed. But Sam *had* changed, and he wasn't sure his life would ever go back to the way it was before meeting Jenny.

"You know, Ron," started Sam, unaccustomed to speaking seriously to his friend, "there are some girls out there that you can't just forget abou—"

"Okay, okay. Sorry." Ron put his hands up in surrender, rolling his eyes. His beer came, and he took a long draw, wiping the foam from his lip with the back of his hand. "She was quite a girl. I get it."

How did Ron know about Jenny?

Sam's eyes narrowed. "What are you talking about?"

"Pepper Pettway. Sex-on-a-Stick. She was one hot piece of ass. And don't get me wrong, classy too. You actually consider the shackles for a chick like that." He licked his finger and pretended to touch something hot. "Zzzz!"

Sam couldn't have been more surprised. Ron thought he was missing Pepper? *Wow.* It made Sam's head spin to realize how off the mark Ron's assumption was.

But he had to hand it to Ron…Sam couldn't think of a more complete prison than a marriage to Pepper. *Shackles.* Yep. His friend had inadvertently nailed it.

"Yeah." Sam gave a short, cynical snort. "Better you than me, brother."

Ron rubbed his index finger on his chin like he was trying to figure something out. Then he pointed at Sam. "She dumped *you*, right? That's why you've been so mopey?"

Sam shook his head slowly at Ron.

"*You* dumped *her*? I don't get you, Sammy. You had

that, and you let it go? You cut it loose?"

"Things aren't always what they seem, Ron."

Ron's expression brightened when he saw the girls make their way into the bistro over Sam's shoulder. He stood halfway out of his seat and waved them over.

Sam stood up and fixed an engaging smile on his face. *At least try.*

"Sammy, this is Sandra," Ron said, gesturing to a grinning, blonde woman whom Sam recognized from his office building. "And this is Kiki."

Kiki smiled, offering her hand to Sam. "Nice to meet you."

"You too." He enveloped her hand, irrationally hating the fact that the last woman whose hand he'd held was Jenny's. Now it was Kiki's. He released her hand gently, telling himself not to be an ass...which just reminded him of Jenny all over again.

This must be what it feels like to go utterly crazy.

Sam raised his eyebrows, gesturing to Kiki's raincoat, but she slipped out of it easily and took the seat next to Sam. He noticed it was a Burberry, possibly custom fitted, and it probably cost a fortune. He couldn't help but wonder how she'd look in a puffy parka with white fur around the hood framing her face.

"Cozy foursome," observed Ron. Sandra giggled and looked up adoringly at him.

Sam turned to Kiki. "So, Kiki, what are you drinking?"

"Champagne," she answered with a brief, refined smile, assessing the small bistro with a calculated glance.

"Sandra?"

"Same! Why not? It's Christmastime!" She giggled again, and Ron asked her about her day. She leaned in closer, and they continued an intimate conversation dotted with several gasps and giggles.

Sam called the waitress over and placed their drink orders. He turned back to find Kiki's elbow on the table, her chin rested on her hand, as she looked him over. Her glossy red nails caught the dim light of the café as they tapped lightly on her cheek. She was pretty. She had almost-black hair and bright-green eyes she made up expertly; she was very thin, and her black blouse set off her pale skin and dark hair. A few weeks ago, he'd have felt eternal gratitude to Ron for suggesting he be the fourth for a setup date with such a beautiful girl.

"So, Sam, Sandra told me you used to date that weather girl? Pepper Pettway?"

He nodded. "We broke up a couple months ago."

"I like that, though."

"You like it that I dated Pepper?"

"Well…she's a nine. And I'm a nine." She chuckled, and it was a throaty sound, likely due to smoking. "You've been, you know, vetted."

"What are you talking about?"

"Oh, come on. Don't play innocent. You rate us just like we rate you!"

"Rate?"

Kiki cleared her throat. "Ummm, lovebirds! *Atencion, s'il vous plaît*!" Sandra and Ron looked up. Kiki flashed Ron a runway smile. "Ron, one to ten, what am I?"

Ron smiled back at her teasingly, raising his eyebrows. "What do I get if I say eleven?"

"Wouldn't you like to know!"

"I *would* like to know."

"It's illegal in several countries," she volleyed back, licking her finger, then touching the space between her cleavage, throwing her head back, moaning lightly.

Ron narrowed his eyes dramatically and breathed in loudly, assessing her. "Ummmm…nine."

Kiki turned back to Sam, victory bright in her eyes. "See?"

"I see," he answered, wondering how in the hell he was going to make it through dinner.

"Oh, come on!" Kiki cajoled, noting his sour expression. "Everyone's doing it! Want me to do you?"

He stared at her like she was an alien life-form. She took that as a yes.

"Brown eyes…not bad. Hmmm…what is that? Reddish-blond hair? Huh. One point off. Ginger's not *'in'* right now." She let her glance sweep suggestively, brazenly up and down his seated body, letting her eyes rest for a long moment on his lap. When she returned to his eyes, she smiled sexily, wetting her lips and pursing them together. "Clearly *fit*. What else? Vice president, right? But not partner yet. I give you…an eight. And a half, 'cause you're cute. Dye your hair or come find me when you're a partner, then I'll give you a nine."

"Kiki, is it? Right?" She nodded eagerly, wetting her lips

again.

It wasn't her fault. It was the sort of flirty game that he would have engaged in a month ago. It would have led to sexy banter and thinly veiled innuendo throughout the meal. By the end of dinner, she'd be trailing her slick red nails up and down his arm, and an hour after that, they'd be skin to skin in his bed.

Again, it wasn't her fault. The thing is…Sam had already found the most fascinating, surprising, sexy girl the world had to offer. He'd found her, and he'd lost her, and it was breaking his heart every second of every day he spent away from her.

"No offense, Kiki, but I can't do this."

Sam stood up, placing his napkin on the table.

He took a hundred-dollar bill out of his wallet and dropped it on top of his napkin. Then he picked up his coat, tossed it over his arm, and walked out of the bistro without another word.

***

When he got home, he took the elevator up to the top floor of his apartment building and walked up the steep flight of gray concrete stairs to the roof. He turned his eyes to the night sky, looking for the stars, and was rewarded with cloud cover and a pinkish-gray city sky. No Cassiopeia, no North Star to "help him find his way," as Jenny had promised. No stars at all.

He had bought a C. S. Lewis book impulsively on a lunch break and found a passage in it that resonated with him. He couldn't shake it now that he'd read it. After the death of his wife, Lewis had written,

Her absence is like the sky, spread over everything.

That's how Sam felt too. There was no respite from his feelings for Jenny, no matter how far away he was from her.

He held onto the railing that surrounded the perimeter of the roof, remembering Jenny at the arch when he had asked her to come to Chicago. She had placed her hand on his arm—*I'm not ready to say good-bye either. I've never felt like this. Never in my life.* And how had he responded to that gift? He had pressured her, judged her, criticized her, called her a coward, and tried to force her hand. For what? For a place *he* could barely stand anymore.

He hated himself.

He hated that he had been wrong: going back to his old life was impossible. Knowing Jenny and leaving her had made it impossible. The hold she had on his heart was unyielding. Even from fifteen hundred miles away, his eyes searched for her in clubs, at church, in throngs of people. Places that used to hold a special energy for him were hopelessly colorless, good for little but useless sentimentality. His hands yearned to touch her, simultaneously resenting and worshipping the imprint of her laced fingers through his. Regardless of the distractions everywhere—work, parties, clubs, girls—his heart ached for her alone with a throbbing, unceasing longing.

And standing on that roof under a pitiable, starless sky, several simple truths became evident to a very changed Sam Kelley.

The first was that he wasn't going to be able to resume

his old life in Chicago.

The second was that what he had with Jenny hadn't been infatuation.

The final one, which his heart had known for some time and his mind was finally obligated to accept with breathtaking clarity:

I am totally and completely in love with Jenny Lindstrom.

***

When Sam told his boss he wanted two extra days at Christmas to spend with his family, Thomas had given him a hard look.

"First it's a day in Montana that turns into three. Then you don't show up to the Christmas party. Lots of clients were looking for you there, Sammy. Frankly, you've been a little moody lately. Your work's solid, but your attitude sucks. How about you take the whole week and make sure you *want* to come back after New Year's, huh?" It was like slap in the face. In a good way. A bucket of ice-cold water, a loud alarm clock, the screech of brakes. A wake-up call. Sam nodded at him, eyes growing wide and hopeful as a liberating awareness flooded him, making synapses fire like crazy in his head, putting together the very beginnings of a plan. *Was it really* that *easy?*

"You know what, Thomas? I'll do just that." He started breathing faster, excitement building.

Thomas had narrowed his eyes, probably realizing he had overplayed his hand, because Sam's face had all the signs of a man who just realized he wouldn't drown if he jumped ship. "Sammy! Don't be rash. Just get your priorities straight."

Sam had chuckled and nodded at his boss with a lucidity—*with a hope*—he hadn't had in two weeks. "That's *exactly* what I'm going to do, Thomas."

He started to leave his boss's office when he turned around, smiling broadly, excitedly, for the first time since he returned from Montana.

"Merry Christmas, Thomas! Thank you, sir!"

***

He had enjoyed spending Christmas Eve and Christmas Day with his family.

More than he had in years. Not that being with his family had necessarily helped him figure out what to do about Jenny, but it was somehow comforting to spend a few days with them. Colleen had arrived with her husband and the girls on Christmas Eve morning and greeted Sam with a shocked and elated hello. Muirin arrived a few hours later with her husband and baby Colin, who was deposited in his uncle's lap and proceeded to take a two-hour nap in Sam's arms.

His sisters had married good men: stable, loving men who doted on their wives and children. Sam found that watching the couples soothed a deep ache inside of him, even as it increased his own personal yearning. Surprisingly, he also found that he was more comfortable with his brothers-in-law than he'd been with Ron or Joe or any of the other single guys he hung out with in Chicago.

He peeked out his mother's kitchen window as Ned followed his daughters outside to make snow angels. At the kitchen table, Scott looked up at Sam, giving him a hard time.

"When's it your turn, Sammy?"

Sam had given his brother-in-law a tight smile, recalling his blunder when he had blurted out *"Someday. With you"* to Jenny.

His gut twisted with regret, remembering Jenny rush out of the courthouse after he'd yelled unforgivable things at her. He'd never apologized to her, and it had been weeks since their emotional farewell. He'd probably have a better chance at converting Ron to the priesthood than having another chance with Jenny at this point.

After Christmas Eve services, the girls had stayed up as late as they could waiting for Santa, but when they couldn't keep their eyes open anymore, they dozed off, and their dad carried them up to bed. Sam, his sisters, their husbands, and his parents gathered in the living room, his dad occasionally stoking a roaring fire, trading stories of Christmases past and passing Colin around to loving arms.

Christmas morning dawned white with sunshine on a new-fallen snow, which delighted the girls almost more than Santa's bounty, and the day was spent opening gifts, sledding down the backyard hill, and eating and drinking way too much. Colleen and Muirin finally left for their respective homes after dinner on Christmas Day. And Sam would head back to the city in the morning.

He was standing on the back patio looking up at the sky when his mother joined him.

"Good night for it," she mused, pulling a thick, wool

sweater around her shoulders and buttoning it up against the cold. "It's clear."

Margaret Gunderson Kelley was still an attractive woman at sixty. She wore her white hair in a neat pageboy held back by a variety of hair bands and kept fit by taking long walks with Sam's dad every morning.

"Not like Montana."

"Well," she said, winking at Sam, "nowhere's like Montana." She nudged her son in the side with her elbow. "So, youngest child, did something happen while you were there?"

"What do you mean?"

"Well, Aunt Lisabet told me what you did for Kristian. The wedding. Standing proxy. Which, by the way, it would have been nice to hear from *you* instead of *her*." She chucked him lightly in the arm before continuing. "Still, I'm proud of you for helping him out. What a nice boy I raised."

"You did okay," Sam conceded, grinning straight ahead in the semidarkness.

"But you're not acting like yourself. Coming home early for Christmas? Staying an extra day? Oh, I'm not saying I don't love every second. I do. We all loved having you here longer this year. But it's not really *you*, son."

He cringed at her words. "I'm sorry about that, Mom."

"Oh, honey, I'm not complaining. You work hard, you play hard. Your job means everything to you." She seemed to hesitate, then continued: "I don't want to pry, but I gather from Colleen that you're not with Pepper anymore."

"Didn't work out." He turned his head to smile at her.

"Don't start crying, now. I know how much you liked her."

She chuckled, shaking her head. "Fair enough. She wasn't my favorite. I wanted more for you. I wanted something deep and lasting and—" She paused, then took his arm and led him to the patio steps. She sat down and pulled him down beside her on the cold, rough concrete. "So it's not Pepper."

He shook his head. "Not Pepper. And about my job," he started, "don't fall over in a dead faint, but I'm thinking about quitting. Downsizing the whole work thing."

His mother's head snapped up. "Should I be worried?"

"Nah. Just thinking it's time for a change."

"Okay…it's not Pepper, and it's not your job. So what happened in Montana, Sam?"

He sighed, rubbing his cold hands together. "I met a girl."

"You don't say."

"It's that obvious?"

"Samuel Gunderson Kelley, you wear your heart on your sleeve. Always have. Always will. And when I see my boy this *melancholy,* I think—no, I *know*—it's got to be about a girl."

"I fell hard, Mom." He sighed loudly, leaning forward to place his elbows on his knees. "I liked her. I really, *really* liked her."

"Sounds like maybe you *more than* liked her, Sam. What went wrong?"

"I asked her to come here."

His mother groaned softly. "I guess that didn't go over

too well?"

"She won't leave Montana. And I mean, I love Montana, just like you do, but—"

"Oh, sweetheart, no." She chuckled, putting her hand on his arm to stop him. "No, no. I don't love Montana."

"Of course you do." Sam looked at her, confusion wrinkling his forehead. "W-We went back. Every year. *Twice* a year. We always went back…"

"I love *my sister.* I love Aunt Lisabet and your cousins. But Montana? No. Oh, Sam, I was—I was glad to go. Relieved. I left *cheerfully.* An opportunity to see the big city with a man I loved? It was a dream come true."

"No, no. Wait, Mom. You left with Dad, but—but…"

She was shaking her head gently, but her eyes said it all. "Sam. *You* love Montana. Always have since you were a little boy. For *me?* It was about family. Not the place. The people. *Only* the people."

Sam's shoulders slumped as he processed this new truth. He had always thought of Montana as "in his blood," an affection he had almost taken for granted as inherited—like brown eyes or reddish hair—from his mother. To learn that she harbored no love for Montana meant that his affection for it was individual. It was not a part of her but solidly a part of him. Not in his blood, perhaps, but firmly in his heart, of his own choice, of his own making.

"Lunkhead." Margaret hugged herself tighter against the cold. "You pressured her to come to Chicago, huh?"

"Yeah. I thought she'd at least consider it. I bought her airline tickets. At the time, it seemed like the only way to be"—he sighed again, angry with himself—"together. I was mad when she said no. I was hurtful. I said…unforgivable things."

His mother nodded slowly. "Unforgivable, huh?"

"Feels like it."

"And you haven't spoken since?"

"Not a peep."

They sat in silence for a few minutes before Margaret nudged him. "Sam, here's what I don't get. You *love* Montana. If you want to be with her, why wouldn't *you* go *there*?"

"My *life* is here. My job, my apartment, friends, family. She comes from this ridiculously tiny town. I couldn't make the money there that I make here. What would I even do in some small town? I couldn't be happy there."

She looked at him. "Is it the *only* town in the entire state of Montana where she could be happy? That seems unlikely."

"I don't know. I didn't ask her to go anywhere else. I pitched Chicago. It didn't work out."

"You know…Bozeman's a great town. Plenty of work there. Helena. Laurel. Great Falls is a nice little city for people who *like* Montana."

"She likes Great Falls," he said, thinking about her original plan to make a life for herself there. "She went to school there. But she chose Gardiner *over* Great Falls."

"I see." She pulled her sweater tighter around her. "I think I need more information. Tell me about this girl."

"Her name's Jenny." He sighed, shaking his head. "It's

no use, Mom. I said terrible things when I left and—"

"Samuel. Tell me about the girl."

He put his hands on his knees and looked up at the sky. He got a good fix on her face in his head and smiled in the darkness. His voice was soft and tender when he started speaking, like how one's voice sounds in one's own head, like a stream of consciousness.

"Her name's Jenny Lindstrom. She's twenty-four. She drinks glögg on Christmas Eve. She doesn't like it that I drink beer, but she says 'men will have their vices,' and she can live with that one. Her mother actually used to say that, but she passed away, and Jenny misses her. Really badly. So badly she needs to be near her family.

"She teaches high school science, and she has a puppy, which is ridiculous, right? A schoolmarm with a puppy. She knows all this stuff about the stars and points out the constellations to anyone who will listen. She quotes Shakespeare and C. S. Lewis out of the blue. She said she's a frustrated English teacher inside.

"The principal at her school, Paul? He really likes her. He's young and good-looking and best friends with her brother. She's got three brothers, by the way, and they're all like these huge, blond stereotypical Swedish guys. Anyway, she says she doesn't like Principal Paul, but I'm sure he's wearing her down.

"She's really beautiful, Mom. She has bright-blue eyes and blonde hair, and she organizes the Christmas pageant and makes a mean omelet. She draws concentric circles on the table with her finger when she's thinking about something. She gets all mad when she thinks something, or someone, is wrong. But she knows how to say she's sorry, and when she does, she means it.

"She blushes all the time. I mean, *everything* embarrasses her, but she's so tough too, Mom. Like really honest and straightforward, and she has this amazing backbone. You know, youngest of four with three older brothers. She gives it back, you know? She's...surprising.

"And smart. Really smart. She knows everything about Yellowstone Park, practically grew up in the park. Her father's a tour guide in Yellowstone. She cleans closets at her church when they need a hand, and she drives the girliest light-blue SUV I've ever seen. She has these beat-up cowgirl boots she wears all the time.

"She braids her hair with flowers for Midsummer just like her mom did. Just like you and Aunt Lisabet and the girls. She likes Christmas movies and hot cocoa and going to the symphony. She loves little kids and wants her own someday. You should have seen her face hearing about the girls and Colin, seeing their pictures on my phone.

"She's got the best heart of anyone I've ever met. She hated that we took the vows for Kris and Ingrid. It was tearing her apart because she thinks you should only say wedding vows once to one person in your life...but she did it anyway because she promised Ingrid, and she believes in keeping a promise to someone she loves, and...and..."

His voice trailed off, lost in the memory of their vows. He had shut down those memories at all costs since returning home, because they were the most visceral of the moments he spent with Jenny. He couldn't bear to remember. But now the floodgates were open, and he closed his eyes against the intense longing that accompanied the memory—her eyes searching his so fiercely across the table for comfort, for support, for—

"Sam?"

"Love," he breathed in a trance, saying the words out loud for the first time. "I love her, Mom. I am totally in love with her."

"Yes," she whispered, "you are."

Uncertainty and panic made him speak faster. "How can I be in love with her when I only knew her for a weekend?"

"Oh, Sam. There's no rulebook. There's no rhyme or reason to love. No logic. No checklist. For some people, it takes a lifetime to find someone, for others, a weekend. For me? A week. You got to know her very well in only a few days. And Sam," she said, putting her arm around his shoulders, "she sounds worth knowing. Does she love you too?"

He rubbed his jaw with his thumb and forefinger. "I don't know. She *had* feelings for me, I know that for sure. She told me. I could see…" He closed his eyes tightly, reviewing their final conversation in his head. "I think I might have blown it, Mom. At the end, I-I might have—"

"Sam?"

"Hmmm?" He looked up at her, searching her face for hope.

She took his cheeks between her cold hands and smiled

at him tenderly. "Sam, when you finally find what you want, you have to claim it. No matter what. Go back to Montana. Go to Choteau or Great Falls or Gardiner. Go wherever you need to go. Figure it out. Don't give up on her yet."

***

He opened his laptop and let it warm up for a moment, pouring himself a beer. After he wrote the email, he would pack a bag, and not just with a change of clothes this time; he planned to stay for a few days, at least. He'd drive out to Midway in the morning and make his way to Great Falls, probably via Minneapolis. It wasn't so bad by plane.

He sat down on his black leather sofa, pulled the laptop onto his lap, and double-clicking on his email icon. He stared at the screen for a moment, thinking about Kristian so far away from Ingrid, so far away from home. *How do I start?* He hadn't written to Kris since the brief email he'd sent from the Billings airport to tell him he was a married man. *Just start typing, man. It'll come to you.*

Chapter 11

When Jenny lost her mother, the sorrow she felt had been overwhelming—paralyzing, even—and her only balm had been the company of her father and brothers. They had come together in unified sadness, negotiating their movements like severely sunburned people sharing a small space, careful not to touch one another, careful not to touch the awful red rawness of their blistered skin. They ate dinner together every night, occasionally in total silence, finding the only possible solace in the common, unspoken heartache that set them apart from the rest of the living, breathing, buzzing world. Being around other people unaffected by their visceral loss took such a lion's share of their daily energy, it was a relief to be quiet with one another at the day's end. Their fellowship of sorrow carried them through those first dark days.

Gradually, Jenny found, with relentless insistence, life demanded that those still living move forward. They spoke more, until they all laughed together one night—more than one of them feeling guilty over their giggles. Little by little, their sorrow became a shared life experience and was woven, bit by bit, into the tapestry of their family. Daily supper became twice-weekly supper, as other commitments and obligations infringed on the family time that became less and less crucial, and finally turned into a Sunday supper as regular life resumed. Red and raw was pink again, healing, and they were living and breathing and buzzing with the rest of the world again.

Silence was replaced by stories of their daily lives, bickering and teasing. The five lives that emerged covered with new skin were changed; they had survived the loss together, but that didn't necessarily mean they were tougher for it. They were scarred. Fear could still permeate moments of Jenny's quiet grief, however bearable now. Unbearable would be losing one of them again.

Sam wasn't a member of her family, which had led her to believe losing him would be bearable.

She was wrong.

When she lost her mother, she read a quote from C. S. Lewis that resonated with her: *"Part of every misery is, so to speak, the misery's shadow or reflection: the fact that you don't merely suffer but have to keep on thinking about the fact that you suffer. I not only live each endless day in grief, but live each day thinking about living each day in grief."* Lewis was just as right now as he had been then, and the passage resonated with Jenny all over again:

Every moment was surrendered to Sam's absence.

The very worst thing about the week after the vows was that after *this* loss—the loss of Sam—Jenny didn't have a fellowship of sorrow with whom to share her sadness and confusion. Her loneliness was exquisite, unparalleled in her life, and thoroughly exhausting. Too much had been lost all at once: her simple, satisfying life; her romantic innocence; her sexual dormancy; saying wedding vows aloud…and all these crucial life changes shared one vital, common element. Sam.

She missed him.

Jenny wasn't raised to be the sort of person to neglect her responsibilities merely because she was harboring personal heartache; she was at school an hour early every day to prepare her lessons and stayed an hour after to straighten her desk and classroom.

She worked on the program for the annual concert and attended all the rehearsals, helping the senior girls choose their carols and the music teacher coach the freshman and sophomore choruses through their pieces, which included several solos and hand motions. She directed the janitor on how she wanted the risers arranged and brought in evergreens cut from a local area of woods to decorate the cafeteria, where they would hold the concert, festively.

She was at church every Wednesday evening to organize the little ones for the pageant. She wiped runny noses and sorted out doves and baby angels, wise men and shepherds. She spent nights at home sewing new costumes until her fingers bled, making halos from wire, white ribbon, and silver feathers with a leaky, angry glue gun that singed her fingers. She crate-trained Casey with a dogged tenacity until the puppy was allowed to wander around Jenny's apartment for limited amounts of time without having an accident. She spent all day Sunday with her father at his small house outside of town, making elaborate Sunday suppers, straightening his kitchen cabinets, and folding his laundry.

She had never been so busy before, but to her frustration, nothing filled that gaping hole of aching loneliness in her life. At night, she drew her knees to her chest in bed, remembering Sam's smile, seeing his face, hearing his voice, replaying his words, yearning for his warmth, his arms, his hands, his breath, his soft lips, his teasing grin, their easy banter. She would cross her arms over her chest and hold herself, remembering his eyes holding hers across the conference table at the courthouse, burning through her to brand her heart until it wasn't hers anymore. And finally, she would weep until she succumbed, mercifully, to sleep.

***

That first week, she didn't see anyone socially, except for one very tearful cappuccino with Maggie one night as she was closing. Maggie must have noticed Jenny swiping at her eyes as Jenny and Casey made their way back from their evening walk, because she had unlocked the door of the café, stuck her head out, and called to Jenny before she could enter the door to her apartment. "Jen! Coffee!"

While Casey scampered joyfully around the empty, dimly lit café, Jenny sat at the coffee bar miserably as Maggie made them two after-hour cappuccinos. Then Maggie leaned on the counter and listened as Jenny spilled her heart out.

"Maggie, this just hurts so much," she finally sniffled, wiping her eyes with a napkin.

"But he wants you, Jen. You refuse to go to Chicago, but you're miserable here. Maybe you should just go. Make it clear it's a visit to see him only, and you'd never consider movin' there. Maybe you'd even like it. Who knows?"

"It wouldn't be any good." Jenny had stirred her coffee, watching the cheerful white foam dissolve into the depths of the cup until it was all a murky brown. "You know when you see two people on a reality show? And they're thrown together in some unlikely circumstance on a deserted island or something, right? And you watch them fall in love, but it's not real. When real life starts up again and the show's over, they try to force each other into their old lives, and it all crumbles. All the magic is somehow lost."

"You don't know for sure that would happen, Jen."

"I do, Maggie. I can't live that life. Dressing up for parties, drinking, living in an apartment, in a city. What would I even do there? I'd be frightened of the city, paralyzed by the strangeness. It would kill the magic."

"Isn't it possible that it's better than *this*?" Maggie had asked, palms open in supplication, gesturing to Jenny's life, her sadness, her longing.

"I couldn't bear to kill it," she had whispered. "I'd rather have the memories. They'll fade. Eventually they'll fade. I just have to keep moving until then."

Maggie had smiled at her then, covering Jenny's hands with her own, the lilt of her soft accent comforting in Jenny's ears. "Then how about a girls' weekend? You and me? Great Falls?"

For the first time since Sam had left, Jenny smiled, grateful for Maggie. She nodded. "Okay."

"Next weekend," promised Maggie. "You and me."

***

It turned out a girls' weekend didn't solve all her problems, but at least it distanced her from them.

Maggie was good company on the drive north, changing the music, pointing at scenery out the window, and making Jenny tell her all about the towns they traveled through. She didn't ask about Sam, and Jenny was relieved not to talk about him. She couldn't escape the near-constant sense of loss she felt, but at least she didn't have to talk about it too, which inevitably brought on more embarrassing, painful tears.

They checked into the Comfort Inn, and Maggie decided to take a short nap before they headed to the Great Falls Symphony that evening to hear "Hallelujah Holidays," which would include the city chorus singing parts of Handel's *Messiah*. Feeling energized for the first time since Sam left her, Jenny couldn't bear to stay cooped up in the hotel room. She bundled up to take a walk and told Maggie she'd be back later to grab some dinner before the concert.

"Jen," started Maggie, pulling back the covers on her bed. "I thought of somethin'. Life is about gray areas. Black and white is more comfortable, but gray is more realistic. Visitin' Sam doesn't have to mean leadin' him on. You don't have to promise anythin'. Hell, you've been upfront about who you are and what you want. You could see him and come back. Just visit."

Jenny zipped up her coat and slung her bag over her shoulder. "Maggie, what good would it do? We'd fall for each other harder, and when I'd have to leave, we'd be exactly where we were before I visited. Exactly where we are now but worse. In that way, I think it *would* be leading him on, Maggie. Unless I was prepared to stay."

She yawned loudly, pulling the comforter up to her neck and snuggling under. "It's not leadin' him on if you're honest. 'I would never move here, but I came here to see you.' I guess what bothers me is by not goin' at all, you're sayin' it's over. And we both know it's *not* over. You can let it die, Jenny. It'll die eventually. But why wouldn't you give it a chance?"

Jenny stared at Maggie for a moment, then looked down her feet in thought.

"Can I say one more thing?"

Jenny looked up and nodded.

"I think maybe you're just scared of leavin'. You say it's about losin' the magic. I don't think that's all of it. You came home to your sick mum. And maybe you're just holdin' on to your da and the boys a wee bit too tightly, Jen. Maybe you think sayin' good-bye to them is worse than sayin' good-bye to Sam. I don't know if that's true or not, but I think it's worth a look."

Maggie flipped over, and a moment later, her breathing was even and deep.

Jenny stood frozen in the same spot for a good few minutes, thinking about everything Maggie said. Then she turned and walked out the door, closing it gingerly behind her.

***

Exiting the front of the hotel onto Tenth Avenue, Jenny

decided to walk down the street to her old alma mater, the University of Great Falls. At an unhurried pace, she enjoyed the activity of the small city. What a difference from Gardiner, which only had a handful of shops. Everywhere she turned, there was something else to see, much of it new in the three short years since she had attended college here. A new Target, Hastings Entertainment, Riddle's Jewelry. She looked in the shop windows, most of them decorated merrily for Christmas with fake buffalo snow and cheerful lights.

By virtue of its location—three hours from Glacier National Park and five hours from Yellowstone—Great Falls wasn't reliant on tourism. This excepted Great Falls from pandering to tourists like many cities in Montana and meant that it had the stores and amenities it needed for its citizens rather than transient visitors. It gave Great Falls a solid, year-round feeling that Gardiner frankly lacked with its heavy reliance on the mostly summer tourist trade. She passed a Starbucks and treated herself to a pumpkin-spice latte, then kept walking, her thoughts naturally turning to Sam, as they always did lately.

How could she have known that the moment he walked into the Livingston Courthouse would be one of the most important moments of her life? She thought of him, so handsome and slick in the little lobby. She'd been so angry at him, and he'd teased her back into a good mood, treating her with such care and kindness when her car skidded off the road, taking her to dinner, staying in Gardiner. She thought of the omelet debacle and how gracious he had been— merry, even, and understanding. She remembered him sitting on the bench at school looking out at the football field, looking so dejected. Jenny smiled. That's when she knew with certainty he liked her as much as she liked him. It had been a revelation.

The cold wind whipped into her face, and she quickened her pace toward the university. Unbidden, her mind turned to his face when she'd opened her apartment door to him the night of the Stroll. He had looked her up and down hungrily and kissed her a few minutes later. She had wanted him to, but the shivers of pleasure she felt at the time had been new to her in every way, surprising and addictive.

She smiled to herself, thinking of his warm hands laced through hers at the Stroll and his stunned dismay when he realized he had blurted out that he wanted to have children with her someday. She hugged herself as she walked along, remembering his wide eyes as he was backpedaling like crazy. Even visiting Yellowstone with him, despite how the day ended, had been magical, she thought, remembering their easy conversation and the story of how his parents fell in love.

For the first time since he left, she didn't cry as she sorted through their memories. She still wasn't sure of herself, but at least her eyes weren't burning with tears on cue. She thought of Maggie's words. Why wouldn't she just go to Chicago? Why couldn't she just go? Was it because she was scared? She swallowed as she evaluated these questions and realized Maggie's words held truth. While she was here in Great Falls, her mother had succumbed to cancer. Lord only knows what could happen if she went as far as Chicago.

Even as she articulated these thoughts to herself, she knew they didn't really make sense. Staying in Gardiner wasn't going to prevent her father or the boys from getting sick or hurt. Sam said Gardiner was where she went to "hide her head in the sand" and "give up." She frowned, walking even more briskly.

How come his words about giving up and selling out haunted her so much? Had she given up? Had she sold out? Was she a coward? Her mother had hidden her illness from Jenny specifically so she would stay in Great Falls and make a life for herself there, but in the end, she'd turned her back on that life.

I went *home to care for Mamma, but I* stayed *home out of fear.*

She had given up on her dreams of a life in Great Falls because she was afraid. And she was holding onto her brothers and father too tightly even now. She was scared to leave them.

Was that the *real* reason she didn't go to Chicago with Sam? Fear? Was she allowing fear to immobilize her?

"No!" she exclaimed aloud, bristling against the weakness of it.

My life is in Gardiner, she reasoned. *My family, my job, my church, my apartment, my friends. It's not about* fear. *It's about being settled somewhere.* But another voice intervened: *Stop kidding yourself. It's about fear, and in your gut, you know it. If you weren't so afraid, you'd see that you could have left your job, your church, your apartment, and your friends, Jenny. You could have left them all behind for Sam.*

Then she pictured the faces of her father and brothers in her mind, and like a punch in the gut, she felt the strength of her fear. She furrowed her brow, walking so fast now, the cold air burned her lungs, and her hands sweated in her mittens, even though it was only twenty-three degrees.

I'm not weak! I'm not the sort of person who lets fear hold dominion over her life! That small, soft voice in her head answered back, *But you did. You pushed him away because you were scared to leave Gardiner.*

Somewhere deep inside of her, she'd determined, consciously or unconsciously, that staying in Gardiner would keep her safe. That being close to her brothers and father meant she wouldn't experience the sort of heartbreak that had accompanied her mother's death.

But it hadn't worked.

Because every day away from Sam made her heart feel like it was breaking.

Could it be that the very choice you made to protect yourself is the one that will cause the worst heartache of all?

She continued into the small campus, walking the familiar paths without enjoying them at all. She brushed some snow off a bench with her mittened hand and sipped the last bit of her now-cold latte. She took off her mitten and wiped a droplet from her lip with her bare finger and let her finger linger there for a moment, remembering the final kiss they had shared after the vows. He had held her flush to his body, unyielding, demanding, and even in the desperation of the moment, she couldn't deny how perfectly they'd fit together.

Her shoulders rolled forward and she crumpled with her chin to her chest, defeated. A searing, certain sadness confirmed without a shadow of doubt that she had made a mistake. In letting Sam go, she had allowed fear to choose her path for her, and she knew with a brutal, heart-wrenching certainty that losing him would be the biggest mistake of her life.

Oh, my God! Help! Help me figure out what to do. Help me have the courage to do it. And please don't let it be too late when I'm ready.

She put her mitten back on and hugged herself. Her spirits lifted with a new, growing patch of peace in her heart, which reinforced she was on the right path to figuring this out.

No more crying now, Jenny. Go home. Have Christmas. Figure out what to do, and then do it.

***

"Children, please listen. Please quiet down. I shouldn't have to say that more than once. Please." Jenny clasped her hands together, a forced, cheerful smile animating her tired face. "That was a very good dress rehearsal. You should feel very proud of yourselves. I certainly am. Give yourselves a hand."

The students clapped and high-fived each other, gathered around Jenny in the cafeteria, which would serve as an auditorium tomorrow night.

"Freshmen, please remember, black pants and white tops. Sophomores, black pants and red or green tops. If anyone needs to borrow something, please see me before you go tonight, and we'll figure it out.

"Sarah, Mr. Ashby wants you to stay after to practice that solo one last time.

"Senior girls, please stop by my classroom tomorrow after third period. We need to figure out once and for all if it'll be 'The Christmas Canon' or 'The Peace Carol' for your encore—we simply don't have time for both. And you need to decide what you're wearing by tomorrow. I see you rolling your eyes, Amanda. Let's be respectful, please.

"Thank you, everyone, for your efforts and for staying late tonight. Please work on those 'Silent Night' verses for our big finale, okay? I'll see you all tomorrow!"

She barely noticed the hum of conversations and giggles as the children shrugged into their coats, faces merry with Christmas cheer. Jenny turned back to the table where she had music and notes in an unruly pile. She sorted the papers into a neat stack, placing them in a folder labeled "Christmas Concert." She turned and waved good-bye to the last teenagers walking out the door of the cafeteria, leaving the room peaceful and quiet after the two-hour-long dress rehearsal with so many active adolescents to corral.

Exhausted, she sat down in the folding chair at the table, rubbing her pounding temples with her fingers and closing her eyes. Trying to stay busy and distracted was sapping whatever strength she had, and she fell into bed at night like an old lady.

Out of nowhere, she saw Sam's face in her mind that morning at church. *Morning, Pretty Girl...*She clenched her eyes tightly against the tears beginning to prickle. *No more crying, Jenny. You promised.*

She crossed her arms over her chest, hands holding opposite arms. She breathed deeply in and out, taking her time, finding her mother's face in her mind and focusing on it. She kept her eyes tightly closed. *Noen elsket meg en gang. Someone loved me once.* But the image of her mother's face faded like a watercolor and was replaced in sharp detail with Sam's, and she saw his eyes—warm and brown, intense and tender—holding hers as she whispered Ingrid's vows. She leaned into the memory, into the selfless, solid reassurance he had offered her that moment.

I miss him.

The pull to be with him—to go to him, if that's what it would take—was getting stronger and more certain with every passing day.

"Jenny?"

She lowered her hands and opened her eyes slowly, remembering where she was. It took her a second to focus on Paul's face in the dim light of the empty cafeteria.

He was squatting down next to her, and Lord only knew how long he'd been there. He looked up at her, regarding her seriously.

She mustered a slight smile. "Hey, Paul."

"Are you okay?"

She nodded, offering him a sad smile. "I'm okay."

He took a deep breath and sighed, tilting his head to the side, assessing her with worried eyes. "It's been almost three weeks since I really saw you smile. I'm concerned about you."

"You don't need to be. I'm fine, Paul. Really, I am. Just

so busy lately with the concert and the pageant at church. I'm just a little tired."

"I stopped in for the last few minutes of the rehearsal. It looked amazing."

"Yeah. I think it's really good."

"Best Christmas concert we've ever had, Jen. Thanks to you." He said this gently and reached over to cover her hand with his. She pulled hers away almost instantly, folding them together in her lap.

He narrowed his eyes for a moment, then looked down, nodding. "Jenny, I know I made things awkward between us. But more than anything, I care about you, and I want to be here for you. You know, I used to be a guidance counselor before I took this job as principal. I'm a good listener. Whatever you need."

I need Sam.

Her eyes brightened with tears, touched by his kindness. She knew his feelings for her were deeper than friendship, but he was setting them aside because he cared for her. "I'm just trying to figure things out."

"Jenny, everything new gets old. It will fade. Eventually. I promise."

She nodded, biting her lip and looking down at her folded hands. Paul's words, meant to comfort her, did just the opposite. She winced as her heart ached at the future Paul outlined for her. She didn't want her feelings for Sam to get old. She didn't want for them to fade.

The days were dwindling down. School break would start tomorrow. Then Christmas. Then…well, she was still figuring out what her next move would be, but she was getting there. In the meantime, she simply missed him.

She whispered, "His absence is like the sky, spread over everything."

"C. S. Lewis?"

She looked up at him, giving him a tired grin. "The very one."

"I hate to see you like this." He stared at her intently, then breathed deeply, standing up and changing the subject. "It's late. Let me take you out for dinner."

She raised her eyebrows, cocking her head to the side with a meaningful look. "No, Paul. I don't think that's such a good—"

He put up his palms face out, interrupting her. "Work colleague. Guidance counselor. Good listener. Family friend. Nothing else. I promise."

Jenny sighed, nodding warily. "Okay. Dinner. Let me go freshen up."

***

It wasn't Paul's fault. It wasn't him. It was just that Jenny didn't want much to be around anyone—anyone who wasn't Sam—and taking her to the Grizzly Guzzle Grill, where she and Sam had dined before the Christmas tree lighting, didn't help either. When Paul pulled into the parking lot, Jenny almost said something but decided it wasn't worth it to leave and go somewhere else.

Lars waved as they walked in, raising his eyebrows in surprise to see his best friend with his sister, and for the second time in three weeks, two Cokes appeared at their table after they sat down.

"I'm really glad we're doing this." Paul smiled at Jenny over his menu.

"Thank you." Jenny nodded politely. "Unfortunately, I think we're giving Lars something to talk about."

"Nah. He knows we're just friends."

They sat in silence for another minute, each deciding what they would have. Finally Jenny put down her menu, and Paul put his on top of hers.

"Jen, I'm sorry you're so down. He had no right to lead you on."

Jenny looked at Paul's handsome face, his coloring so much like her own. His eyes were earnest and worried. *It would be so much easier if I could just love you, Paul.*

"He didn't lead me on. He didn't make any promises he didn't keep. He *asked* me to come to Chicago."

"You said no?"

"I did." Jenny took a sip of her pop.

"I was sure that he…" Paul's eyes narrowed, staring at Jenny in surprise. He shook his head in confusion. "I don't understand, Jenny. You seem so sad."

"I *am* sad. I don't want to be in Chicago. But that doesn't mean I don't want to be with Sam." Jenny sighed, watching her finger make circular motions on the table. "His life is there."

"And yours is here."

She nodded slowly, resigned. "My family is here."

They placed their orders, and Paul talked animatedly about Upper Slide and the first few weeks of ice fishing.

Jenny generally made it out there with the boys once or twice during the season but knew there was a whole community of folks who spent every available moment up at the lake all season. It was composed of some very colorful characters. Listening to Paul, Jenny smiled a few times and even chuckled once.

"There it is!" Paul exclaimed in triumph, smiling back at her. "A Jenny giggle."

She looked down and sipped her drink. "Well, you accomplished the impossible, Paul. You should be very proud."

"Jenny, if you'd let me—"

"Don't," she said sharply, wincing at the tenderness in his tone. "You promised."

Her expression closed instantly, and any momentary cheer was quickly extinguished as they returned to awkward silence, and she was relieved when dinner finally arrived. She thought about the meal she and Sam had shared at this very table a few weeks before. He had blundered his words, telling her he wanted to have children with her someday. She'd been so shocked, and he'd looked so appalled at the slip. She sank into the memory for a moment, smiling absently.

"What are you thinking about?"

Jenny looked up, smile fading.

She sighed. "Sam. He wasn't always as smooth as he seemed. I loved that."

Paul's voice was hard and annoyed when he muttered, "You only knew him for a weekend, for God's sake."

Jenny stared at him, hamburger midway to her mouth. She set it down on the plate, and her lips tightened into an angry line. "What does *that* mean?"

"It means…" He opened his palms in supplication. "It means—"

"Get over it?"

"I'm not trying to be insensitive."

"You're doing a pretty good job, though."

"Okay, Jenny. Yes. That's what I want to say: get over it. He's not from here. He clearly didn't have your best interests at heart. He turned your whole life upside down in four days. I'm not sure why he still deserves your—your *devotion.*"

She nodded, folding her hands on the table in front of her. "He deserves my devotion because he was *able* to turn my whole life upside down in four days."

"I don't underst—"

"Not that you have a right to demand answers about my life, Paul. But it means that if I cared for him less or if he cared less for me, he wouldn't have been able to make that kind of impression."

"So what, Jen? What do you *want*? Do you *love* him? Is that it? After knowing him for a long weekend, you're *in love* with him?"

She gasped and held her breath, her eyes widened, and her mouth opened loosely—she had a revelation. It was the missing puzzle piece, the cause that could make Chicago the effect. Her eyebrows knitted as she stared at the table, and out of the blue, she beamed, exhaling until her lungs were empty, looking up at Paul with a radiant smile.

"Yes." She started laughing, nodding, tears brightening her eyes. "Yes." She swiped at her eyes, nodding. "Yes. After knowing him for four days, I am totally and completely in love with him."

He looked at her like she had lost her mind. "I don't think you're thinking clearly, Jenny."

She smiled at him, her eyes alive and full of hope. "Yes, Paul. I am." She looked down at the table and then tried out the words again in a whisper. "I love him. I *love* him."

Paul took his napkin off his lap and tossed it on top of his plate, over his half-eaten food. His face was pinched and humorless. "Well, good for you, Jen. What the heck's keeping you *here*?"

She grimaced and swallowed as fear rose up inside of her unbidden. Fear. Her family. *What if she went to Chicago and something happened to one of them? How would she live with herself?*

"Jen, what're you going to do?" he insisted.

"I don't know yet." She worked her jaw as she had seen Sam do. "But this isn't a life. This is the shadow of a life. My dad and Lars are constantly in the park. Erik's always helping them. Nils has his hands full with the business. They all have *lives* here." Her forehead creased in thought, and her eyes were wide when she looked back up at Paul. "Is it possible I'm *only* staying here for Sunday suppers?"

"It's possible. Losing your mom was really hard for you, Jen." He folded his hands on the table, sighing in defeat. "You know what? All right, Jenny. I promised you I'd be your friend tonight, so let's talk. And just a little disclaimer? This is definitely your *friend* talking, because encouraging you to go for this guy feels all wrong for me as a man." She met his eyes, biting her lip, desperate for some guidance, even from an unlikely source. "Here's what I think: You're devoted to your family. You have been for as long as I've known you. Especially after your mom passed. It would take a lot of courage for you to go. But you have that kind of courage, Jenny. Even if you're not sure you do, I am. As long as Sam loves you the way you deserve to be loved, then you should be able to find that courage inside of you."

She nodded at him, and he continued, shaking his head, a sour expression on his handsome face.

"May as well throw the game at this point," he muttered, meeting her eyes with decisive intensity, using his guidance counselor voice. "Use your head, Jenny: Gardiner and Chicago aren't the only two places in the whole world to choose from. Maybe if you'd give a little, he would too. Sometimes love means making a compromise."

What he said made a lot of sense. Her expression softened as she thought about how hard it must have been for him to set aside his personal feelings and counsel her.

"There's someone out there for you, Paul."

"I wish she was you."

"She's not."

"Can I ask you something?"

"Fire away."

"If I'd..." He looked at her, his big, blue eyes serious and pleading. "If I'd spoken up sooner...if I'd asked you to take a walk with me some Sunday evening after supper and held your hand and told you how I felt, if I hadn't waited so long…would it have made a difference?"

She reached across the table and touched his hand gently, overcome by the wistful yearning in his voice. She shook her head. "No, Paul. It wouldn't have."

He withdrew his hand from hers on the excuse of adjusting his glasses. "Well, I guess we'll never know, Jen."

"*I* know. I promise you'll know someday too. We're too much alike, Paul. You need someone to challenge you too. That wouldn't have been me. I promise I wouldn't have made you happy, and I care about you too much to let something like that happen."

He cocked his head to the side like a Lindstrom and smiled at her, and she saw the littlest bit of hope in the smile. That's when she knew he would be all right. She didn't know why or how or with whom, but she was confident a man as good as Paul had a great love in store for him, and she smiled back at him, knowing she would have her treasured friend back again one day.

Treasured friend. Something in those words jarred something in the back of her mind. *Treasured. Treasure.* Something her mother used to say. Suddenly she remembered and blurted it out: "For where your treasure is, there your heart will be also."

"Where'd that come from?"

"I don't know. I think it's something my mamma used to say." She smiled at him with confidence and joy. "Sam's my treasure. My heart's in Chicago. As soon as Christmas is over, I'm going to go find it."

***

The Christmas pageant wasn't perfect, but no Christmas pageant is ever perfect. The baby Jesus—Martha Johnson, one year old—cried bitterly at the affront of being held by the strange fifteen-year-old girl portraying Mary. Mrs. Johnson ended up sitting on a stool between Mary and Joseph, rocking the cradle for a pacified Martha, who sucked on her bottle and gazed lovingly at her mama. A couple of the doves of peace got into a shoving match, which ended in Dove A falling into the Angel of the Lord, who lost her halo and ended up singing "The Glory of the Lord" with a sad, bent wing. Otherwise, not bad. Not bad at all.

Jenny had chuckled from the first pew where she was directing the children and prompting their lines. Her heart was lighter since her conversation with Paul, but she knew she still needed to talk to her pappa about her decision to head to Chicago, and she didn't know how he would react to the news. Aside from the fact that he might object to Jenny "chasing" a man, she was sure he wouldn't approve of the sheer distance.

After church, Lars brought the Christmas tree to her pappa's house, and they decorated it, sipping glögg and snacking on Swedish candies and cookies. Dinner would come later.

Once the tree was up and trimmed, Erik turned on a Christmas movie, and the boys settled in front of the TV. Jenny's father grabbed his pipe and headed out to the front porch swing. Jenny gulped. *Now or never.* She shrugged into her parka and followed him out the door.

"Can I sit with you, Pappa?"

"It's cold, Jenny-girl."

"I don't mind." She sat down beside his reassuring warmth. "Why do you still smoke outside?"

"Your mamma thought it was a *disgraceful habit*." He said this with her familiar inflection. "Men will have their vices, Jen."

Jenny smiled. "They will, Pappa."

Her father puffed, and rings of sweet-smelling tobacco smoke rose into the air, over the banister of the porch, floating away to the mountains that existed in the darkness beyond. "You got something on your mind, *min dotter*?"

"I do."

"You been sad lately, Jen. I been waiting for you to talk to me."

"Ah, Pappa. I don't want to bother you."

"You're my youngest child. My only girl. You don't bother me. Why you been sad? The fella from Chicago?" She turned in surprise to look at his face. "You think an old man doesn't notice when his daughter falls in love?"

She gasped, eyes widening. "Wh-what? H-How did you know?"

"Well, I meet him in the church, and I see your eyes, Jenny-girl. I see your eyes when he says him intentions is pure. I see you glowing."

"Why didn't you say anything?"

"What good is it that I know it if my Jenny don't?"

"I love him, Pappa."

"Yep."

"I have to go to him."

"Yep."

"Chicago."

"…yep."

She paused. He didn't fight with her. He didn't demand assurances or promises from her or remind of her place and propriety. He just rocked quietly next to her, occasionally taking the pipe out of his mouth to tap it.

"Pappa, I'm scared." She whispered this admission.

He breathed in. "I was scared when I meet your mamma. Prettiest girl at Midsummer. Flowers in her plaits. Would have followed her to China, Jenny. Would have followed her to hell. Wouldn't have mattered. Might as well just have up and died if'n I couldn't be with her."

Her father wasn't one for flowery statements. Tears filled her eyes, and her face crumpled at the simple poignancy of his words. She bowed her head so he wouldn't see her glistening eyes.

"Scared is okay. Hiding isn't. We're strong people, Jenny. Can't hide here in Gardiner. Life wants to be lived."

She nodded beside him, still trying to swallow down the enormous lump in her throat. Gratitude, fear, hope. She felt his arm around her. Her father wasn't a big talker, and he wasn't a big hugger. She leaned into him, resting her head on his shoulder.

"I know the gal we raised. You be scared. It's okay. But it's time to start moving, Jen. If the fella from Chicago's the one, you go. Your mamma had big hopes for you. Been waiting to see when you'd get moving again. Glad to see it happen."

"I'll be back, Pappa."

"Jenny-girl, I told you. I know the gal we raised. You'll *always* be back."

Jenny nodded against her father's shoulder, feeling the weight of the world lift off her shoulders and join the smoke of her father's pipe, floating out into the mountains far away.

"I love you, Pappa."

He breathed in sharply and nodded once, patting her shoulder awkwardly.

"It's Christmas Eve. We got to make the dinner, Jen." He leaned forward, giving her a moment to readjust against the back of the swing. Then he stood up, tapping his empty pipe against the porch railing. "I'll go get it started. You come when you're ready and give your old pappa a hand."

As he left, he put his hand on her head for a moment, his big palm splayed out over her blonde hair. His hand moved, and she felt him kiss the top of her head and linger there for a moment. Then he turned, and she heard the door open and shut behind him.

She used one foot to push off, curling her legs under herself, swinging gently back and forth in the dim light of the porch, staring at the endless expanse of the black Montana sky. Her feelings were sorted, she had her father's blessing, and her decision was made:

She loved Sam.

She had the courage.

For better or for worse, she was going to Chicago.

And she wasn't coming home until things were settled.

***

Christmas was over.

Carols had been sung.

Pageants had been performed.

Relatives in Bozeman had been visited.

The morning after Christmas Day dawned bright and cheery, and Jenny woke with purpose and determination.

She decided to buy her tickets to Chicago first, before writing to Sam. Regardless of his answer when she suggested a visit, she was going to Chicago to see him. She wasn't giving up on him without a fight. Her laptop needed a second to boot up; she hadn't been using it much lately. She put on the percolator to make some coffee and let Casey out of her playpen, waiting for her coffee to brew.

She wasn't expecting anyone, so she was surprised by the knock on her door. The first thought in her head was *Sam!* And even though there was no earthly reason to imagine Sam Kelley would suddenly arrive in Gardiner to see her, her shoulders slumped in disappointment when she found Erik standing outside.

"Heya, Jen," he said, smiling at his little sister.

"To what do I owe the pleasure?"

She walked back into the living room, and Erik closed the door behind him and followed her.

"Ah, Casey! Look at you, big girl!" He reached down to scratch behind her ears, then pulled her onto his lap, taking a seat in Jenny's easy chair.

Jenny headed into the kitchen. "Coffee?"

"Yep."

Jenny poured two cups, straightening her back. She knew how her brothers felt about Jenny leaving Gardiner for Chicago. Against her mother's wishes, they had brought her back from Great Falls, and even though she was grateful for their interference then, she really wasn't interested in hearing it now. She was a grown woman, and if she wanted to go halfway across the country chasing the man she wanted, well, they just needed to get the heck out of the way.

She stirred a little milk and sugar into Erik's cup as he liked and headed back into the living room. "Weren't you helping Pappa with a group today?"

"Got a few minutes. Wanted to talk to you."

"Could have talked to me yesterday, Erik. We were together all day."

"True enough. But I wanted to say something just to you. Just me to you without Lars and Nils butting in."

She plopped down on the loveseat across from him, eager to get this conversation over with so she could get rid of Erik and have time to clear her mind and sort her thoughts before writing her email to Sam.

She put her coffee cup on the table and faced him squarely. "So?"

"Pappa told us you're going to Chicago." His blue eyes, so similar to hers in shape and color, held hers seriously.

She wouldn't be cowered. "That's right."

"For Sam," he confirmed.

She tilted her head to the side, eyeballing him, then nodded curtly, feeling huffy.

He breathed in deeply, about to speak, but Jenny

decided she had had enough. "You know what, Erik? I get it. I'm the little Lindstrom sister, and you think I have no business chasing after a man in Chicago. And you're afraid I'm going to get my heart broken. So I am sure you drew the short straw, and the boys sent you over or whatever. But it's *my* life. *Mine.* And while I appreciate the protective thing you three have going here—"

"Wanted to wish you luck, Jen."

Jenny stopped short and stared at her brother with her mouth open. This was the last thing she expected to hear. "You what?"

"I just wanted to come by and wish you luck with everything."

Tears filled her eyes as she looked at Erik's face, so open and genuine, and she realized how much it meant to her to have his support, his blessing. She bit her cheek to keep from crying and barely whispered, "Luck?"

"You used to have a lot of heart, Jen. That first time the boys went to get you up in Great Falls? I know you told them to go to hell forty ways from Friday. I also know the second time they went up to get you, you had to come home because of Mamma. You had no choice. But I wasn't with them, Jen. Neither time. Wasn't with them, because I hated what they were doing.

"Gardiner isn't for everyone. Isn't for you, and it might surprise you to know that it isn't for me either. Pappa, Nils, and Lars? They love the park. They'd go on in there every day and wander around whether they got paid for it or not. And I love the park, Jen. You know I do. But it's not everything for me. It's not what I want. It's not enough. Maybe we both got scared of leaving, you and me. I don't know.

"But I know I got woke up watching you, Jen. All that heart suddenly came back to you, and I got to thinking…well, I think *Sam* woke you up. I think that's what happened. You know how I feel about being tied down to some gal. It's not for me, that's for sure. But I'm happy for you.

"So I just wanted to wish you luck, Jenny-girl. You're my family, and I'm sorry to see you go far away, but I sure do understand." He stood up, placing Casey on the floor, cocked his head to the side, and gave her a stern look. "And one last thing. You got your heart back. Good. Now don't get it broken, *lillesøster*."

Jenny launched herself across the room and into her brother's arms, resting her head on his shoulder and loving the sturdy strength of him so close to her. When she leaned back, Erik swiped at his eyes and cleared his throat.

"Got to go to work."

Jenny nodded. "Thanks for this, Erik."

He nodded back at her and headed for the door, then turned back before he twisted the knob to leave. "Heya, Jen? Wherever you end up? Let me know. Might be looking for a fresh start too."

"Wherever I am, Erik, there will always be room for you. *Elsker deg.*" Love you.

"*Elsker deg også*, Jen," he whispered, holding her eyes before closing the door behind him.

***

With her father and Erik on her side, Jenny knew Nils and Lars would come around. She smiled to herself, wondering what Erik wanted for his life, wondering how long he had felt quietly dissatisfied with Gardiner, as she had. *What a lot of wasted time.* She wished they had been able to share their feelings and find strength in one another's longing for more than Gardiner had to offer.

She sighed, and Erik's words replayed in her head: *All that heart suddenly come back to you, and I got to thinking…well, I think Sam woke you up.*

Sam woke me up.

She knew that Erik, who was generally so wary of love, was right. The part of her that found love, the part of her that knew the mesmerizing sweetness of passion, the part of her that finally found the courage to leave Gardiner—that part of her was asleep until she met him, until loving him and being loved by him awakened her.

She clasped her hands together and closed her eyes, her heart overwhelmed with gratitude and joy to know love's transforming power in her life. *Now please don't let me be too late. Please don't let him have moved on. Please, please let us still have a chance to be together.*

She settled on the loveseat, typed in her email address and password, and felt tingles of nervous energy in her belly. She was about to open a second browser to search for airline tickets when she noticed an email from Ingrid in her in-box, sent six hours ago. Surprised and curious, she decided to read Ingrid's email before buying her tickets.

Dear Jenny,

Merry Christmas to my best friend. I am guessing you had a traditional Svenska Christmas Eve with your dad and the boys, and I imagine you reading this the day after Christmas. How was Bozeman? Did your crazy, weird uncle try to kiss you under the mistletoe again? I hope you had your running shoes on!

Kristian had a message from Sam that mentioned you two had an intense weekend together. Kristian says that it's not our place to get involved, and I think he'd be mad I was writing to you. (Then again, he knows me so well, part of me wonders if that's why he forwarded Sam's message to me in the first place.) We don't know exactly what happened between you two, and I don't even know if you want to see him.

But I know you, Jenny-girl. You've never given your heart away. I am wondering if you gave it to Sam. Based on what he told us, I am thinking you did. And on that suspicion, I need to tell you something:

Sam's in Great Falls. Right now. He's spending the rest of the week there, at the Triple Peak Lodge. Kristian's grandparents used to own it. It's somewhere between Great Falls and Choteau. He heads back to Chicago on New Year's Day.

What you do with this information is up to you. If whatever was between you two is over, I guess you delete this email and get on with your life. If it's not, stop reading, get off your ass, and drive north, girl.

Here's what I know, Jen...being away from Kris is awful. Being apart has made me realize how precious a gift it is when we are together. Don't let this slip away if it's the real deal. *I* can't be with the man I love. But there is no good reason *you* can't.

Drive safely.

We love you,

Ingrid, Kristian, and Baby S.

Chapter 12

Sam stared at the roaring fire sitting on the edge of an easy chair, his elbows on his knees and his hands folded. It was good to be back at the Triple Peak after so long.

He'd arrived the day before yesterday, and if he wasn't positive then, he was more and more certain that his life was finally on the right track. Being back in Montana was soothing and exciting at once, and as Sam strenuously considered a permanent move to the state he had always loved, his heart felt lighter than it had in weeks.

His job interview today at Davis Financial had gone predictably well.

Sam knew his education and experience overqualified him for the open position, but surprisingly, they wanted to venture into some really interesting, cutting-edge financial solutions and were willing to give him some latitude in hiring talent for his own team and rolling out the program at his own pace and discretion. It would have been another five or six years before MTA would have offered him anything close, and even then, his ideas would have been bogged down in the bureaucracy of a large company.

No, there weren't going to be many posh client dinners here in Great Falls, but his subtle understanding of the office culture—mostly based on watching a mass exodus of people at 5:01 p.m. while he was still being interviewed in a glass conference room—indicated quitting time was quitting time, and the employees of Davis were encouraged to get home to their families in lieu of late nights at the office. It was exactly what Sam was looking for. They asked him for an answer by January 2, and Sam was ninety percent sure of his answer.

The outstanding ten percent rested on Jenny's unaware shoulders.

He planned to go see her tomorrow, and he hoped and prayed that her heart would still be open to him. But he would be lying if he said he wasn't worried. He was. She hadn't reached out to him in any way since she had run out of the courthouse in tears. He wasn't certain she would welcome him back into her life.

That's okay. As long as there's even the slightest sliver of hope, I will take the job in Great Falls, and I will court her properly, driving down to Gardiner every weekend until she softens. I will do anything to have her in my life. I love her.

He had taken a walk around Great Falls after his interview, trying to see the city through new eyes. It wasn't a bad little city: shopping areas and restaurants, big stores, small boutiques, and the university. He meandered through the unfamiliar paths of the university, dusting the snow off a bench to sit for a few minutes and imagine Jenny going to school here. He had visited Kristian once in his senior year, but it was a short weekend that had included a visit up in Choteau, so he didn't have vivid memories of the campus.

He began his walk back to his hotel, passing a store

called Montana Sapphire. As he walked by, the brilliant gold of the setting sun bounced off something in the window so brightly, it blinded Sam for a moment in his walk. He backed up and took a look in the window, noting the offender was a light-blue gem cut into a star shape, mounted on a platinum band. He stared at it for a while, knowing full and well his unexpected impulse to buy it was ridiculous. He didn't even know if she would speak to him and he was looking at engagement rings? *Keep moving, Sam.*

He walked down two more blocks before turning around, walking back briskly, and entering the store.

"The light-blue ring in the window?" he asked, gesturing to it.

"Oh, yes. The North Star model. It's not a sapphire, sir. It's a star-cut diamond. Unusual, right? For a special lady. It has eighty-six facets, and this particular ring is one-point-five carats and has a color rating of H. Do you want me to price it for you, sir?"

He ended up buying it. Truth be told, he'd been sold by the words *North Star* and couldn't seem to leave the store without it. He didn't have a finger to put it on yet, but he hoped maybe one day—someday—once Jenny had forgiven him, he might have the chance to give it to her.

Back at the hotel, he had stuffed the small box in his suitcase, feeling foolish. He didn't even know where the impulse to make such an impractical purchase had come from.

It's just that life felt so *possible* in the last day or two. Leaving Chicago. Moving to Great Falls. The hope that he could win Jenny back and have her in his life. *Possible.*

The fire was warm against his skin, so he leaned back into the comfortable softness of the easy chair, closing his eyes, enjoying the din of conversation in the lobby of the lodge, the smell of the crackling fire, the soft classical music being piped into the room.

"What a surprise! Are you staying here too?"

The hairs on the backs of his arm stood up because the woman's voice sounded so much like Jenny's, but this was his mind playing a trick on him, just as it had at those nightclubs in Chicago when his eyes had seen Jenny in every blonde woman he beheld. He kept his eyes closed. It wasn't her voice. It was merely another woman whose voice sounded like hers.

"Sam?"

His eyes flew open at the sound of his name, and he jolted forward like he had been shocked.

There she was…standing before him:

Jenny.

A massive lump formed in his throat as he stared up at her, willing her to be real, *desperate* that she was really here.

"Jen?"

Her wide blue eyes were bright with tears. She nodded at him.

"It's me."

"Jenny!"

He leapt up and grabbed her around the waist without permission, pulling her against his chest roughly. Closing his arms around her, his fingers curled into fists on her lower back, handfuls of her sweater bunched in the clawlike grip of his fingers. He rested his cheek against her head, working his jaw, feeling a tear slip from his eye and trail down his face into her hair. Her arms looped around his neck, and he closed his eyes with a sigh.

After weeks of aching longing, suddenly, miraculously, he was holding her again.

Say something! Say something, Sam!

But the lump in his throat wouldn't allow it.

Anyhow, words would have just been in the way.

***

Jenny closed her eyes, resting her cheek against his chest, hearing the frantic thumping of his heart and the ragged unevenness of his breathing.

His arms were around her so tightly, she couldn't even lean back to look at him. He had looked at her almost like she was an apparition, like it was impossible for her to suddenly appear before him. And then he'd grabbed her and held her, and nothing—nothing in her entire life—had ever felt so right.

In that moment, Jenny knew she would never willingly live another day of her life away from Sam. Almost losing him once was enough to prove to her that—like father, like daughter—she would follow him to China, she would follow him to hell, she would rather die than be without him. It didn't matter *where* she was, as long as she was with him.

He finally leaned back, his eyes were glistening.

His beautiful eyes, his beloved face.

He held her face with a stark intensity in his eyes that

almost frightened her. He must have seen her swallow nervously, because he tilted his head to the side, and his face softened, searching her eyes, then dipping his head to kiss her.

When his lips brushed against hers, her eyes filled with tears again and fluttered closed. Her fingers caressed the skin on the back of his neck as he moved his lips softly over hers, and that heavenly heat bubbled up from the depths of her body, radiating out from her middle until a wave of requited love fell over her, and the terrible, aching loneliness of the past few weeks faded away like the darkness of a nightmare when you wake up in the bright light of a brand-new day.

He leaned back, breathless, like he was still in the throes of a dream, then leaned his forehead against hers.

"How did this happen?" he murmured.

"Ingrid."

He loosened his grip around her body but found her hand, clasping it in his as he pulled her down onto a small loveseat in front of the fire.

"Tell me." He seemed to drink in her face, searching her eyes, using his knuckle to brush away her last errant tear.

"She wrote to me two days ago. She knew something had 'happened' between us and told me you were going to be up here for New Year's." She tilted her head to the side, smiling at him as another wave of love made her cheeks warm. "I was already packing for Chicago, so—"

"Chicago? Are you going to Chicago?"

She nodded at him, taking a deep breath.

"I'm going wherever you are, Sam." She released his

hand and opened her palms, gesturing to the lodge. "Isn't that obvious?"

He breathed in, biting his lower lip and stroking his chin with the thumb and forefinger of his free hand. "Hmmm. Chicago, huh? Well, that's too bad…"

This was too forward. He's back with Pepper, or he's moved on, or—

"…because I'm moving to Great Falls."

It was her turn to be shocked. "Wh-what? What are you talking about?"

"I figure if the woman I love needs to be in Montana, then I need to be in Montana too." He smiled at her, shaking his head slowly as his eyes brightened again. "Jenny, I love you so much."

She gasped and closed her eyes, bowing her head as her tears burst forth in torrents.

He pulled her into his arms, and she rested her wet cheek on his shoulder, soft sobs racking her body. He rubbed his hands up and down her back, whispering, "It's okay, Jenny. It's going to be okay now, Pretty Girl."

She took a deep breath, and her tears ebbed away, leaving her exhausted and happy, processing this news.

"You're really moving to Montana?"

"That's why I'm here. I interviewed for a job yesterday, and it's mine if I want it. I was going to drive down to Gardiner tomorrow to see if there's any way you could forgive me for being so awful to you at the courthouse and see if…see if…"

She put her palm on his cheek, and he turned slightly to press his lips into her palm.

"See if what?" she whispered, loving the sight of his bowed head kissing her hand.

He looked up at her, and his eyes were serious, searching hers, looking for the answer to an unasked question. Finally, he smiled at her and spoke in a gravelly whisper: "Come up to my room?"

She swallowed, eyes widening. *This is it, Jenny. This is the man you love asking you to come up to his hotel room.*

She swallowed again and looked down at her lap, her heart racing with unease: the last vestiges of the discomfort she used to feel around men, worries of maintaining propriety, sheer nerves at the thought of giving herself to him. She closed her eyes and severed those old worries from her current train of thought with a single, unforgiving blow.

He loves me and I love him. Our future begins now.

"Okay."

He smiled at her with heartbreaking tenderness, seeming to understand, with perfect clarity, everything in her head and in her heart. He took her face between his hands and kissed her lips gently.

"You take my breath away," he murmured against her lips, then he kissed her again, this time more deeply. Any lingering unease dissolved as she melted into him, wanting him, needing him, desperate for his hands on her body, for the heavy warmth of his weight pressing against her.

"Trust me," he whispered close to her ear. "I promised your dad my intentions were pure."

Her breath caught. "So you're *not* going to try to seduce me?"

He leaned back, looking surprised for a moment, then chuckled, nodding. "Actually, I am. But I need to do something else first."

First? What is he up to?

He grabbed her hand and pulled her to the elevator with him. Lacing his fingers through hers, she could have sworn she felt his tremble before their palms were finally flush. The elevator doors opened, and he pulled her toward his room. He took a keycard out of his back pocket and slipped it into the reader, which flashed green, then opened the door, letting her precede him into the room.

It was beautiful, decorated in creams and tans, with a large, log cabin–style bed dominating the room and a small sitting area in front of a fire. The fire must have been recently lit, and it glowed cheerfully behind glass, casting the whole room in a warm, golden, dreamy glow. She noticed a sliding door on the other side of the room that led outside onto a rustic balcony. She gestured to it. "Do you mind if I…"

"Sure. Go check it out. I have to get something."

Jenny crossed the room, taking a deep breath as she passed the big, plush bed. She slid the door open and stepped onto the small balcony. It was ink dark, but she knew there would be snow-covered mountains in the distance in the morning when she woke up next to him: three peaks to be exact. She leaned her arms on the railing and breathed in the cold Montana air, closing her eyes, feeling full, feeling grateful.

"Jenny."

When she turned around, Sam was on one knee before her.

"Sam!" she gasped, covering her mouth with her hands, fresh tears stinging her eyes.

In one palm, outstretched to her, was a small open box, and inside the little box was a ring with a light-blue star-shaped gem. She still had her hands over her mouth, but her eyes flicked up, slamming into his.

"Jenny Lindstrom." He swallowed nervously but held her eyes with enduring love and tenderness. "*Noen elsker deg nå. Og han er velsignet. Someone loves you* now, *Jen. And* he *is blessed.* I love you. Will you marry me?"

She dropped her hands and started laughing and crying at the same time, nodding because she couldn't make words. He took her left hand and held it, staring up at her, his question still waiting for an answer.

"Yes!" She laughed with wonder as he slipped the ring on the fourth finger and kissed it. "Yes, yes, yes, I will marry you."

He stood up, and she put her hands on either side of his face, tilting her head to the side like all the Lindstroms and admiring her ring. "I love it. It looks like a star."

"And I love you."

He smiled at her the way he would smile at her forever, like no woman walking on the earth had ever been, or would ever be, loved as much as Jenny Lindstrom Kelley.

"*An ever-fixed mark,*" he told her, "so you'll always find your way back to me."

"Shakespeare," she murmured with wonder. Then she

smiled. "I love you, Sam. I'm going to love you forever."

He smiled and put his arms around her, lifting her off the ground and lightly swinging her around before leaning back to look at her beloved face. As he lowered his head to kiss her, Jenny had one final thought before she gave herself totally to Sam, and it was the same one she had the first time she ever saw him, on the day he walked into the courthouse four weeks ago:

This is Sam, the man I'm going to marry.

THE END

EPILOGUE

Two Years Later
Great Falls, Montana

Erik Lindstrom carefully taped up the last box and carried it out to his car, setting in on the backseat and slamming the door shut. The trunk was already full to bursting; he'd have to return to Jenny and Sam's place in a few weeks to pick up the rest of his stuff. Maybe he should have rented a U-Haul, as Jenny had suggested.

He looked up to see Jenny walking down the stairs to the driveway with Sam beside her, their hands linked together. Erik wanted nothing less than a devoted spouse for his sister, but at the same time, Jenny and Sam's lovey-dovey ways made him uncomfortable.

Erik didn't have much faith in love.

He liked a pretty girl just as much as the next guy and had no problem with short-lived flings and mutual pleasure. It was love he didn't trust. He didn't want any part of it. *No, sir. No how.*

"You're going to drive carefully, *Minste?*"

Jenny's feet crunched over the gravel driveway as she approached her brother, dropping Sam's hand to wrap her arms around Erik. He was grateful for the warmth of her embrace. He might not believe in *romantic* love, but he had plenty of space in his heart for his family.

"Of course, Jen." Erik glanced down at her still-flat belly with brotherly concern. "I don't want you worrying about me. Just grow a nice little Lindstrom for all of us to love on, okay?"

"Kalispell feels like a long way away after having you around all year. We'll miss you, Erik," said Sam, putting his arm around his wife.

Erik nodded at his brother-in-law with an easy smile. "You know I'll be back, Sam. Lots. At *Midsommardagen*, for sure."

Jenny grinned, crossing her arms over her chest and leaning back into Sam. Suddenly her eyes flew open and she pressed the heel of her palm against her forehead.

"I almost forgot!" She smiled at Erik cajolingly, pushing a strand of blonde hair behind one ear. "I need you to do me a favor. Can you stop in Choteau for me? On your way north? I need you to pick up something from Ingrid."

Ingrid and Kristian had recently moved back to the United States and lived halfway between Great Falls and Kalispell in Choteau.

"Aw, Jen," protested Erik, giving her a sour look. "Is this really necessary? I'm eager to get up there. I meet with my supervisor at five so I can start work tomorrow."

"Yes, it is necessary, and it's the least you can do after being my houseguest for a year." She gave Erik her best no-nonsense glare. "You'd best get moving, *Minste*."

Why couldn't Erik say no to her? There was something

about his sister…and Ingrid too, for that matter. His heart had a veritable wall of ice around it when it came to any other girl in the world, but those two had always managed to get around it, the pair of them. Like a couple of human blowtorches.

He nodded grudgingly and kissed Jenny on the cheek before shaking Sam's hand good-bye.

As he pulled out of their driveway, he looked back in time to catch them kissing before they turned and sprinted back into the house, Sam pulling Jenny eagerly behind him up the steps and into the house. Erik rolled his eyes, but a quiet voice in the back of his mind wondered,

What would it be like to love someone as much as Sam loves Jenny?

He grimaced, annoyed with the direction of his thoughts. There was no doubt as to the answer. He knew it as surely as he knew his name, as surely as the sky was blue:

Like hell. That's how.

He sighed, shaking his head to clear it and rolled down his window. Turning up the music, he drove north and smiled at the long stretch of open road ahead, ready to start his life's next chapter…

Erik Lindstrom's story continues in:
SWEET HEARTS
(available on March 23, 2020)

ALSO AVAILABLE

from Katy Regnery

a modern fairytale
(A collection)

The Vixen and the Vet
Never Let You Go
Ginger's Heart
Dark Sexy Knight
Don't Speak
Shear Heaven
Fragments of Ash

THE BLUEBERRY LANE SERIES

THE ENGLISH BROTHERS
(Blueberry Lane Books #1–7)

Breaking Up with Barrett
Falling for Fitz
Anyone but Alex
Seduced by Stratton
Wild about Weston
Kiss Me Kate
Marrying Mr. English

THE WINSLOW BROTHERS
(Blueberry Lane Books #8–11)

Bidding on Brooks
Proposing to Preston
Crazy about Cameron
Campaigning for Christopher

THE ROUSSEAUS
(Blueberry Lane Books #12–14)

Jonquils for Jax
Marry Me Mad
J.C. and the Bijoux Jolis

THE STORY SISTERS

(Blueberry Lane Books #15–17)

The Bohemian and the Businessman
The Director and Don Juan
Countdown to Midnight

THE SUMMERHAVEN SERIES

Fighting Irish
Smiling Irish
Loving Irish
Catching Irish

THE ARRANGED DUO

Arrange Me
Arrange Us

ODDS ARE GOOD SERIES

Single in Sitka
Nome-o Seeks Juliet
A Fairbanks Affair
My Valdez Valentine
Kodiak Lumberjack

STAND-ALONE BOOKS:

After We Break
(a stand-alone second-chance romance)

Frosted
(a stand-alone romance novella for mature readers)

Unloved, a love story
(a stand-alone suspenseful romance)

**Under the sweet-romance pen name
Katy Paige**

THE LINDSTROMS

Proxy Bride
Missy's Wish
Sweet Hearts

Choose Me
Virtually Mine
Unforgettable You
My Treasure—all new!
Summer's Winter—all new!

Under the paranormal pen name
K. P. Kelley

It's You, Book 1
It's You, Book 2

Under the YA pen name
Callie Henry

A Date for Hannah

ABOUT THE AUTHOR

 *New York Times* and *USA Today* bestselling author **Katy Regnery** started her writing career by enrolling in a short story class in January 2012. One year later, she signed her first contract, and Katy's first novel was published in September 2013.

More than forty-five books and three RITA® nominations later, Katy claims authorship of the multititled Blueberry Lane series, the A Modern Fairytale collection, the Summerhaven series, the Arranged duo, and several other stand-alone romances, including the critically acclaimed mainstream fiction novel *Unloved, a love story.*

Katy's books are available in English, French, German, Hebrew, Italian, Polish, Portuguese, and Turkish.